For the staff of Café Diem,
without whom I would write many fewer books

THE
HOLLOW
PLACES

T. KINGFISHER

TITAN BOOKS

The Hollow Places
Print edition ISBN: 9781789093308
E-book edition ISBN: 9781789093315

Published by Titan Books
A division of Titan Publishing Group Ltd.
144 Southwark Street, London, SE1 0UP
www.titanbooks.com

First Titan edition: November 2020
10 9 8 7 6 5 4 3 2 1

A CIP catalogue record for this title is available from the British Library.

Printed and bound by CPI Group (UK) Ltd, CR0 4YY.

THE
HOLLOW
PLACES

1

Nobody ever believes me when I tell them my uncle Earl owns a museum.

They start to come around when I explain that it's a little tiny museum in a storefront in Hog Chapel, North Carolina, although there's so much stuff jumbled together that it looks bigger than it is. Then I tell them the name and they stop believing me again.

It makes for a good icebreaker at parties, anyway.

My uncle runs the Glory to God Museum of Natural Wonders, Curiosities, and Taxidermy.

Most of it is complete junk, of course. There are things in the cases that undoubtedly have MADE IN CHINA stamped on the underside. I threw out the shrunken heads when I was fifteen and found identical ones for sale at the Halloween store. But the wall of Thimbles of the World is real or, at least, contains real thimbles, and all the Barong masks are really from Bali, and if the Clovis points were chipped out in the seventies instead of thousands of years ago, they were at least still made by a human with a rock. The jar of MYSTERY PODS?! on the counter are the cones from a *Banksia* plant, but they're a mystery to most people, so I guess that counts.

And the taxidermy is real, insomuch as it is genuine taxidermy. That part of the museum has eleven stuffed deer heads, six stuffed boar heads, one giraffe skull, forty-six stuffed birds of various species, three stuffed albino raccoons, a Genuine Feejee Mermaid—which I keep trying to get him to rename because I think it's probably racist, or at least he could put a sign up explaining the context—two jackalopes, an entire case of dried scorpions, a moth-eaten grizzly bear, five stuffed prairie dogs, two fur-bearing trout, one truly amazing Amazonian river otter, and a pickled cobra in a bottle.

There's a lot of other stuff, too. That's just the ones on the first floor. I'm leaving out the things in boxes, and some things are hard to count. How do I classify the statue of St. Francis of Assisi with the carefully stuffed and mounted sparrows perched on his arms? And I'm not really sure whether the scene of tiny taxidermy mice in armor riding cane toads counts as one thing or as six mice and two toads. They're in the case with the armadillo purse (and do I count that as clothing or as taxidermy?) and a mug that may have been used by Elvis Presley. The mug has an

American flag on it. Uncle Earl put an album sleeve behind it and a large sign proclaiming that Elvis came to the Lord before he died. I'm not sure if that's true, but Uncle Earl firmly believes that every celebrity he likes came to the Lord before they died. I think this is so that he can picture them partying with angels instead of being hellbound.

Uncle Earl believes strongly in Jesus, Moses, the healing power of crystals, the Freemasons, the Illuminati, that aliens landed at Roswell but the government is suppressing it, secret histories, faith-healing, snake-handling, that there is an invention that will replace gasoline but the oil companies are suppressing it, chemtrails, demon-possession, the astonishing powers of Vicks VapoRub, and that there's proof that aliens contacted the Mayans and the Aztecs and probably the Egyptians, but the scientists are suppressing it. He believes in Skunk Ape, Chupacabras, and he positively adores Mothman. He is not Catholic, but he believes in the miracle of Fatima, visions of Mary appearing on toast, and he is nearly positive that the end times are upon us, but seems to be okay with this, provided it does not interfere with museum hours.

Uncle Earl also likes nearly everyone he's ever met, even the ones who believe in none of these things. If you made a Venn diagram of the saved and the damned, the damned would all be outside Uncle Earl's personal circle. He doesn't like to think of people he knows being in hell.

I tried pointing out once that the nice tourist couple he'd

just talked to for forty-five minutes were Muslim.

He said that was fine. "There's a lot of Muslims in the world, Carrot." (My name is Kara, but he's called me Carrot since I was two years old.) "God wouldn't send all those good people to hell."

"A lot of people would disagree with you."

"That's fine, too."

It's hard to argue with Uncle Earl. He can believe in too many things at the same time, without any apparent contradiction.

"Dr. Williams at the coffee shop says the earth is billions of years old."

"Could be," said Uncle Earl. "Could be. Creation took seven days, but I don't know how long a day is for God."

"But you've got a sign in the case with the prairie dogs that says the earth is four thousand years old."

"It's a quote from the Reverend James Smiley. It's attributed down at the bottom. If it's wrong, it's on him. I'm not here to judge. The visitors can decide for themselves what they want to believe."

"What if they decide wrong, though?"

"God forgives a lot," said Uncle Earl. "He has to. We all do a lot that needs forgiving."

I gave up.

When I was a kid, my classmates asked if I thought the museum was creepy. Some of the taxidermy was old and kind of battered, and you turn around the wrong corner and there'd be glass eyes staring at you. One of the albino raccoons had a particularly unpleasant grin. But, no, I never found it creepy. I grew up in it. I was sitting behind the counter taking people's donations when I was so young that I needed to sit on a phone book to reach the cash register.

(Years later I realized that I could probably have won instant fame from my classmates if I'd made up a story about the museum being haunted by the ghosts of the stuffed animals, but it didn't occur to me at the time. Oh, well. Opportunities lost.)

The sign out front of the Glory to God Museum of Natural Wonders, Curiosities, and Taxidermy mostly has small print, but the word WONDERS is large, so most people call it the Wonder Museum. There are a lot of jokes—"I *wonder* what Earl was thinking," "I *wonder* where he gets this stuff." They stopped being funny a long time ago, but we all smile politely anyway, in case the person saying it has money.

To answer the second question, Uncle Earl gets the stuff at flea markets or estate sales or on the internet or he makes them himself. He dabbled in taxidermy for a long time and he has lots of friends on the internet. People like Uncle Earl.

To answer the first question, I don't always know what he's thinking either.

∗

There was a time, when I was sixteen and working at the Wonder Museum for a summer job, that I tried to argue with him. I was angry at everything because this is the natural state of sixteen-year-olds.

"You believe in evolution," I told him. "You just don't know it."

"Well, I don't know about that." He pushed his glasses up on his nose. "Doesn't seem right, us coming from monkeys."

"Look, you believe that babies take after their parents, right?"

"Of course. That's just genetics, Carrot. For example, your momma always liked to argue, and look at you now."

I favored this with a snort and plunged onward. "And you believe in survival of the fittest, right? That fast antelope live long enough to have babies and slow antelope get eaten?"

"Sure, Carrot."

"That's evolution, right there. That. Those two things together."

Uncle Earl shook his head sadly. "Doesn't seem right," he repeated, "us coming from monkeys."

I threw my hands in the air and stomped into the back to rearrange the armored mice.

A few weeks later, shortly before I was done with summer break, he informed me that he had come around on evolution.

"What?"

"Thinking you must have been right, Carrot." He nodded. "Seems like we must have evolved." He waved a finger at me. "Only thing that explains Bigfoot, isn't it?"

I stared at him. I did not even know where to begin.

"Yep," he said, taking my silence for agreement. "Bigfoot's the missing link, all right, so you figure we gotta have a chain in order to have a link missing. I'm gonna update the sign in the prairie dog case."

He smiled at me beatifically and I went and got him the sign from the prairie dog case so that he could remove the words of the Reverend Smiley. Even at sixteen, I was learning that you had to pick your battles.

Eighteen years to the day after Uncle Earl accepted Bigfoot into his life, my marriage ended.

It would be a better story if I had walked in to find my husband, Mark, in bed with my best friend and dramatically told him to never darken my door again. But it was just two people who got married too early and had a long, slow slide into comfortable misery. I can't even say that it was my idea. It simply hadn't occurred to me that I could leave him or that he could leave me, and it was rather surprising to find out how wrong I was.

I felt a lot of panic because I had no idea how I was going to support myself—he had the better job, with health insurance—but the rest of the emotional stuff got a lot easier.

He offered me the house, which I couldn't have afforded to keep. I declined.

Which is how I found myself, at thirty-four, staring down the barrel of moving back in with my parents.

I love my mother. I cannot live with her. We are too much alike. If you have ever seen those photos of two deer who get their antlers locked together during a fight, dragging each other around until they both starve to death, you have a pretty good idea of how my mother and I get along.

Our optimal living distance is about two hundred miles. This is close enough that, in an emergency, I can drop everything and get out to see her, but limits random visiting. Since we are both aware of the whole locked-antlers problem, we can manage short bouts of family togetherness, then retire back to our respective corners to recover.

Moving back in with her was a more upsetting prospect than the divorce. Freelance graphic design just doesn't pay a lot, though, and it was going to take me months to save up a deposit on an apartment. I actually contemplated lying and saying I was living with a friend and moving into a room at the YMCA, but it turned out that even the Y had a waiting list.

Jesus Christ.

So I packed. I had a pretty good system: pack for an hour, cry for five minutes, pack for another hour, rinse, repeat. I was grimly throwing my books into boxes—I was taking the Pratchett, dammit, and he could buy his own—when the phone rang.

It was Uncle Earl.

That in itself was unusual. Uncle Earl liked the internet a lot, but he wasn't great on the phone. He called on my birthday every year, but that wasn't for months yet.

"Hi, Uncle Earl. What's up?"

"Hi, Carrot. It's your uncle Earl."

"Yes, I . . ." I closed my eyes and leaned against the bookcase.

Pick your battles. "How are you doing, Uncle Earl?"

"Me? Oh, I can't complain. The gout came back last month, but the doctor's a real nice lady. Museum's doing well."

I realized that I'd derailed him and waited.

"Heard you were having a rough patch, Carrot."

"Well, these things happen." I had an immediate urge to downplay the divorce, even though I had been sobbing furiously about an hour earlier. "I'll manage."

"I know you will, hon. You were always tough as an old boot."

From Uncle Earl, this was highly complimentary. I laughed. The tears were still a bit too close, so it came out strangled, but it was a laugh.

He hemmed and hawed for a minute, then said, "I'm sure you've got plans already, but I wanted you to know, I cleaned out the spare room at the museum last year."

"What?"

"The spare room in back," he said patiently. "Next to my workshop. I know your mom's probably real excited to have you back home"—this was a profound lie, and we both knew it—"but you know, with the gout, I don't get around as easy as I used to right now, and if you wanted to stay here for a bit, I thought I'd offer."

"Uncle Earl." I could feel the tears starting up again and pinched the bridge of my nose.

"It's no trouble," he assured me.

"I would love to stay there," I said, all in a gasp. My mother lived sixty miles from Hog Chapel. My ex-husband had visited the Wonder Museum once and told me the place was "kinda freaky," so all my memories of the Wonder Museum were good ones, without him in it. I could wander around the dusty cases and pet the stuffed grizzly and make the armored mice reenact the end of *The Empire Strikes Back*.

Hell, I could actually catalog the damn collection and earn my keep.

"Really, Carrot?"

"Really."

"Great!" I think he might have been as surprised as I was. "Then I'll get some new sheets for the bed. Just let me know when you're headed down."

I thanked him a few more times and hung up, and then I cried on the bookcase for a while.

When I finally stopped, I wiped my eyes, then I took all the Lovecraft and the Bear and left Mark with the Philip K. Dick because I never liked androids anyway.

2

I moved into the Wonder Museum on a rainy Monday afternoon.

The museum is closed on Mondays since Uncle Earl stays open all weekend to cash in on the tourists. Hog Chapel would love to be like the town of Southern Pines, an hour east, but can't sustain quite so much quaintness. There's one famous golf course that brings people in, and a retirement community for wealthy seniors, who bring their grandkids into downtown on weekends, but that's about it for big money. The rest of the population is mostly tiny organic farmers looking for cheap land, and extremely earnest hippies who want to talk to you about biodiesel.

Every now and then the small-business bureau suggests changing the name from Hog Chapel to something more enticing, but it never passes. Who wants to live in Pinestraw or Pine Needle or Happy Pines or Sunset Pines anyway?

As it is, downtown Hog Chapel can reliably sustain one coffee shop, one diner, a hardware store, and two junk stores with pretensions of being antique shops.

The Wonder Museum does okay. Uncle Earl bought the building dirt cheap decades ago, so while it's not a cash cow, it doesn't have many expenses. It's sandwiched between the coffee shop and a boutique clothing store. The boutique clothing store goes out of business approximately once a year, whereupon someone buys it, changes out the name and the scented candles, and proceeds to gently lose money for another year.

When I drove my aged Subaru up, the boutique was named Glad Rags and had a mannequin dressed like a flapper. Judging by the signs advertising 30 percent off everything, I expected the shop would soon be changing scented candles again.

Uncle Earl came out to meet me, despite the rain. He's not a terribly physically demonstrative man, but he hugged me and said, "It'll be okay, Carrot," while I snuffled on his shoulder.

I didn't have that many boxes. Most of them were books. I have always been one of those who rhapsodized about the book as a physical object, but having to pack and carry the boxes was enough to make me want to throw over physical books altogether and just live on an e-reader.

I'd left Mark the furniture. I had no place to put it. I had my clothes, a couple of pictures I'd taken off the walls, my laptop, and a couple of coffee mugs. And refrigerator magnets. I had been collecting refrigerator magnets whenever I traveled anywhere, and damn if I was leaving my ex souvenirs of cities he hadn't visited.

Uncle Earl wanted to help, but his gout was bad and he kept having to stop and rest his foot, so I pretended I was too tired to unload and just grabbed a couple essentials.

"Your room's through here," he said, once I'd gotten those out of the car. He limped through the back hall, which was hung with posters announcing the anniversary of the Mothman sightings—"Fifty Years of Terror!"—and a random assortment of small-animal skulls wired to a kayak paddle. (Why a kayak paddle? you ask. Look, if I could explain this stuff, it wouldn't be the Wonder Museum, okay?)

My uncle may well have cleared out the room last year, but the coat of warm-yellow paint on the walls was brand-new. The room still smelled of it, even though a fan was in the doorway to blow some of the fumes out. The bed was an antique with elaborately lathed corner posts higher than my head, ridiculously imposing and faintly absurd, given that it was only a twin bed and had a green comforter decorated with little pineapples.

On the wall opposite the bed was the mounted head of a Roosevelt elk. Roosevelt elk are massive animals, nearly the size of horses, and this one had a rack of antlers like tree limbs. I took one look and started laughing in recognition.

"Oh my God! Uncle Earl, is that Prince?"

"You always were fond of him." Uncle Earl sounded a trifle embarrassed. "Thought you might appreciate the company."

I laughed again, walking up to my old friend.

When I was five or six, I saw *Bambi*, because this is a baffling thing that parents still do to their children. I had not cried, but I had stared huge eyed at the screen while Bambi's mother died. But the figure that really impressed me was Bambi's father, the Prince of the Forest.

(Incidentally, if you haven't read the book, by Felix Salten, there is an incredibly weird scene where the Prince shows Bambi the body of a dead poacher to explain to him that humans can die, too. Everybody goes on about how disturbing *Watership Down* is as an animal book for kids, but it doesn't hold a candle to *Bambi*.)

The next time I went to the Wonder Museum, I walked up to the mounted elk head and shouted, "Prince!"

My deer-identification skills were not strong at six. My mother, being that sort of person, explained that elk and deer were different species and this wasn't the Prince.

Uncle Earl, being the sort of person *he* was, waited until my mother had gone next door and told me that elk were even greater princes of the forest than deer, and that this elk would be honored to be called Prince.

The next time I came back, the plaque next to the elk had been changed, and it now read:

"PRINCE"

Cervus canadensis roosevelti

Even at a young age, I was aware that he was doing this partly to be kind and partly to make sure both my mother and I could be right. At a much later age, it would occur to me that my mother had been Uncle Earl's sister first, and he probably had a lot of experience in working around her inexhaustible need to be correct in the face of adversity.

It was good to see Prince again. I hugged Uncle Earl. "You didn't have to do this. Thank you."

"It's what family's for, Carrot. Anyway, I'll work you hard while you're here. Don't you worry about that."

He tried to look stern and failed miserably. I excused myself to go to the bathroom and only cried a little while I was in there, mostly because of the kindness, and a little out of sheer relief.

∗

I went to bed early, exhausted from the drive and the emotions, and slept like the drugged dead. I didn't even get up to use the bathroom.

I woke up and did not have even a moment of confusion about where I was. The last few weeks, sleeping in the living room, I would wake up and stare at the ceiling and wonder why I wasn't in the bedroom, and then the divorce would come crashing back down on me all over again. But here I woke up, and even though it was dark, I smelled paint and I saw Prince's antlers in the thin sliver of light from the door and I knew exactly where I was.

I had to fumble for my cell phone to see what time it was. Eight fifteen. Early for me, but if I was going to help run the museum, I had to get used to getting up early. We opened at nine. I got up, showered, threw on clothes, and padded out to the front, where Uncle Earl was setting up the point-of-sale system.

"Morning, Carrot," he said. "I brought doughnuts."

I looked over at the box of Krispy Kreme and reminded myself that I was back in the South, where our cultural food is deep-fried. Sure, great wars are fought over the proper sort of barbecue, but everybody finds common ground on the hush puppies. And Krispy Kreme. It's as close to a religious pilgrimage as you can make in this part of the country. (Go a bit farther south and Graceland fills this ecological niche, but not in the Carolinas.)

I took a doughnut and bit into it. It was made of air and glory.

"You want to run next door and get us some coffee?" asked Uncle Earl. "I'd go, but . . ."

I took note of the way he was sitting on the stool and got a suspicion that it wasn't just gout bothering him. His back was straight, and I could see a brace under his clothes.

"Back bugging you, Uncle Earl?"

"It's fine."

"Fine like it's fine, or fine like it hurts like hell but you don't want to complain?"

His lips twitched. "Well, more like the second one. Went out on me a few weeks back. Still twinges sometimes."

"Jeez. Didn't they give you meds?"

He shrugged carefully. "The ones that work make me foggy. Always afraid I'll fall asleep in front of the customers."

I paused on my way out the door to get coffee. "Well, if you want to take one tomorrow, I'll be here and make sure you don't."

I almost expected him to turn me down—Uncle Earl would let you cut his leg off rather than complain—but he said, "I'd like that, hon," and I had a sinking feeling that he was in a lot more pain than I thought.

✳

The Black Hen coffee shop next door was ostensibly owned by a woman named Martha, but her brother Simon was the barista. I assume he got off shift at some point, but I never saw him leave. Simon was interesting. He dressed like a thrift-store Mad Hatter, with fingerless gloves and strange hats. He looked exactly the same now as he had the last time I had been here, five years ago, and exactly the same as he had when I'd first met him, nearly a decade ago. Simon had to be nearly forty, if not older, but he looked about eighteen. Somewhere, a portrait was probably aging for him.

Uncle Earl and I drank free at the Black Hen because Uncle Earl owned the whole building, and I think he took at least half his rent in caffeine. Simon loved the Wonder Museum and came over sometimes with interesting skulls, also in lieu of rent.

"How've you been, Simon?" I asked, flopping down in one of the chairs while he filled up a carafe for me to take back.

"I'm good," he said. "I hear you're not so good."

"Divorce."

"Ugh. Do I need to kill him?"

Simon was approximately half the size of my ex, but it was an arresting mental image. "No, but you're sweet to offer. I'll manage." (*I'll manage*, I said, as if I weren't still bursting into tears at inconvenient moments once or twice a day.)

"Aww. You're better off. Men suck."

I raised an eyebrow.

"Sorry, it's the eye talking." He put my coffee on the counter.

". . . the eye," I said.

"Oh, you haven't been around for a while! Yeah. Turns out my left eye's got some rare form of color blindness that only women get. So they think I'm probably a chimera and ate my twin in the womb and it's actually *her* left eye."

I sipped the coffee. It was extremely good coffee. "Huh."

"The optometrist got very excited."

"I bet."

"Sometimes I see weird shit with it."

Knowing Simon, *weird shit* could encompass anything from

ghosts to auras to invisible aliens performing in a barbershop quartet. I thought about asking if he'd seen anything in the Wonder Museum, but given that it was wall-to-wall weird shit, how would he even tell?

After a minute, because I am incapable of leaving things alone, I said, "Is it just the left eye?"

"Well, it's hard to tell. I'd have to get everything tested individually, wouldn't I? I mean, my pancreas could be female. How would I even know?"

I had never before contemplated the gender of my pancreas. I gazed into my coffee.

"How's the museum?" he asked.

"Seems to be doing okay. I'd like to try and catalog some of the things, maybe update the website while I'm staying here."

"Hoo, good luck." Simon shook his head. "Better you than me."

A man who had devoured his twin in the womb and was now carrying her eye around in his head was pitying me. That seemed as if it should be a good metaphor for my life, although I'd be damned if I could make sense of it. I took the carafe of coffee, clutched my own cup, and headed back to the museum.

✽

A couple of early tourists showed up to tour the museum, promptly at nine. I unlocked the door and waved them in.

"Welcome to the Wonder Museum!"

"I love this place," one of them confessed, a shaggy-haired woman with a bull ring in her nose and a T-shirt that said I ❤ CHICKENS. "It's the best. I bring all my friends here when we're in town."

"Glad you think so!" I said cheerfully.

The little knot of tourists vanished up the stairs, their voices drifting after them. "Wait until you see the taxidermy. . . ."

I swept my eyes over the displays, packed to bursting with . . . stuff. Contemplating the cataloging job ahead of me was like standing at the bottom of Everest and looking up. "Do you have any kind of inventory system?"

"Oh, yes," said Uncle Earl. "For the T-shirts and the bumper stickers and the mugs."

"But the museum exhibits?"

He frowned. "Well, *I* know what they all are . . . mostly . . ."

There is probably a phrase that strikes more fear and terror into the heart of someone attempting to take an inventory, but I do not know it. But looking at Uncle Earl's hopeful, slightly worried face, I could not say it aloud.

"Spreadsheets," I said. "We will do this with spreadsheets. And stickers."

I pulled up a fresh one and wrote #00001 in the first box, then wrote *Prince—mounted Roosevelt elk head*. I went into the back, took a photo with my cell phone, then plugged it into the spreadsheet. Uncle Earl had a bunch of tiny price-tag stickers, for putting on the coffee mugs. I wrote #1 on one and affixed it to the back of Prince's plaque.

"One down," I muttered, looking around me. "Another couple million to go."

I got to work.

3

A week later, we were settling into a routine. I got up just before the museum opened. I ate whatever Uncle Earl brought in—muffins or doughnuts or whatever. I went next door, got coffee for both of us, and then Uncle Earl sat at the till and I did all the jobs that required mobility—fetching mail, putting out the signboard, restocking the stickers and the coffee mugs. Somewhere around lunch, he'd send me out for sandwiches at the diner, and I'd spend the rest of the afternoon cataloging.

When we closed up at six, he'd say, "Good job today, Carrot. Don't know what I did without you." Then he would go home and I would go next door to the coffee shop and leech on the Wi-Fi. If I could think of something fun to say, I'd update the museum's social media. I had grandiose visions of overhauling the web page and doing more with it than the occasional blog post about the history of Feejee Mermaids, but I hadn't quite gotten there yet. And you had to be careful when you posted pictures of skulls and taxidermy because there were always people who wanted to tell you that this made you a murderer and the moral equivalent of Ed Gein. My internet armor had been built up in the fanfic battlegrounds and was thus impenetrable, but Uncle Earl was a gentle soul, and I was afraid that someone might hurt his feelings.

Most of my time was spent designing people's logos and wedding invitations and sending them off to clients, while Simon slung coffee and told me rambling stories about his childhood in Florida. This sounds boring. It was not. I would be head down in a project, letting the words flow over me, and Simon would casually throw out that his parents had been religious-party clowns on weekends, or that he had nearly been eaten by an alligator on two separate occasions. I would jerk upright, startled, and say "Wait, *what?*" and then Simon would explain how his sister had fought the alligator off with a lawn dart, and I would stare at him and wonder how he had survived to adulthood. (I asked him about this once. He said he'd never expected to live this long and now he was just happy to be here. Possibly that explains why he seemed so absolutely content to be a barista and live over the coffee shop. I think he genuinely expected to keel over on the espresso machine one day and be buried with a steamer in his hand.)

At some point, the coffee shop would close. Simon never

kicked me out, but when he'd turned the sign to CLOSED, I'd finish up what I was doing and head back next door. If I sat in a particular spot against the wall downstairs—directly under the kudu head, next to the portrait of Pope John Paul done entirely in sunflower seeds, I could still get Wi-Fi, so I'd check various forums, eat the other half of my sandwich from lunch, then congratulate myself on not stalking my ex-husband on social media to see if he was appropriately miserable.

(Mark was not appropriately miserable. He was posting platitudes about life being full of possibility and moving bravely into the unknown. Dammit, I can't believe I spent so much of my life on a man who would unironically post the line "Today is a gift, that's why we call it the present." And in Papyrus, too.)

Sitting alone in a darkened building full of dead animals, fake shrunken heads, and, of course, His Sunflower Holiness might have been creepy if I wasn't used to it, but it didn't feel that way. Even when a passing car would splash its headlights through the window and the glass eyes of the animals would catch the light, it didn't bother me. Sure, they briefly looked alive, but so what? They had a kind of benevolence, like stuffed and mounted guardian angels. Uncle Earl's basic kindness infused every corner of his beloved museum.

It was a kind place. It was beginning to feel like home. I could feel it working its way into my bones, and that worried me a little, because a few months ago I had been a graphic designer with a house and a husband, safe and stable, building up a career a little bit at a time. My life had stretched out in front of me, not terribly exciting but *comprehensible*.

Now I was on a completely different track. I had barely any money, my job prospects were awfully thin, and stability was starting to look like a room with a stuffed elk head and a portrait of Elvis over the bed.

It's only been a week, I told myself. *You get at least a month to recover from your marriage before you have to start worrying that you're a slacker.* Which was all the excuse I needed to pull up some suitably smutty fanfic and go to bed.

✳

The UPS guy came in with a box the next morning, shoving the door open with his shoulder. Uncle Earl started to get up, winced, and I hurried to grab the pad and sign for it so that he wouldn't have to.

"Got a new helper, I see."

Uncle Earl nodded. "This is my niece, Car— Kara."

The UPS guy tapped the brim of his hat. "I'm sure we'll see each other plenty." He headed back toward the door. "At least until your donors slow down a bit!"

"Not much chance of that," I muttered, glaring at the box. I'd been working all week, including most of the day we were closed, and I felt as if I'd barely made a dent. And here was *more* stuff coming in.

Oh, well. I took the job on myself, after all.

"Let me photograph these," I said, getting out my phone, while Uncle Earl unpacked the box. "For the catalog."

"Okay, Carrot."

He pulled newspaper-wrapped bundles out of the box and laid them on the counter. "From my old friend Woody," he said. "He haunts estate sales and sends me things. I like his because he always includes the provenance when he can find it."

Woody's gifts were eclectic, to say the least. The first bundle was a bag of leg bones from Soay sheep, barely as long as my hand. "Soays are tiny," said Uncle Earl. "Up to your knee, maybe." The next two were modern primitive carvings of birds with their beaks gaping open and strange, flopping fish in their mouths. Then a lynx skull — "We can always use more skulls" — a blank book made of banana leaves, and a woman's face molded out of fish-skin leather.

"Oh, fish leather," said Uncle Earl wearily. "You have to keep it in the cases or Beauregard gets it." Beauregard is the latest of the Wonder Museum cats, an immense tabby with a skull like a fist. He had come up briefly when I was unpacking, headbutted me in the shin, and slouched off. Beau is excellent at catching the mice that might gnaw on the edges of the taxidermy and has a personality like a benevolent feline Genghis Khan.

The final object in the box was wedged crosswise to fit. It was a wooden carving, about the size of my forearm. Uncle Earl unwrapped it on the counter and paused, slowly crumpling the newspaper in his hands.

"Yech," I said. "That's a creepy one."

He picked up the card and read, "Carved corpse-otter effigy, Danube area, circa 1900."

"Corpse-otter?"

"That's what Woody says. . . ." Uncle Earl slid off the stool and actually came out from behind the counter to study the carving from both sides. "What a strange piece."

The carving was fairly crude, but you could still tell what it was. One side was an otter, turned with belly toward the viewer, head tilted up. The skull was too broad for any otter I'd ever seen, and it had a distinctly un-otter-like expression, but the tucked paws and long tail were unmistakable.

From the other side, it was a dead body. You could tell by the crossed arms and the wrapped shroud that covered everything. The artist had scored lines that had been filled with dark dye or simply with years of dirt, which clearly indicated tightly wrapped cloth. The corpse's head was at an odd, broken-neck angle, to match the otter on the other side.

"That's messed up."

"It's a bit weird, yeah." Coming from a man wearing a T-shirt proclaiming BIGFOOT LIVES!!!, this was quite a statement. He turned the carving over a few times. The carved lines seemed to squirm under the fluorescent light.

Beauregard sauntered up and eyed the fish leather hungrily.

"Well, we've got space in the raccoon case," said Uncle Earl. "Masks with masked bandits."

"And the carving?"

"Put it over by the otter, I guess." He fished out the keys. "Would you mind, Carrot?"

I took the mask and the carving and the keys and headed upstairs. Beau followed, trying to look as if he were just interested in me as a person and not because I was carrying a delicious-smelling art object.

There are at least three raccoon cases, so I picked one that wasn't too cluttered. Raccoons are easy. But the stuffed Amazonian otter was the pride of the Wonder Museum.

Amazonian giant otters get around six feet long and weigh seventy pounds. They're huge, bigger than wolverines. The natives call them water jaguars.

Even by those standards, this one was a monster. He was closing in on eight feet, and Lord only knows what he weighed when he was alive.

They're also super-endangered. My uncle's otter was a donation from an old trophy hunter who had lived up at the retirement village until recently. His kids all thought trophy hunting was revolting—I'm not saying they're wrong—and he couldn't sell his trophies because all his taxidermy was from years ago and didn't have all the various certificates you need to have to prove it's legal to have endangered-species skins. Nobody would buy them on anything but the black market. So this old guy was living in his little senior-living condo, the walls covered in mounted heads and skulls, facing the fact that when he died, his kids were going to throw all the animals in the trash.

"It was real sad, Carrot," Uncle Earl had told me on one of my visits. "He talked to all the heads like they were his friends. Asked me to keep his animals from winding up in the dumpster. So he donated them all to the museum and I promised to do my best."

He did, too. The wildebeest skull hangs on the wall behind the cash register, and kudu and blesbok and whatnot from this guy are scattered all through the museum. And the otter.

I still don't approve of trophy hunting, but the thought of the old man talking to the animal skulls, all alone in his room, was sad enough that I couldn't muster a lot of outrage. If there was a sin there, he'd obviously done a lot of penance. Honestly, it reminded me a bit of that fairy tale "The Goose Girl," where the severed horse head gets nailed to a wall and the heroine talks to it every day. That kind of bleak down-at-the-bone enchantment.

I'd say that Uncle Earl was an unlikely fairy godmother, but he'd certainly swooped in and given me the gift of a spare room, so maybe it wasn't that unlikely after all.

A lot of the taxidermy gets nicknames eventually, not just Prince. "Move Bob to cover the hole." "See if Tusky will fit there." "Dust Corky's horns, will you?" Bob's the wildebeest, Tusky is a boar. Corky is the male kudu, from Corkscrew, which is what the horns look like.

The otter doesn't have a nickname. It's just *the otter*. It's the crown jewel.

I dropped off the leather mask, much to Beau's disgust, and proceeded to the otter. It gazed past me with wet black eyes. The creature's mouth was mounted open, showing the heavy canines. It's not a smile or a snarl. It's just a businesslike showing of teeth.

I nodded respectfully to the otter and looked around for a place to put the carving. There was a shelf up against the wall with a couple of tacky porcelain windmills. I took them down, put the carving on the shelf, and wandered around looking for a place to stick the windmills. I finally found a gap under the Thimbles of the World and called it good.

My hands felt vaguely greasy. I'd say it was some kind of malicious taint from the otter carving, but realistically, given how suddenly eager Beau was to sniff my fingers, it was probably left over from the fish leather.

I would have lingered over the otter but I heard someone on the main floor ask if we had a particular shirt in XL, and I went to go rummage in the back so Uncle Earl didn't have to.

*

I was starting my third week at the museum when Uncle Earl didn't come in one morning.

He called me, so I didn't have time to worry.

"Hi, Uncle Earl."

"Carrot? This is your uncle."

I closed my eyes. His voice was a bit weaker than usual;

it wasn't the time to teach him how caller ID worked. "Are you okay?"

"Well, I'm afraid it's my knee, hon. Can't walk real well right now. Can I ask you to open the museum for me today?"

I assured him that I would, that he should stay home and stay off his knee, and insisted that he call the doctor.

"You're a real blessing, Carrot. God must have sent you to take care of me."

I avoided saying that God could have just sent an email instead of my divorce, and I made my uncle promise to take it easy.

Running the Wonder Museum single-handedly was not much more difficult than helping Uncle Earl with it, except that I had to be up front to talk to the tourists instead of wandering around cataloging things. I used the downtime to work on my most recent gig, which was a logo design for a customer who wanted the logo to have everything, including—I am not making this up—a feather because his mother's maiden name had been Featherstone and he'd started the company because she believed in him.

Still, it was money.

Uncle Earl was back the next day, but two days later, he was out again. Monday I hauled off and drove him to the doctor myself.

He limped out of the back looking gloomy. "They want to do surgery," he said. "Soon as they can. But not on my back. On both knees. They said I'm walking funny because of my bad knees and it's throwing my back out."

"Yikes. Okay."

"I'd be out for weeks, Carrot. I can't ask you to watch the museum while I lay in bed."

"You can and you will. Call Mom. She'll take care of you while you're recovering, and I'll watch the museum."

A week later, Mom came down to drive Uncle Earl to Charlotte. I hugged him and told him to focus on getting well, that I'd take care of everything. He went over how to pay the power bill for the fourth time, then Mom gave me a fond, exasperated glance and shooed him into the car.

"I know you'll do great, Carrot," he said, rolling down the window. "You call me if you have any problems. God bless you for doing this."

I still didn't believe in Uncle Earl's God, but he believed, and that's all that mattered. I gripped his hand, then Mom started the engine and they drove away.

I waved after them, then drove back downtown, unlocked the front door, and turned the sign to OPEN. The eyes of the mounted animals shone in the light and His Sunflower Holiness beamed down at me benevolently.

It was the one-month anniversary of my arrival at the Wonder Museum.

4

Everything went well, at least for a few days. There were the usual sorts of problems—Uncle Earl had told me how to pay the power bill but not the water bill, which took me nearly an hour to sort out, and then the point-of-sale system needed an update, and doing that took the computers down for two hours, and I had to make out receipts by hand for T-shirts and coffee mugs. An update came out for the website that broke every link, and I had to go through and update them by hand. And Beau groomed the grizzly bear's left hind paw until he threw up, because old taxidermy is preserved with nasty chemicals. I assume this was revenge for not letting him eat the fish leather.

The first major crisis occurred on the Thursday after Uncle Earl left, when I was doing my sweep to make sure nobody was left in the museum after closing and discovered a hole in the drywall in the otter room.

The hole was jagged and irregular, about a foot and a half long. Probably one of the tourists had put their elbow into the wall. None of them had come around and apologized for it, though.

I swore under my breath. Not even in charge for a week, and some idiot was wrecking up the joint. . . .

"Well, better the wall than the otter," I muttered. The hole was in the back wall of the museum. The shelf that had been up on the wall had fallen down. I couldn't remember what had been on it—ceramic windmills? I didn't see any broken ceramics on the floor, but maybe the guilty tourist had shoved them under something else and fled.

It occurred to me, as I stared at the hole, that I wasn't sure how to patch it. I could spackle nail holes and dents and whatnot, but this was something else again. Major home repairs had been my ex-husband's job. Anything bigger than a Dremel scared me.

I went next door to the coffee shop to mooch on the Wi-Fi and look up how to patch drywall.

Okay, that's not entirely true. I went to check up on various social media, maybe have a rousing argument with someone about a particular fanfic ship, and then look up how to patch drywall.

My ex was posting inspirational quotes again. I swear I wasn't looking for them, they just came across my timeline anyway. I know, I should just have unfollowed him, but it felt petty.

We were having a Friendly Divorce™. Probably some people really have those, but in our case it felt as if we were locked in a competition over who could be publically most gracious to the other. Ha ha, no, I'm not bitter, why would you think that, no, my teeth always lock like this when I smile, I don't know what you're talking about. . . .

"How's it going?" asked Simon.

"Ugh. One of the customers knocked a hole in the wall, and now I have to figure out how to fix it. And my ex is posting pictures of . . ." I paused. "One of his coworkers with her hands all over him. Huh." That son of a bitch. It had been a month! A *month*!

"Need any help?"

"An alibi," I muttered.

"You were with me the whole time."

I set the phone down. *No, no.* We were divorced. He was allowed to have relationships. I could have one, too, if I wanted. With . . . err . . . well, Simon definitely was not interested in anything I had to offer, but presumably someone else. There were straight men in Hog Chapel. A couple were probably even under sixty. "I don't suppose you have any spackle lying around?"

Simon rolled his eyes, or possibly his eye and his late twin's eye, however that worked. "I am the *god* of spackle. Wait until we close and I'll come help you patch it up."

"It's a big hole. I think the goop will just fall through."

"Oh ye of little faith."

So I waited around until closing, and Simon flipped the little sign on the door, counted out the cash register, then vanished into the back. He reemerged with a tool kit and a sack full of mysterious home-repair objects.

"Christ," he said when he saw the hole. "Did they offer to pay for it?"

"I don't even know who did it. Nobody fessed up, and you know Earl doesn't have cameras." (Cameras were expensive, and why spend money setting up a CCTV system when you could spend money on a life-size statue of Mothman?)

"It's gonna need the big patch put in." Simon frowned. "I'm gonna need to find a stud."

"Don't we all," I said, not quite under my breath. Simon grinned.

He took out his phone, turned on the screen, and stuck it into the hole, angling it to the side, then peered into the hole. "Let's see where the . . ."

He stopped.

He turned the phone the other way and turned his head to look.

"No stud?" I asked after a few seconds.

"Um," he said. "Carrot, you might want to take a look at this."

Simon backed away from the hole and held his phone out to me. He sounded calm, but it had a strange, brittle edge.

My heart sank. There would be leaking pipes or exposed

asbestos or something. Something *expensive*.

I shone the light through the hole.

There were no leaking pipes. There was no stud.

I was looking into a dark hallway that vanished out of the circle of light, in both directions.

"Ugh." I pulled my arm back. "Isn't this over the coffee shop? Isn't there supposed to be more of a wall?"

Simon looked at me. "I don't think you quite understand. That's not the coffee shop."

"Well, it's not the museum. Did somebody wall up a room between us?"

Simon looked skeptical. "I don't think there's enough space, is there?"

"Don't look at me, I just work here." I frowned at the hallway. It looked as if it was made of concrete, which was weird given that it was on the second floor of a brick building, but then again, I was working in a museum with a sunflower seed portrait of the pope, so who was I to talk about weird? "Hmm. Do you think you can take out a big enough chunk of wallboard for us to go through? I'd like to see where it goes."

Simon gnawed his lower lip. "Yeah, but my patch kit isn't gonna work to close it back up. I'll need to go buy actual wallboard."

I dithered for a minute, but curiosity won out. This wasn't just a crawl space, this was clearly a full-size hallway. Presumably the ends were blocked off, but if we could get even a couple square yards of usable space, that would give us room for another couple displays. And room in the Wonder Museum was always at a premium.

"Open it up," I said. The chance of more room was worth the few bucks to patch the hole.

He pulled out a power tool of some description. A saw thingy. Like I said, home improvement is not my skill set. A few minutes of muttering about the charger and fooling with batteries, and then he made four bold cuts in the wall, chopping a doorway three feet wide and tall enough to step through if we ducked our heads.

"Mind the floor," he said. "There's a soft patch in the floor over the coffee shop, and if this attaches to it, it might be rotting out."

"God, I hope not." I had a flashlight app on my phone and shone it into the hole. The floor looked like concrete. Did that mean it was solid, or that I was going to ride a slab of broken cement down two stories and into the basement?

Well. Nothing ventured . . .

I stepped through into the hallway.

It was quiet. That was the first thing I noticed. It was very, very quiet, more so even than you'd expect from the Wonder Museum at night. No car noises came through the wall. Even the soft hum of electric motors, the one you stop hearing after about thirty seconds, was silenced.

Simon stepped through after me, holding his top hat in one hand. He settled it back on his head and adjusted the brim.

I shone my cell light down the corridor and whistled. It went much farther than I expected, at least thirty feet, before hitting a wall. "Holy crap. This must go clear to the end of the block."

"In both directions," said Simon, checking the opposite way. "Shit. Do you think we found . . . I don't know, part of the Underground Railroad or something?"

"The building's from 1907, Simon. I'm pretty sure the Underground Railroad stopped before that." (I wish I could say that I was an expert at local history, but there's actually a big brick in the outer wall with 1907 stamped on it, and I passed it every time I went to get coffee.)

He thought for a minute. "Moonshining tunnels?"

"*Now* we're talkin'."

I set out in the direction of the coffee shop. The concrete wall had been painted, but the paint had chipped off and fallen away so that the only thing left were scaly patches of navy blue.

The floor didn't echo at all. It also didn't feel particularly unsteady, thankfully. I glanced over my shoulder to make sure that Simon was following.

"Right behind you."

"Good. This is eerie."

"Hell yeah." He grinned. "There was an abandoned mental hospital in the town I grew up in. We used to get high and go sneak into it."

"And?"

"Oh, that place was creepy as hell. Peeling linoleum and

weird rings on the walls and empty elevator shafts. Plus it was totally haunted by dead inmates."

"How do you know that?"

"How could it *not* be?"

". . . You make a valid point."

We were about ten feet from the end of the corridor when I saw that I'd been wrong about its being the end. There was a gap in the right-hand wall. It wasn't a dead end, it was a ninety-degree turn.

Simon and I both slowed down as we approached the turn. I don't know what we were expecting. Monsters, maybe. Empty elevator shafts.

No, it was just more corridor.

"Along the outer wall of the coffee shop, do you think?" I said.

"There's windows in that wall."

"Oh. Hmm." I played my light down the corridor. "Maybe . . . uh . . . we went up, somehow? We're just under the roof?" The concrete had felt level underfoot, but I was coming up short on other explanations.

"It's only a two-story building."

"Well, maybe we didn't go as far as we thought and this is in between the two buildings."

"Maybe there was a shit ton of black mold in the crawl space and we're both lying on the floor hallucinating," said Simon.

"Pretty consistent hallucination."

"I mean, assuming you're actually seeing this and I'm not hallucinating *you*."

"If we're both hallucinating, then we might as well keep going," I said, stepping forward.

Another twenty or thirty feet on and the corridor opened up suddenly.

I stopped in the doorway, slowly playing my light across the room.

It was circular. It was at least forty feet across. The walls were concrete, scraped and marked with graffiti. The floor was also concrete, but a thin layer of grit and watermarks made wavy lines across it, as if it had flooded sometime in the past.

And there was just no damn way that it was in the Wonder Museum.

5

"I'm being very calm about this," I said to Simon. "I want you to notice that."

"Consider it noticed."

"You're being very calm, too."

"I'm getting really invested in the black-mold thing."

"This can't possibly be over the coffee shop, can it?"

"I mean, it's got to be. Right?"

"You just said a minute ago that you didn't think it was."

"Yeah, but then you changed your answer, so now I have to change mine."

I inched out into the room. The floor crackled underfoot, not in a concrete-collapsing way, but in a multitude-of-twigs-and-small-pebbles way.

"Looks like water got in," I said.

"Yup."

"Have to find it and put some buckets out. It might flood the main building." Part of my mind had seized on the fact that I was responsible for taking care of the building and was not going to let that go, even if the building had a completely impossible set of hallways and a room in it.

Simon did not answer me, probably because he was reading the graffiti on the wall, or trying.

"You know this language?"

I looked. I didn't. Parts of it looked familiar, but not all of it. "Dunno. Cyrillic, maybe?"

"Soooo . . . Russian moonshiners?"

"Sure, why not?"

"Because it makes no sense?"

"Take it up with the black mold. I'm just a hallucination, remember?"

"Yeah, okay." He flashed his light on the ceiling. "Grating up there."

I looked up at it. Fifteen feet up, rusted nearly through. Looked like an air vent of some sort. Presumably that was where the water got in, but I couldn't see anything but darkness through it. "Huh."

It had to lead to the roof of the building. Or, at least, it had to if we were still pretending that this was physically possible. Simon's black-mold theory was starting to gain some ground.

"There's a door over there," he said. I had to shine my light on him in the darkness to see where he was pointing. Opposite the hallway

We walked over to the door. The crunching under our feet sounded incredibly loud in the silence.

The door was metal. It looked industrial, all rust and flaked paint. It had several heavy bolts on it, but they'd rusted into a solid mass of oxidized iron.

"Where do you think it goes?" I whispered.

"No idea," Simon whispered back. I don't know why we'd lowered our voices. It just seemed like a good idea.

"Should open over the street, shouldn't it?"

"Carrot, we should be standing *over* the street right now. We're way past where the building ought to end."

I bit my lip. He wasn't wrong. "Do you think we can open it?"

He looked at me. "Do you think that's a good idea?"

"What do you mean?"

"Come on, there's a hallway that can't exist and a giant locked door at the end. Do you *want* to get eaten by monsters or open a portal to hell or whatever?"

"It's not a *giant* door," I whispered back. "It's a perfectly ordinary door."

"With like fifty dead bolts!"

". . . Three. Three dead bolts."

He looked at me. He looked at the door. He said, "Come on, let's go back to the coffee shop and I'll make us Irish coffees and we'll discuss this like people who don't die in the first five minutes of a horror movie."

I yielded to the logic of this.

We backed out of the room. Somehow the darkness hadn't been quite so bad when we didn't know the door was there. Simon kept his light on the door, which was good. I'm not saying that I thought it might open if we weren't watching it, but . . .

Hell, I don't know what I'm saying.

We turned back down the corridor with the hole and I let out a shriek to wake the dead. Eyes were looking back at me, glittering flat green in the light.

Simon jumped back, his shoulder hitting me, and I fell against the concrete wall, adrenaline screaming through my veins.

"Myyeh?" said the owner of the eyes.

"Christ—*fuck*—it's the cat," said Simon.

"Dammit, Beau, you nearly gave me a heart attack." I scooped him up, still light-headed from the shock. He permitted this indignity but dug his claws into my T-shirt just far enough to let me know that further liberties would result in significant bodily harm.

"Myeh!"

"I thought we were gonna get eaten by brain goblins or something," said Simon.

"What're brain goblins?"

"No idea. That's just what I thought when I saw the eyes. 'Oh, shit, it's brain goblins.'"

"It's my fault." I stepped back into the museum and set Beau down. "Should have closed up the hole. Let's move something in front of this so the cat doesn't get into it again. Or the tourists, for that matter."

This was easier said than done. I wound up tacking a batik tapestry over it. It belled out toward me, as if air was coming out of the hole. Well, that wasn't so strange. Clearly, water was coming through into the one room through the vent. I went and found a poster of Elvis with a cardboard backing and hung it over the tapestry, which helped some. I didn't want tourists getting lost in the hallway.

We went down to the silent coffee shop and Simon started a pot of coffee and pulled whipped cream out from the mini-fridge under the espresso machine.

"You thinking black magic or aliens?" asked Simon, while the coffee brewed.

"We could flip a coin," I said, because the alternative was to scream at him to shut up, that there was nothing there and none of it had happened. This seemed excessive and Simon did not deserve to get yelled at.

He took out a coin. "Heads for aliens, tails for black magic."

"Why does it have to be black magic? Can't it be neutral magic? Magic with no significant moral imperative?"

Simon rolled his eyes, caught the coin in midair, and slapped it on his wrist. "Good news, it's aliens."

"Shouldn't we have flipped for black mold first?"

"The coin gets mad if you ask it too many questions."

"Ugh. Don't you have a better source of divination?"

"We could order Chinese food and ask the cookie."

"That's . . . no, that actually sounds like a great idea." I punched in the number for Panda Palace and recklessly spent my last gig's earnings on beef lo mein and broccoli and pork fried rice.

I had to drive to pick it up. (Simon graciously threw himself on my Irish coffee.) As I pulled away, I stared up at the top floor of the building. Was it really only two stories? Could it be two and a half? The brick facade was stairstepped at the top; maybe you could hide another corridor in there. That didn't explain how we could have walked so far forward, but maybe it wasn't that big. Maybe it was one of those buildings they make with odd angles so that you think you're going straight, but you're really veering sideways and it's all optical illusions.

It had to be something like that, didn't it?

The alternatives were . . . well . . .

Black magic or aliens?

I didn't believe in either one. Uncle Earl, I knew, believed in both.

I wondered which one of us was right.

✱

"Okay," I said, stabbing my fork into the pork fried rice, "what do we need to explore the hallway?"

"Oh, God, we're really doing this." Simon stared at his beef lo mein as if it might save him.

"Don't you want to?"

"Obviously I want to, I just feel like one of us should say 'Don't go in there!'"

"We're not in a horror movie, Simon."

"How do you know?"

"Because one of us would have to be spunky and virginal."

Simon digested this for a moment. "I'm spunky."

I gave him a Look.

". . . Fair. We'll need flashlights, I guess. Better ones than our phones."

"And a tape measure," I said. "Or at least a string."

He looked blank.

"So we can measure how long the hallway is. That way we'll know if it's impossible or . . . I dunno, if it's a weird optical illusion or something."

"Yeah, okay." He nodded. "That's not a bad idea. Maybe it's just like a hall of mirrors, and we're not going as far as we think we are."

Despite his protests, he was still saying "we." I was glad of this. I did not feel any urge to explore the concrete hallway by myself. I might not believe in black magic, aliens, Bigfoot, or brain goblins, but people who go exploring alone in haunted houses get horribly murdered.

Horror movie or not, the hallway was starting to feel a lot

like a haunted house that had somehow been grafted onto my uncle's museum.

"Do you think Uncle Earl knows it's there?" I asked.

"He's never said anything about it. And I can't imagine him just walling off space and ignoring it. Not when he could be using it for exhibits."

I pointed my fork at Simon. "Yes. Exactly."

"So *when* are we doing this?"

I frowned. "I dunno. Tomorrow night?" Tomorrow was Friday. Given the choice between being stuck in the museum on a Friday night, looking at social media about how my friends were out partying, and trying not to spy on my ex-husband's life, I would much rather explore a haunted house.

Apparently Simon had the same amount of social life that I did, because he nodded. "Yeah, that's fine. I'll kick off a few hours early."

"Your boss won't mind?"

He rolled his eyes. "My sister's always telling me to take more time off. I tell her I don't have anything to do, might as well make money, but, eh. You know how they are."

"Only child," I said.

"Lucky you."

I thought of my mother and the possibility of having another sibling to blunt the intensity. "We may have to agree to disagree on that one. Anyway—tomorrow at . . . seven? Will that work?"

"It's a date." He fished out one of the fortune cookies. "Here, let's see if cookiemancy works any better than the coin."

I snapped apart my cookie. The fortune said "The journey of a thousand miles begins with a single step." "Ugh. Platitude cookie." I tossed it aside. "You do any better?"

"'A business opportunity is coming your way.' We should probably have stuck with the coin."

"Oh, well." I picked up my leftovers and my new Irish coffee. "Tomorrow at seven. Be there or be square?"

Simon, possibly the least square human being I knew, just raised an eyebrow at me and shook his head.

✱

At 7:00 p.m. the next day, we assembled with flashlights, string, and a tape measure. Simon had a thermos of coffee. He said it was medicinal.

He had dressed for exploration in camo cargo shorts, black fishnets, a pair of stomping boots that would fit in a mosh pit, and a top hat with a pheasant feather on it. His T-shirt read SILENT NIGHTCLUB.

In my Wonder Museum T-shirt and jeans, I felt distinctly underdressed.

"Have you told your uncle there's a portal to Narnia in his museum?" Simon asked as we climbed the stairs to the otter room.

"No. He has surgery tomorrow and I don't want to worry him."

"You think he'd worry?"

"I think he'd come back here, knee or no knee, to see what was going on."

We stepped through the hole and into the hallway. I had taken the precaution of locking Beau in the bathroom, a crime for which I was going to pay heavily in feline scorn.

"Which way?" asked Simon.

"You're asking me?"

"It's your museum."

"Ugh." I turned to the left. "Well, we haven't gone this way yet."

Simon turned on his flashlight and followed.

If nothing weird was going on, except maybe for optical illusions, we should have been behind the upper story of the boutique. I was no longer quite willing to swear that nothing weird was going on.

The corridor went—you know, I don't know how far it went. It didn't seem as if it went that far, but distances were clearly a little wonky at the moment. I didn't break out the twine and measure it, anyhow.

It ended in another door, but this one stood halfway open. The room behind it seemed very dark.

Simon and I stared at the door.

"I liked the abandoned mental hospital better," he said a bit plaintively. "It had linoleum."

"If you want to bring some linoleum next time, I won't stop you."

"Ha."

I took a step forward, then another. Brain goblins did not leap out and eat me. I touched the door.

It was stuck in place, but open wide enough to get through. Unlike the other door, this one had a metal grate inset into it, which had wept rust in long red streaks.

I slid through, light held in front of me.

This was a small room, smaller than my bedroom in the museum. It had a single bed and a metal cupboard. Empty tin cans littered the floor. Something in the corner looked like a fifty-five-gallon oil drum.

The beam of light crossed the floor to the mattress and up.

There was a dead body on the bed.

6

I let out a squawk and backed up. "Oh, shit! *Oh, shit!*"

Simon said, "What?" Then he caught sight of the body. "Shitshitshit!"

I had the hysterical thought that I'd already *said* that, and then we both clutched each other's forearms like two teenagers in a haunted house.

The body did nothing. The body had not done anything for quite some time, by the look of things. It was mostly bone, with bits of blackened skin lying patchy and tight over the forehead, the teeth exposed. Hair clung in a ragged halo around the head. The mattress had a dark, spreading stain in the outline of the body.

Five years old? Fifty? Five thousand?

The clothes had survived better than the body had, but I

couldn't see their original color under the layers of dust.

"Well, at least he doesn't smell," said Simon, after a few minutes had passed and the body hadn't jumped up and attacked or done the Macarena or whatever dead bodies in impossible bunkers did when they were disturbed.

"Uncle Earl had a skeleton that sorta looked like this," I said. "Except it was fake."

"I don't think this is fake."

"Me neither."

Look at how calm we are, I thought. *Super calm. Two responsible adults, being calm. And responsible.* I took a deep breath. "Well, we have to call the cops, I guess."

"What?" Simon's head shot up. "No!"

"There's a dead body! You have to call the cops when you find a body!" I waved my arms and set the beam of light bouncing over the ceiling.

"No! You can't call the cops! Carrot— I—uh—"

There are generally only two reasons people don't want the cops called, and since Simon was whiter than mayonnaise, I could rule one of them out. I sighed. "What are you doing?"

"I'm not *doing* anything! But I've got an outstanding warrant in Florida."

I rolled my eyes. "You haven't been back to Florida for twenty years! Come on, the statute of limitations has expired on everything except . . ."

I ran through a mental list of Simon's possible crimes.

Murder seems unlikely, although I guess I can't rule it out. Kidnapping's even less likely.

"Dealing LSD," he said.

Yeah, okay, should have seen that one coming. So much for us being responsible adults, I guess. . . .

"I was young!" he said defensively. "It was that or sell my body!"

"I'm not judging. How much did they catch you with?"

"Two pounds."

"Two . . ." I had to clutch the doorframe. "Simon, they sell that stuff in like micrograms! Milligrams! Whatever! How the hell did you have *two pounds*?"

"It was on sugar cubes," he said glumly. "And you know they go by weight when they're trying to prosecute you."

"How the hell did you get away?"

"I had very skinny wrists when I was nineteen. Slid 'em right out of the handcuffs and ran like hell."

I pressed the heel of my hand to my forehead. "Okay, but . . . dead body!"

"And if the cops come out, it'll be a murder investigation and they'll start looking very seriously at us to make sure we didn't murder anyone, and I'll wind up in prison for the next thirty years with a cellmate who won't even give me a courtesy reach-around!"

I groaned. He probably wasn't wrong. And if I was being honest, I didn't really want the Wonder Museum shut down for a month on my watch while the cops tore apart the walls getting into the bunker. And Lord knows what they might impound on the way . . . such as the taxidermy that was a bit too old to have papers. . . .

Frankly, I wasn't even sure what you were supposed to do when you had an impossible hallway in the walls. Did you call the police to report that the laws of time and space were getting broken?

"Fine. No cops."

Simon visibly relaxed. I turned back to stare at the dead body.

"Nothing got at him," I said finally. "No scavengers." I thought of deer dead by the side of the road on the way into Hog Chapel, surrounded by flapping black vultures. Nature's cleanup crew.

They hadn't cleaned up this guy.

"Yeah, but what killed him?"

I looked around the room. Empty tin cans. Fifty-five-gallon drum. The top was off and it was empty, but if there had been water, presumably it might have evaporated. It wasn't *that* humid. "Heart attack? Suicide? Starvation?"

"Isn't that a bloodstain on the mattress?"

I took a step forward. "Um. I . . . uh . . . think that was . . . goop."

"*Goop?*" Simon sounded strained.

"Well, when he died, he would have . . . um . . . I mean, he probably decayed a bit, and it had to go somewhere." I shone my flashlight under the mattress. There was a black, greasy-looking stain on the floor. It had bubbled up with fungus in places. I didn't want to think about what the fungus had been feeding on.

I thought Simon might have a serious freak-out, but he was made of sterner stuff. Probably being nearly eaten by alligators all those times helped. As long as a large reptile wasn't hanging off your leg, life went on. He just nodded and looked around the rest of the room. "No more doors. I guess this is the end of the hallway."

"I'm starting to think it's less of a hallway and more like a bunker," I said. "This is survivalist shit, isn't it? Eating out of tin cans and whatnot."

"He could have been a prisoner."

"The bolts on the door are on *this* side."

Simon grunted. "Fair. I've just got prison on the brain right now."

"Don't worry. No cops."

"Thanks, Carrot."

I ran my hand through my hair. By my watch, it had been about ten minutes. It seemed like it had been about a year, but discovering a dead body, even a very old one, tends to distort one's view of time.

"Okay. Now what?"

"Now I want a drink," muttered Simon.

I had no better ideas at the moment, so we went back down

the hallway toward the hole, which is when I made the second alarming discovery of the night.

"Um," I said.

"Huh," I said.

"Simon?" I said.

He lowered the thermos. "What?"

"Look at the hole from this side."

"Uh . . . it's the museum?"

"No, not *through* the hole. Look at the *edges*."

He played his flashlight along the edge of our makeshift entry and swore softly under his breath.

We had been so astonished by the hallway yesterday that we hadn't bothered to look closely at the hole. I suppose if I'd thought about it at all, I thought there was a stretch of drywall in the hallway that Simon had chopped through to get in.

The concrete stretched in both directions, with a rectangle sliced neatly out of it.

"It's got to be plaster." Simon grabbed the edge of the hole with his free hand. "Look, it's only wallboard thick. There's got to be a layer of plaster over it and it only looks like concrete."

"So cut it with your saw thing. Just cut another inch out."

He muttered to himself. "I don't need a saw, it's just wallboard. Pocketknife will work, if you don't mind it being ugly."

I shrugged. "You're the one patching it."

Simon took out his pocketknife, set the edge against the hole, and tried to saw upward.

Absolutely nothing happened.

"Fuck," he muttered after a few seconds, checking the blade. "It's not going. Maybe I'll get the saw."

"Try from the other side," I suggested.

He pushed Elvis aside, stepped into the museum, and sliced a ragged semicircle out of the wall.

"What the hell . . . ?"

I watched as the point of his knife emerged through the concrete and cut a wavering arc. The bit of wallboard fell down, hit the ground, and went *thud*. Bits of gravel fell off it.

Even I know that an inch of cut wallboard does not go *thud*.

"Yeah, it's concrete." My voice was very calm, for someone who was watching the impossible happen in real time. I reached down and picked up the chunk. It had the same cross section as the bit that Simon had cut, but it was longer than my hand. Longer than Simon's knife blade, come to that.

"Cut just a bit on your side," I ordered. "And catch it."

Simon ducked his head and gave me a puzzled look, but cut a thin slice and caught it as it fell. It lay in his hand, a shred of plaster-coated board, nothing much to look at.

On his side, the wall was made of plaster and wood pulp and whatever else walls are made of.

On my side, it was six inches of stone.

I turned the concrete over in my hands and quietly relinquished the notion that I was dealing with reality as I understood it.

"So about that black mold," I said, handing him the chunk of concrete.

Simon turned it, looked at the edge of the hole, and I watched him come to the same realization that I had. He looked up at me, looked down the hallway toward the body, and said softly, "Shit."

In one sense, this was a relief. If this wasn't reality, then I didn't need to call the cops about the dead body. Their jurisdiction ended at the hole in the wall. The dead body was the responsibility of . . . someone else.

Somewhere else. The next world over. Another plane of existence.

In another, much larger sense, my brain was screaming hysterically that there was a hole in the world.

The funny thing was that I'd been thinking all along that the hallway was weird and it might be unnatural and toying with the idea of its being . . . someplace else . . . but it turned out that playing with that idea in my head and sitting there with a chunk of impossible concrete in my hand were two different things. The difference between thinking vaguely that a stretch of road was awfully dark and you hoped there weren't any deer on it, and the sudden flash of eyes in the headlights and the scream as you stand on the brakes and try to stop.

Have you told your uncle there's a portal to Narnia in his museum?

If this were Narnia, I'd expect more fauns, and maybe some Turkish delight. And I don't even like Turkish delight. The first piece I had tasted intensely of rose, which means it tasted the way Head & Shoulders shampoo smells, and I have never gotten over that association.

. . . This was probably not the best time to be thinking about shampoo.

The chunk of concrete hadn't turned back into wallboard when it passed through the hole. I had no idea what that meant, or if it meant anything at all.

"What do we do?" asked Simon.

I rubbed the back of my neck and looked around the hallway. Even though absolutely nothing about it had changed, it felt suddenly more sinister. If this *was* another world or dimension or whatever, maybe things were different. Maybe it had monsters that didn't make a sound before they ate you. Maybe things just appeared out of nowhere and snatched you away.

"I don't know," I admitted.

"We could close the hole back up," he said a bit doubtfully.

"Could we?"

"I mean, I can get a drywall patch. . . ."

"Right, but . . . no. That's not what I mean." I waved my hands. "If you put up a patch, does it become concrete over here? Or is it just going to be drywall?"

Simon blinked. He reached up and touched the edge, as if looking for an answer. "I don't know."

"I don't know either. If it's just drywall, though, couldn't something just break it down?"

"Like what?"

"I don't know! Something! Whatever killed that guy!"

"You said he died of starvation!"

"I said maybe! I don't know! I'm not a doctor! He could have died of all kinds of things!"

Simon's face disappeared from view as he rested his forehead against the museum wall. "We could fill the hallway with concrete?"

"Errr . . ." This seemed a little drastic. I had visions of wet concrete slopping out onto the floor.

"You could stand on that side and see if it turns to concrete as I patch the drywall?"

My vision changed to myself being walled up alive, "Cask of Amontillado" style, watching the hole slowly fill in. *For the love of God, Montresor!* "Oh, no! What if it closes off for good once you've patched it? I'd be stuck in . . . in wherever this is."

Simon's shoulders sagged.

After a minute he said, "Let's cover the dead guy."

"What?"

"The dead guy. I'll get a sheet."

"How will that help?"

"It won't, but I'll feel better. I can't stop thinking about the fact there's a dead body there. It's really distracting. Plus . . . you know . . ." He scuffed his foot. "You cover dead bodies."

He was right, and at least it was a problem we could fix, unlike the hole. "Yeah. Yeah, okay."

Simon left and I stared at the hole. I didn't want to turn my back on it. Where did that other door go? What was on the other side?

Could there be another dead body there?

I gnawed on my lower lip. Another *live* body?

Had we uncovered . . . I don't know, a serial killer's lair? Someplace he was leaving his victims?

Serial killers aren't magic. They can't make holes that turn drywall into concrete.

Okay, what if it's a serial killer from another dimension? I had a vision of a movie poster like some of the ones in the Wonder Museum. *Hannibal Lecter from Dimension X!*

. . . Jesus effing Christ.

I was mulling over the implications of extradimensional serial killers when Simon returned with a sheet. It had little flowers on it.

I looked at the flowers, then up at him.

"Look, it's clean," he said defensively. "And I don't think he cares."

I doubt he cared about much anymore, but Simon obviously cared about covering the body, and he was right. When he'd dropped the sheet over the bones and stepped back, I felt better, too. It was . . . well, there was still a dead body, but it felt less urgent, somehow. (How exactly there was urgency to a body that had been dead so long he'd turned to bones, I don't know. Humans aren't logical about death, okay?)

We closed the door behind us. It squealed, but it closed.

"So what do we do now?" Simon shone his flashlight down the hall. "Try to wall it off?"

"There's still another door," I said.

"The door that's locked from this side to keep whatever's over there *out*?"

"Yeah, that one."

I expected Simon to argue. Possibly I was hoping that he would argue. But he groaned and stomped around the hall for a few minutes, then said, "Okay. But this is how people die in horror movies, you know."

"You're not the teensiest bit curious?"

"I'm incredibly curious! I've just *also* seen horror movies!"

I waved my hands. "Probably the dead guy locked it."

"And he'd rather starve to death than go through it? That doesn't bother you at all?"

I was starting to regret that I'd ever suggested starvation. "We don't know that. Maybe he was old. Maybe he knew he was dying and just wanted to die in peace without his relatives bothering him."

"A giant bolted metal door seems a little excessive just to keep out your relatives."

"You only say that because you don't know my mother."

"I'll give you that one."

"We'll be fine. We won't touch anything that looks like a giant egg sac."

He folded his arms. "And no wicker men."

"*Positively* no wicker men."

"And no clowns."

"Jesus, if there's clowns, I'll keel over on the spot and save them the trouble."

"And we turn around if anything seems even the least bit creepy."

"What, more so than the dead body?"

Simon muttered to himself. "I gotta go get my tools. Wait right here."

He went downstairs, still muttering, but I was pretty sure it was mostly for show. This was much more mysterious than an abandoned mental hospital, and he couldn't possibly be immune to the excitement. I felt like an explorer standing on the brink of some impossible discovery.

Maybe there won't be anything, I warned myself. *Maybe it'll just be another dead-end hall. For all you know, this place isn't very big.*

Hell, for all I knew, the universe was full of little pocket worlds made of two rooms and a connecting hallway and not much else. It wouldn't make any sense, but what about this made sense?

I swept my flashlight around the hallway again and noticed something near the wall. It looked like a piece of wood, right under the hole in the drywall on the hallway side. We'd been stepping over it without realizing it.

I bent and picked it up. It looked familiar.

It was the corpse-otter carving.

I had a bad moment when I thought that maybe it was another one, and that the creepy little carving had somehow reached out and called to another one like itself, but then I saw the sticker on the underside, with #93 on it. It was the same one. I'd cataloged it myself.

#93 - Corpse-otter carving, circa 1900, from Danube – gift from Algernon "Woody" Morwood.

I slapped my forehead. Of course, the damn thing had been on the shelf that had been hanging askew on the wall. I remembered moving the ceramic windmills the day it arrived. Then I'd forgotten all about it. When the tourist had knocked the hole in the wallboard, it must have fallen through onto the floor. We'd been looking up, not down, so we'd missed it.

"Christ," I muttered, stepping back into the museum. "Give me a heart attack, why don't you." I set it on top of one of the raccoon cases. Not a great display spot, but it'd do until we could get the wall fixed.

Simon came back, carrying his tool kit. "This is stupid," he said, more to thin air than to me. "This is maybe the dumbest thing I've ever done, and I dated a Baptist boy once."

"How'd that work out?"

"'Bout like you'd expect. He got off hard on self-loathing. I think he's a Republican lobbyist now."

There did not seem to be much that I could say to that. I led the way through the hallway.

No, not the "hallway." The bunker.

The room at the end was the same as it had been. Nothing had changed. We moved our lights over the walls, looking for anything we'd missed, but all we saw was graffiti.

"I don't think it's Cyrillic," said Simon. "Look, this bit's . . . squiggly. And this over here is in different handwriting."

I looked at the one he'd indicated. It looked kind of like the bubble writing that we girls had done in grade school, all the big loops and *i*'s dotted with hearts. It was hard to read, but it didn't look like the same letters as the other graffiti. A different alphabet? Or just handwriting so stylized I couldn't make it out?

Hell, maybe it's like tagging and there's letters in there somewhere, but it's nearly impossible to make out.

"Huh," I said. "I suppose that means there was more than one person down here?"

"No body."

"Maybe they left."

"Or got cannibalized."

"Jesus, Simon . . ."

"What? It could happen!"

I rubbed my forehead. "Unless he ate their clothes, too, no."

"Okay, okay. That's fair." Simon set his tools down in front of the door and examined the rusted lumps that had been bolts at some point in their careers.

I couldn't get the thought of cannibals and serial killers out of my head. "Should we bring some kind of weapon?"

"Outstanding warrant, can't buy a gun. You?"

"Never touched one." I had a vague feeling that guns were not exactly point and shoot. You had to load them, right? There were hammers or bolts or safeties or something.

"You ever stab somebody?"

"No. Have you?"

"Well . . . I was holding a sword once and my sister was chasing me and she tried to kick me and stabbed herself in the leg. It was a whole thing." He went back to work on the locks.

"So swords are out."

"I'd prefer it."

I gave up on the thought of weapons. What was I going to do with one? Self-defense wasn't exactly my strong suit anyway. I took aikido for a while but mostly for the exercise and to get out of the house.

I reached out and touched a bit of wall. Rough, with sharp bits of flaking paint. Dry to the touch, which didn't surprise me. It looked as if there had been water once, but then everything had dried out. Probably why the skeleton was still intact, even if the tin cans had turned to crumbling rust.

I wondered idly what the labels on those empty tin cans had looked like. Had they been in this odd not-Cyrillic, too? Or the bubble writing?

"Okay," said Simon. "I think I've got it."

"You can work the bolts?"

"*Work* is a strong word." He took out a hammer and a flathead screwdriver, set the edge under the first rusted bolt, and whacked the back of his makeshift chisel with the hammer.

The lump of rust came partly away from the door, with flat sheets of dried paint attached to it. He hit it again and it fell off the door and landed at his feet.

The rest of the bolts came off just as easily. The screws holding them in place were nothing but rust.

"I'm a little afraid that when I pull on the door handle, it'll come off, too," admitted Simon. "This thing is like . . . rusted solid around the edges. I might have to take the hinges off."

"Can you loosen up the edges?"

"Mmm." He crouched down on the ground and slid the screwdriver into the crack there. "Maybe . . ."

The tapping of his hammer echoed in the room. I rubbed my arms. It was cooler than I liked in the room.

Hey, if it's still here in summer, we can totally save on air-conditioning. . . .

"Best I can do," said Simon finally, stepping back. He put his tools back in the toolbox, took the handle in both hands, and began to pull, cautiously.

The handle wiggled in his hands and I think both of us held our breath, but finally, with a long groan of metal, the door began to open. Light poured through the opening, and I think both of us cried out in surprise.

Then the handle fell off.

"Ha!" Simon tossed the handle down and shoved his hands

into the narrow gap. I jumped in beside him, dropped my flashlight, found a grip without razor-sharp rust to bite into my fingers, and the two of us pulled.

The door screamed and squealed on its hinges, but it opened another few inches. Just enough to wiggle through, if the two of us turned sideways and didn't mind rust smears on our clothes.

The light blazed strong as daylight, illuminating a narrow slice of the room.

"Whoa." I picked up my flashlight and turned it off. "That's bright."

A dozen thoughts tried to crowd into my brain at once, about how it was night and if there was light, it must be artificial (but maybe it was the streetlight out front, maybe everything was still normal, maybe this wasn't *really* another world), which meant that there was someone alive and changing lightbulbs, which meant . . .

I clamped down on the thoughts. It felt like panic. *One thing at a time. You'll figure it out when you get there.*

"There's a lip around the door," said Simon, reaching out. "Like an air lock or something. All the way around. No wonder we couldn't see the light through the cracks."

I nodded, sucked in my gut, and squeaked through the door.

There was a little landing beyond, and a set of stairs. At the top of the stairs, another door stood open. Beyond it, all I could see was white.

I crept up the stairs, hearing Simon work his way past the door behind me. Three steps below the top, I could see out the door. I put my hands on the top step to steady myself.

The whiteness was the sky. The air was thick with fog, drifting over the surface of sluggishly moving water. I was crouched inside a doorway on a tiny, hump-shaped island, covered in thick green grass.

I knew this because from the door, I could see dozens of other tiny, grassy, hump-shaped islands, vanishing into the mist.

7

Will it sound strange that the thing that bothered me most was the daylight?

It couldn't be daytime. It was dark outside. And I hadn't gotten on a plane and flown for hundreds of miles, crossing out of night. There simply hadn't been enough *time*.

I thought I had believed in a different world when I'd held the concrete. But a piece of concrete is a small thing. The sun is the *biggest* thing. Now I was feeling that different world on my skin, even if I couldn't see the sun through the thick white mist.

It'll burn off soon, I thought, and then, like an echo, *at least, it would in my world*.

I had always had mixed feelings about Narnia, mostly because of the heavy-handed lion-Jesus allegory. I suddenly had very strong feelings that C. S. Lewis had not spent nearly enough time on the sudden realization, when moving between worlds, that nothing could be taken for granted. Maybe fog hung around all day here, even when the sky was bright. Maybe there was no night, or maybe this was what night looked like. Maybe gravity stopped working here on Tuesdays.

It was strange and quiet. The landscape looked deeply unnatural to me, all those strange, rounded islands. They were too evenly spaced, like gravestones. I thought of European barrows, the low, artificial hills where ancient people buried their dead.

"O . . . kay . . . ," said Simon, crouching beside me. "Okay. That was . . . not what I was expecting."

After my first, bewildered impression, I saw that a few larger islands were scattered among the tiny islands. These were flatter, more natural looking, covered in short shrubs with silvery leaves.

"Osier willows," I said, pointing. "At least if they're the same as in our world."

Simon gave me a look. "You're a botanist now?"

I snorted. "No, I did a logo design for a guy who sold woven-willow baskets. Withyworld LLC. I did about a thousand variations on willow patterns for him, and he could *not* make up his mind. I have looked at more willow photos than God."

"Does God look at a lot of willow photos?"

"He does if he's a graphic designer. Do you think we can get to one of those other islands?"

"Depends on how deep the water is." Simon climbed out and stood on the edge of the island. The grass stretched out in front of us, maybe three feet or so, then dropped off sharply. Algae softened the line, but it looked unnaturally squared off.

"I think this is part of the bunker," said Simon, crouching down. "Look, there's steps down there, too."

I stepped up beside him and looked down. Sure enough, there were slick green stairs under the water, stepping down three or four feet, then vanishing into the mud.

"I can't tell how deep it is." Simon tapped his forehead over the eye that may or may not have belonged to his dead twin. "Depth perception's hard."

"We'd be wading. At the very least. Depends on how deep the mud is."

"If we climb up on top of this one, maybe we can get a better view."

I nodded.

The island was, as I had guessed, another of the tiny barrow-like islands. Once we were actually standing on it, it looked like an elongated teardrop. Silt had piled up on the backside, probably from upstream, and presumably that was why the grass was growing so lushly over it. It was wet and slick underfoot, and we had to go up on our hands and knees.

At the top, barely six feet wide and maybe ten feet long, we stood up.

Downstream, the landscape was what we'd seen. Dozens of the tiny islands, though from this height, they were teardrop shaped as well.

Simon turned to look upstream and his breath went out of him as if he'd been kicked in the chest. Filled with sudden dread, I turned.

There were more islands upstream as well. All of them identical, green with grass, spaced like graves.

Set into the side of each of those other islands was a single metal door.

"Holy . . ." Simon shook his head. "I . . . dude . . ."

"There's so many."

"Yeah."

"Do you think they're all bunkers like this one?"

"I don't know. Seems likely, doesn't it?"

"*Why* would there be so many?" I turned in a slow circle, trying to count all the little islands. If the ones downstream had doors as well . . . that was thirty, forty, fifty bunkers. And that's just what I could see before the fog brought the curtain down.

A bird called somewhere over the water, and both Simon and I jumped like we'd heard a gunshot. Then we both laughed. It was a killdeer, the sort you see in fields and parking lots all over North Carolina, dragging its wing and pretending to be injured. "*Kildeeeeee kildeeee kildeeeee . . .*"

"I guess that's the same as back home." Simon exhaled. "Glad it's not a crow."

"Oh?"

He shrugged, looking embarrassed. "I feel like the crows here would be weird. Too smart, maybe."

"Huh." I thought about that. It didn't make a lot of sense, but then I thought of the great mobs of crows that gather sometimes at twilight, cawing at each other, and thought of all those crows sitting in the willows on the larger islands or perched across the barrow islands . . . yes, all right, maybe I could see it.

I scanned the mist-covered horizon again. The islands vanished into it, growing paler and less distinct, an exercise in atmospheric perspective. One or two had willows growing over them, which should have broken up the monotonous regularity and made the scene less strange, but didn't.

"This is so bizarre," said Simon finally.

I shook my head. That it was clearly daylight here was still messing me up, more than it should have. My internal clock had shorted out and was blinking 12:00.

The dozens of tiny islands and doors weren't helping.

A couple of the doors were ajar. One or two seemed to be all the way open, or perhaps the doors themselves were missing.

"Do . . . do you want to go look in one of the others?" I asked finally. "I think we could get over to that one island behind us. It doesn't look too deep." That island had no door, being more of a sandspit with willows on it, but from there, I thought I could probably get to a couple other islands without having to swim.

"It's not that I really want to," said Simon, "but what are we going to do? Spend the rest of our lives wondering what's behind door number one . . . number two . . . number fifty . . . ?"

"I don't know that I want to explore fifty." I gnawed on my

lower lip. "We don't have to go if you don't want to."

Simon groaned. "I sort of want to, I just want to complain about it."

"Were you like this in the abandoned mental hospital?"

"Oh, you have no idea."

"Right." I started toward the edge of the island.

"Wait." Simon caught my arm. "Before we go out there, I want to do something. I need you to hold the flashlight."

I raised an eyebrow, but he was already heading back down the steps.

He dug around in his tool bag and pulled out a dead bolt. It was new and shiny looking.

"Where'd *that* come from?"

"Got Holderfield to go get it for me." (Holderfield is one of the regulars at the coffee shop.) Simon picked up the drill. "And a concrete bit, just in case."

"You knew we were going to open this door," I said, holding the flashlight steady as he applied lock to doorframe. "You argued with me, but you brought this along?" I'm not sure if I was more exasperated or amused.

Simon snorted. "Your uncle says nobody's ever won a fight with you. I figured I'd lose." *Wrrrrrrr* went the drill.

"Hey!"

"He says it in a very complimentary fashion." *Wrrrrrrrrr.*

The lock was installed in short order. He swung the door back, nearly closed, to check the alignment, then pulled it open again. *Skreeeeeekkkkk.* "All right. If we run into zombies or Godzilla out there, this'll hold them for . . . I dunno, a good thirty seconds."

"That's comforting. I'm feeling very comforted right now."

"It's what I do."

We finished up. He set down his toolbox and I rolled up my jeans, prepared to wade the river.

"Are we going to be able to find this one again?"

I glanced around. I didn't have any good way to mark the opening, but the islands weren't quite identical. "No willows on this one. Just downstream from the one with two big bushes on top."

"Fair enough."

On the first step in, the water was cold, but not frigid. Not like the warm ocean on the Carolina coast, but not icy mountain stream, either. Chilly. The concrete steps were slick with algae, but the next step down into mud, it was . . . well . . . mud. My hiking sandals sank in and squelched.

Simon removed his boots, tied them around his neck by the laces, and followed. "Gaaah."

"It's not so bad once you get used to it."

"Yeah, that's what my first boyfriend said about anal."

"*Simon.*"

"What?"

I knew if I looked at him, he'd be grinning like a shark, so I kept my eyes on my feet. Truth is, I was glad for the distraction.

My sandals had vanished into the mud. Trying not to think about Simon's love life was better than waiting for something to bite my toes. Otherworldly piranhas, maybe, or leeches.

I didn't see any fish, or even any bubbles of the sort that would make me think some small creature was lurking in the water. It was still quiet. Our voices, even kept low, seemed to echo over the whole river. The splashing as we walked sounded like gunfire.

The nearest island was a flat sandspit covered in willows. I was glad to step out onto it and see my feet again, even if they were crusted in mud and algae.

"Do you think we can get some horrible disease from the water?" Simon asked.

I considered this. "Like dysentery, you mean, or giardia? I think you have to drink the water for that."

"I was thinking about that one you can get from wading in stagnant water with the wrong kind of snail, and then five years later your liver falls out."

"That is not a real disease."

"Hand to God. I mean, maybe your liver doesn't fall out, exactly, but it stops working. It's like a snail parasite that eats human liver. Also, isn't there that one worm?"

"Guinea worm. They've about wiped that one out."

"They've about wiped that one out *on earth*."

I opened my mouth, then closed it again, because I had no response for that.

The sand looked like . . . well, *sand*. Nothing proclaimed it as having alien origin. A bunch of rocks had broken down into a bunch of smaller rocks and then into this. Apparently geological process worked the same in Narnia or Oz or whatever this was.

The willows were either osier willows, as I'd thought, or a close otherworld relative. The silvery leaves looked exactly like the ones I'd stared at and drawn and stared at some more. They rustled in the wind. A hissing rustle, layered and complex, the sound made by thousands of leaves moving against each other. The kind of thing that you'd describe as a *susurration* or *murmuration* if you felt like busting out the fifty-cent words.

Simon stepped up beside me and looked around the sandspit. The water flowed by silently, but the willows whispered on and on and on.

If you faced downstream so that you couldn't see all the doors, it was pretty. Soft mist, rolling water, silvery leaves. I tried to dredge up some of the excitement I'd felt before. I was standing somewhere completely alien, completely unknown. There was so much possibility, just waiting to be explored.

In the concrete hallway, which was arguably far creepier than a pleasant island full of shrubs, I had been excited. Now what I felt was more like . . .

Dread, I thought, acknowledging it to myself for the first time. *This is dread.*

It wasn't the fact that I was suddenly in another world. I had either made peace with that, or I had convinced myself that I was probably completely out of my mind and I might as well go along with the internal logic.

No, it was something about this place itself.

If you play video games, sometimes you'll encounter a bug where you suddenly fall through the world. Something goes wonky and the landscape that is pretending to be solid suddenly isn't. And you fall through and suddenly you see that the whole virtual world is just a skin a pixel deep, and you're looking at it from the back, like a stage set viewed from behind. All the shapes are still there, all the rocks and mountains and trees, but inverted. You can stand inside things that looked solid just a minute ago and look up through trees that are suddenly chimneys.

I was getting the strangest feeling that the willows were somehow like that. If I dug one up, it wouldn't have roots, it would just be attached to the sand, a thin willow-shaped skin made of the same stuff as the islands and the river. As if the willows and the river were . . . not artificial, exactly, but behind them was something vast and hollow.

Hollow, but not empty.

This is ridiculous, I told myself. *You're just freaking out because this is all so strange, and blaming it on the willows.*

I scuffed at the sand with my foot and dug a small hole. The sand was damp and became wet barely an inch down.

Well, what had I expected? The sand and the willows weren't *really* a single pixel deep.

Physically, maybe not, I thought, digging at the hole.

But some other way. If I took a step wrong, would I come out behind . . . everything?

"What's up?" asked Simon, looking down at my feet as I dug at the sand with my heel. "And what's with the funnels?"

"Eh?"

He pointed with one stockinged foot. He had hairy toes. "There."

I followed his foot and saw a little cone-shaped depression in the sand. It was bafflingly familiar for a moment, then snapped into place.

"Ant lions!" I said, snapping my fingers.

"Huh?"

"They're a bug. Eats ants. They make those little funnels in the sand to catch the ants when they fall in. You see them all over Texas."

"Oh!" Simon stepped carefully around the funnels. "We called 'em doodlebugs in Florida. Yeah, I know what you mean."

I nodded. My mother-in-law's yard in Texas had been full of them. And I was never going to have to go back there for Thanksgiving and listen to my ex-husband's relentlessly successful sister recount her triumphs ever again.

The wave of relief that hit me was absurd. Apparently I'd hated those holidays more than I'd ever realized.

Besides, I thought, *I bet that smug twit with her perfect kids never went to another world. I win that one.*

That the ant lions would dig in such wet sand was odd, but

maybe they had aquatic ants here. There's supposed to be ants that live in weird rafts in South America and climb trees when it floods. No reason you couldn't have swimming ants in Narnia.

My gleeful malice toward my former sister-in-law dispelled a great deal of the dread, which may be the only good turn she ever did me. The willows swayed and rippled as if small animals were moving through them, but it seemed to only be the wind at work.

"We can reach that bunker from here, I think," I said. "Without too much wading."

"Are you sure it's a bunker?"

"No, but I don't know what else to call it." I lifted my hands helplessly and let them drop. "For all I know, every one of these has a hole that leads to a different planet."

"God, I hope not," muttered Simon. "One's hard enough to deal with. Fifty would be entirely too much."

"You think there's only fifty?"

"You think there's more than fifty of these doors?"

I looked around, over the chest-high willow bushes. "I have no idea. There's too much fog. They could go on for miles."

"Or this whole world could be about a hundred yards across and walled in by fog."

I stared at him and he waved his arms. "We don't know! I don't know! Why does it have to be the size of our world? For all we know, it's teeny!"

"Then where would the water come from?" I asked. "Rivers have to have a source."

"Rivers in *our* world do."

I groaned. I wasn't completely willing to abandon my understanding of geography just yet. "Look, we can get to that other . . . whatever it is . . . and look in the door."

As it turned out, we couldn't. The door was closed tight, and when we pushed against it, it didn't give even a fraction. Rust had formed a thick scab around the frame. I frowned at it. "If we had a crowbar . . ."

"Maybe." Simon shook his head. "Look, some of the other doors are wide open. We should go look in those before we waste time prying this one open."

This seemed logical. I looked around to make sure I could still spot our door easily. The last thing I wanted to do was lose track of our entry point. There it was, grass on top, the island with two willows just visible beyond it. No problem. We waded laterally to another door. This one was close to the riverbank, but the water was deeper getting to it. My jeans got soaked to midthigh and I started to shiver.

The door stood open. I pulled my flashlight out of my pack and shone it down the steps. At the bottom, the door was ajar.

Several inches of water stood in the room below, with a slurry of dead willow leaves on top. I shone my flashlight over the still water, not wanting to step down into it. Simon joined me on the threshold, balancing on the single step.

"I'd rather not walk in that," I confessed.

"Me neither."

The flashlight revealed a doorway on the opposite wall, door askew on its hinges, sagging drunkenly against the frame. Rust had eaten away at the bottom. The water continued on behind it. We'd be wading through sludge, full of God knew what.

If there was a portal to somewhere else in there, it wasn't immediately obvious. Honestly, I felt relieved. One extra world, as Simon had said, was more than enough.

"Go back, try another one?"

"Yeah."

There wasn't another one in easy reach. The shore was closest, although, for all I knew, it wasn't really a shore but a much larger island. All I could make out were the willows vanishing into the mist and one or two larger trees that were hunched over, as if to get out of the wind.

"Well, we can test your theory about the world being a hundred yards wide. . . ."

"As long as we can still get back home."

I pointed to our bunker. "Right there."

"Then lead on," said Simon, so I did.

It wasn't a long way, although one unexpected undercut left me soaked to the hips. I was glad I'd put my phone in my backpack when I started to wade. (It had no signal, which didn't surprise me. I'd snapped a couple of photos, which all came out looking like a vague misty river with some lumps in it. As proof of a trip to another world went, it wasn't much. I could just as easily make them into postcards, claim they showed the Loch

Ness Monster, and sell 'em at the museum for a buck apiece.)

We stood on the shore, looking back toward the bunkers. They all looked nearly identical, differing only in whether the doors were open or closed, and by how much. More were closed than open, from what I could see. I had no idea if that meant anything or not.

"Do we go upstream or downstream?" asked Simon.

"No idea. But let me mark this spot, first. Everything looks too much alike." I was having a memory of the Wood between the Worlds in the Narnia books, where every pool led to a different world, and all of the pools were identical. You had to mark your pool or else you might never find it again. I didn't have a good way to mark our bunker and I still knew which one it was, but I didn't want to let it out of my sight and risk losing it for good.

I didn't *think* that each bunker led to another world, but what did I know? Better to mark our place.

The detritus washed on the beach from the river included several stout sticks. I found one with a fork in it and jammed it into the sand so that it stood upright. "There," I said. "Ours is the second one out on the left-hand side."

Simon nodded gravely.

The river had cut away the bank here, and it was a scramble up to the top. From the top, our view was increased by . . . well . . . very little. There was still fog. I felt drops of water falling on me, but I couldn't tell if it was rain or if the fog was just getting thicker. A chunky fog, my dad would have called it. The kind you can get your teeth in. (My dad says about twenty words per year, on average, and is completely overshadowed by my mother. He must have spent one year's allotment on chunky fog for me to remember it now.)

At the top of the bank were more willows. There was also the sort of widely spaced grass you find on sand dunes, and a lot of bare sand and gravel. Ant-lion funnels were scattered across the sandy bits. Mostly, though, there were willows.

I heard the killdeer again, but it only called once and then went silent. No insects. That probably didn't mean anything. My extensive research into willow leaves didn't include whether a bug ate them, and anyway, I couldn't imagine most bugs would be out and about in the fog. Even the ant lions were probably taking the day off.

I was so glad to see a tree that wasn't a willow that I made for the first one I saw through the fog. It was about twelve feet tall and hunched over like an old woman.

It had shaggy, furrowed bark and splotches of lichen on the trunk. It smelled like cedar, but that's as much as I could tell you.

"Well, they have plants other than willows here," I said.

"I'll make a note of it." Simon unscrewed the cap on his flask and took a slug of coffee and whiskey, possibly toasting the existence of the non-willow.

Another couple droplets of rain or chunky fog splattered my face and arms. "I think it's starting to rain."

"Not like we can get much wetter." Simon glanced at his rolled-up pants and soggy fishnets. His look had gone from Safari Mad Hatter to Bedraggled Drag Queen. He was still wearing it better than I did.

I gazed up at the sky, which looked exactly like the rest of the fog, only straight up. A fogdrop splashed on my forehead and ran down the sides of my nose.

"Is that a rock?" Simon pointed. "It looks like a dark blob to me."

For once it wasn't his eyesight. It looked like a dark blob to me, too. A vague, rectangular shape, the opposite direction from the river. We made our way toward it.

It was a school bus.

Buried axle deep in the sand, tilted a little to one side, it was utterly recognizable and utterly out of place. Willows had grown up and through the back bumper, and rust had crept up the sides from the wheel wells. It had been there for a while, though in this damp, rust probably didn't take long. Still, it read SCHOOL BUS in the right place on the front and BYRICOPA COUNTY PUBLIC SCHOOLS on the side. And there's nothing that looks like a school bus except a school bus.

Except . . . except . . .

It was the wrong color.

Honestly, if it had been blue or something, it might have been easier to take. I would have shrugged and said that perhaps the school buses in this world were simply blue. But this was just close enough that it was jarring. School buses are usually goldenrod, and this one was a shade darker, with too much orange to it. Carrot colored.

I'm a graphic designer, I notice these things. If it had been paler, I could have chalked it up to bleaching in the sun, but not this. Also, the font they had used for SCHOOL BUS was a serif font, not sans serif. It was pretty chunky, still easy enough to stencil on, but . . . serif.

I had a suspicion that when we went back to the museum, if I looked up *Byricopa County*, I wouldn't find anything.

Simon looked at me and I looked at him. Then I shrugged and picked my way across the sand to the bus.

The sand was full of the same little ant-lion funnels as the tiny beach. Some of them were quite large, the size of a saucer. I skirted around those. Whatever insect had made them probably couldn't eat a person, but I suspected it could give me a nasty pinch, and I didn't want to risk the possibility that this world had ant lions that could bite through a sandal.

The bus door was on the side tilted down, and it was open. The inside was empty—just rows of seats, in the fake green leather familiar to school buses the world over. Apparently the universe over.

I opened my mouth to say something—I've forgotten what—and the sky tore open with a ripping sound and began to pour rain.

"Jesus," muttered Simon as we both ran for the empty bus.

Thunder crashed overhead. The rain came down in a solid sheet, like standing in the shower.

Simon's top hat gave him a measure of protection, so his hair was only soggy. I was drenched from head to toe in the three seconds it took for me to reach the bus door.

"Well, at least we've got someplace to sit," I said, moving toward the green leather seats.

"Don't!"

The note of panic in Simon's voice was so real and immediate that I froze in place. "What?"

"Don't sit there." He took off his hat and shoved the lank strands of wet hair out of his face.

I looked at him, puzzled, then back at the rows of seats. "Err . . . what's wrong?"

"I don't know." He put his hat back on, hunching his shoulders a little. "Just . . . don't sit there."

You can, if you find yourself in a strange world, ignore the intuition of your friend who devoured his twin in the womb and is seeing the world with one of her eyes. You would probably be foolish to do so, but I suppose it's an option that you do have.

I was not feeling quite so foolish. I sat down with my back against the front wall, near the driver's seat. Simon sat down beside me. We stared at the long rows of green seats and waited out the rain.

8

I know I dozed off. It's probably a good thing. Because I was half-asleep, what I saw seemed like a dream at first, so I didn't do anything stupid, like leap up screaming.

In my dream, I was still sitting in the bus, knees drawn up, head leaned back against the dashboard, under the complicated set of handles that the driver would use to open the door. I was looking down the center aisle of the bus, except that the seats were no longer empty.

They were full of children, except the children were *inside* the seats.

I could see them moving under the green leather, distending it as they pushed forward against it. It molded to their faces and shoulders, drew tight around their fingers as they reached out through the leather. Were they trying to get out? I couldn't tell.

They might simply have been moving restlessly, as children do, climbing over the seat backs and turning and talking to each other, waving their arms and poking each other.

It wasn't until Simon's hand closed over mine that I started to think it wasn't really a dream.

"Carrot . . . ," he said quietly. His nails dug into my palm.

The fake leather made groaning, whispering sounds. At least, I hoped like hell that it was the leather. Otherwise the children were talking to each other in voices of old springs and creaking fabric and . . . no, it had to be the leather.

I seemed to be moving impossibly slowly as I turned my head. "You see them, too," I said just as quietly.

He nodded.

I looked back to the children trapped in the seats. I don't know if they heard us or simply sensed that I was awake, but they began to move more violently. Fists punched against the leather. I watched one girl—I was nearly sure she was a girl— pull her knees up against her chest. The green leather molded itself over her arms as she leaned forward, hugging her knees. I could see the individual barrettes in her hair, the bracelet wrapped around one thin wrist, but the way the leather pulled tight across her face left her with blank eye sockets and a lipless, tented mouth.

This is real, I thought sluggishly. *This is really happening. I am here and this is not a dream.*

Simon's nails dug deeper into my palm, but I barely felt it.

It occurred to me, belatedly, to drag my eyes to the driver's seat. The driver's seat, which was *right beside me.*

Stillness. The seat was still exactly the same as it had been.

And yet . . . I don't think it was empty. I had a powerful sense that if I looked at about head height and somehow looked—I don't know, *sideways*, or *through*, I would meet the eyes of someone sitting there. Someone made up of the empty space that I was looking through.

The school bus driver hadn't abandoned the kids, but whatever had happened to the driver had been . . . different.

"On three," Simon breathed. "One . . . two . . ."

On three, we both threw ourselves out of the bus. The rain had let up to a drizzle, but I didn't care. I would have plunged into a rain of fire to be off that bus.

The rain had cleared up a great deal of fog, which is probably the only reason we didn't get separated. We tore through the willows. Simon's boots banged against his chest as he ran, and he was probably going to have massive bruises there. (He told me later that he didn't even feel it, which didn't surprise me at all.)

The willows slapped at us with thin stems and long silver leaves. In retrospect, either of us could have fallen and broken our legs or our neck, but we just collected thin red welts and leaves stuck to us.

It was still so *quiet.* Even with the fog lifted and our breath coming in gasps, even with my heart hammering in my ears, it was unnaturally silent. As if there was nothing in the world but wind and water and willows and two terrified people and a school bus full of . . .

Ghosts? Spirits?

I had the feeling again, of things waiting on the other side of reality. The kids had been on the other side, pushing against the world. And the driver. The driver had been there. I couldn't *see* them, but there had been someone *right there*, and whatever had separated us had been as thin as a single pixel.

Don't think about that. Just run.

We reached the river's edge.

And stopped.

And stared.

"Where's the stick?" gasped Simon. "*Where is it?*"

"Never mind the stick, where's the *beach?*"

The narrow sand-and-gravel beach was gone. The river had swollen under the heavy rain. Only a few feet, but a few feet was all that had been needed.

Our tracks were gone. The stick pointing to our door was gone.

"Shit," Simon whispered. "Which one's the way home?"

The bunkers all looked the same. From this angle, all the open doors looked the same. The islands were all nearly identical little green mounds. We could see much farther now, for all the good it did us. The opposite shore of the river looked exactly like this one. It was also a lot farther over than I'd thought, and there were a *lot* more bunkers than I'd thought.

Second one out. Left-hand side. From where?

We're in the woods between the worlds and we've lost track of which one is ours. . . .

I tried to clamp that thought down before it could get much further. "Let's think about this logically."

"I'd like to panic for a minute, if it's all the same to you!" snapped Simon. "There were things in that bus! Ghosts or—or something! I don't know! And the stick's gone and now we don't know how to get back and we're going to be stuck here with that bus full of whatever the hell it was!"

I waited. Honestly, I was rather glad he was panicking, because if he hadn't, I was going to. Panic was definitely called for right now, but for some reason, if there's two people, only one of you panics at a time.

He put his face in his hands and breathed heavily for a few minutes.

I gazed upstream to give him a little time. The fog had cleared, but the clouds were still steel blue, and they had cracked open to let beams of light through, the kind that look like an inspirational postcard. But the beams were coming through at a low angle and dusk was starting to pool under the willows. The eerie, regular shapes of the bunkers looked like . . . like . . . I wracked my brain for a comparison that wasn't *gravestones* or *teeth* or something worse.

Egg cartons?

. . . Yes, all right. Egg cartons. Sure.

For some stupid reason, all I could think was that if it was light here, it was dark at home, so if it got dark here, it must be getting light at home, and that meant that pretty soon I'd be late opening the museum and I'd be letting down Uncle Earl. Which was ridiculous, because Uncle Earl would never blame me in a million years, but that made it worse.

Get a grip, I told myself grimly. *If you can't find the right bunker, you'll not only not have opened the museum, you'll have left a door to Narnia open in his wall. That's much worse.*

Shit, and you left Beau locked in the bathroom, too. I winced.

No, no, he can drink out of the toilet. When I don't answer the phone, Mom will come over to yell at me and she'll let him out. And maybe discover the hole in the wall.

Please, God, if you love me, don't let me be stuck in this horrible alternate Narnia with my mother.

Simon finally straightened and put his palms on his legs. "All right," he said tiredly.

"Better?"

"Not particularly."

"That bus . . . ," I started to say, and stopped.

He held up a hand. "Let's . . . not. Not right now. I can't. After we're home, maybe. Now what?"

"Well, look." I waved to the line of bunkers. "We know it's one of the ones that's a little back from the shore, right? It was the second one out, with just grass on top. And it has to be one of the ones with the door partway open. So we just have to check those until we find the right one."

Simon frowned. "Assuming we're standing in the right spot."

"What?"

"The right spot." He waved his hands. "Look, my vision isn't great. Is this where we were before? This all looks the same to me, and I wasn't paying attention to what direction I was running."

I opened my mouth to say that *of course* it was the same spot, then closed it again.

Was it? The riverbank looked the same up and down its length. That twisted tree might have been the oak we saw earlier, but there was another one off in the distance. We were near a bend in the river, but the earlier fog meant that I had no idea how close to the bend we should be. There had been two shrubs on top of an island in a line behind ours, but I suddenly realized that the concept of a line depended very much on where you were standing. That island over there had three willows, but from the other side, would it look like two?

Simon's vision was good enough to read my expression. He muttered, "Fuck," took his top hat off, and dragged his fingers through his hair.

"There can't be that many that have open doors." I stepped down into the water. "Come on. I want to get out of here before it gets dark."

✳

We waded to five of them, and the water definitely felt deeper, but I couldn't be sure if I was going too far or if the water had risen or if I was just paranoid. Two had closed doors at the bottom. We could see those without going down the steps, which saved time. Three were open. The first two were all the way open and clearly not ours. The last one was open partway, but when I ran the light over the gap in the doorway, it became obvious that it wasn't ours because of the six inches of standing water in the bottom, and the kind of algae that indicated it wasn't a recent development.

If we'd found one that had another portal in it, I'd have been seriously tempted to just go through it. Maybe it would be like a subway stop and we'd come out a couple of blocks away from the Wonder Museum. And if it wasn't, if we wound up in . . . I don't know, Tibet or Uganda or somewhere where we didn't speak the language, we could presumably find an embassy, and we wouldn't be near that horrible bus.

What if you found a portal and it wasn't to earth, it was to the world the bus was from? What if it went somewhere else? How would you know?

Fine. We should only take a door to the Wonder Museum.

But there were no portals. Looking through the doors showed only damp concrete, not the friendly lights of the Wonder Museum. No big holes in the walls that led to some clearly different space. Maybe our entry was the only one, and somehow the unknown tourist had knocked a hole in the fabric of reality with his elbow.

"Look," said Simon, "it's going to be dark really soon. We're not going to find the right one. Let's take one of the ones with the closed doors, get down in the stairwell, and stay there for the night."

"The closed doors? But if something comes after us, we'll be trapped."

"And if we take one with an open door, something could come out of the bunker at us. At least this way, we've only got to watch from one direction."

I thought of a dark, yawning hole at my back, sitting there through the night, waiting for something to come out of the blackness. . . .

"Yeah," I said. "Yeah, okay. But let's try one more."

We slogged out into the stream again.

❉

The next one had a door standing ajar at the bottom. I shone my flashlight through the gap, hoping against hope . . . and my hopes were immediately dashed. The opposite wall did not have an opening, and there was a chest-high wall between the wall and the door, with bits of rusted rebar standing out from the top. Not our bunker.

I sighed, turned, and that's when I saw movement over Simon's shoulder.

I dropped instinctively down on the steps, yanking Simon down with me. He didn't yelp or make any kind of sound, just went flat beside me. Later, I would think that Simon's life had prepared him for this sort of thing rather better than mine had prepared me.

A figure came out of the gloom. They seemed to be standing on the water at first, but it rapidly became obvious that they were standing in a small boat, poling it along, like a gondolier.

They looked human enough. They didn't have tentacles or extra arms. They wore a faded shirt and loose drawstring pants, in a style that could be five or five thousand years old. I couldn't see well enough to make out things like zippers. Or pointed ears, for that matter.

They poled the boat along without making any more noise than the soft splash of the pole. If I had to guess—male, mid-forties. Seamed brown face, black hair under a broad hat, nothing that would stand out as being from any particular region in our world.

But despite how normal they looked, that feeling came rushing back, the one I'd had before, that I was watching a thin skin of reality stretched over something vast and hollow. As if the boatman and the river and maybe even the sun piercing the clouds were all paint on a flat canvas, and if I had the right sort of knife, I could cut through that canvas and see what lay beyond.

The boatman poled the boat past, the pole creaking gently in the water. They never even looked at our doorway, at the two of us crouched in the shadows on the stairs.

It's just the aftershock of the school bus, I told myself. *There's nothing inherently wrong with the boatman. It's just paranoia.*

It didn't matter what I told myself. I did not want the boatman to see me, and that was all there was to it.

The boatman passed off to our right and was gone. We listened to the sound of the pole until that, too, was gone.

There was no question of going back out. The man would see us. And maybe he was fine, maybe he was a perfectly normal human, maybe we'd tell him about the bus and the kids under the seats and he'd be horrified. Or maybe he'd yell "Outlanders!" and pull out a gun and shoot us as aliens.

Hell, we *were* aliens, weren't we? This wasn't our world.

Maybe he'd open his mouth and nothing would be inside but willow branches, and the leaves would spill out like flat green words. . . .

Fuck. I didn't know where that thought came from, and I didn't like it one bit.

As if the darkness had followed in the boat's wake, the river was rapidly turning the deep French gray of dusk. (It's a color Designers use it a lot. When you see gray, but with some warm brown in it? That's French gray.)

The wind was rising. I could hear the willows rustling. *The wind in the willows*, but without Ratty and Mole and Badger to lend some practical, earthy advice to the scene.

Shit, if a giant talking rat showed up, I'd probably scream bloody murder, so maybe it was for the best.

"I guess we're spending the night here," I whispered to Simon. "Door or no door."

He nodded glumly. "Guess so. Well, let's see what's down below . . . maybe there'll be a room that's more comfortable."

We descended the stairs without any enthusiasm. I looked over my shoulder a few times. Nothing but river and darkening sky. I almost wished the killdeer would call again, just so that there would be a sound of some kind to break up the heavy silence of the sky and the movement of the willows.

The room below was in the same poured-concrete style as our bunker. It did have a hallway leading off it. It wasn't opposite the door, but set into the right-hand wall. The chest-high wall we'd seen earlier was an odd construction, dividing the room down the middle, like a privacy screen maybe, or a way of denoting two rooms. It was open on both sides.

I shone my flashlight over to the left side. Markings on the wall caught my attention, and I raised the beam of light higher.

On the left-hand wall, in letters eighteen inches high, someone had scratched:

They Can Hear You Thinking

I went to my knees. I went slowly, as if I had just decided to sit down, but I could not have stopped. My heart was hammering as if I'd been running, and I could actually see my blood pulsing in my eyes, a rhythmic sparkle in time to my heartbeat. My mind was a screaming blankness.

"Fuck," said Simon softly. "Fuck, fuck, fuck." He grabbed my shoulder. "Carrot . . ."

"This is bad." I sounded so calm when I said it, too.

"Yeah, it is. Stay with me, Carrot."

Gradually the panic receded. It's not that I was less scared, but kneeling on concrete isn't fun and there was gravel under my knees, and I started to think about how much it hurt, and if I was thinking about the pebble digging into my right calf and the way that one of my sandal straps was twisted under my foot, I wasn't thinking about . . . about whoever They were. The ones who could hear me thinking.

If They're listening right now, they know a lot more about my sandals than they did before, I thought, and then I began to laugh soundlessly.

"Carrot, if this was a movie, I'd slap you to snap you out of it, but I don't think that actually helps, because if you've been slapped, then you just have something else to be hysterical about, don't you?"

"It's fine," I said hoarsely. "I'm fine. I mean, I'm not fine, but I'm . . . yeah, okay."

"It'll be okay. As long as only one of us freaks out at a time."

"I'll do my best." I gestured at the wall. "What . . . who do you think . . . ?"

He took a deep breath. "I don't know. Maybe it's just some crazy person writing crazy shit."

I'd meant *Who do you think They are?* but I didn't try to

clarify. It's not as if he was going to know. He knew exactly as much as I did, no more, no less.

The kids in the bus could hear you thinking? Or people like the man in the boat? Or something we hadn't met yet?

the willows it's the willows they hear you thinking they're listening right now and rustling their leaves and talking to each other

I bit down on my lip and concentrated very hard on the rock under my knee.

"Come on." Simon helped me to my feet. "Let's go look farther in."

"Farther in. Yes." *Don't look at the wall. Look over there. There's another hallway to explore.*

My appetite for exploration had vanished. I wanted to go home. If I didn't get home soon, the museum would be closed for tourists. I'd let Uncle Earl down. Or something would kill us, and then he'd find a gaping hole in his wall and go through it and find the same thing we had, and then whatever had got us would get him, too.

I had to not panic so that I could get home and save Uncle Earl from this awful willow-filled Narnia.

"I hate this," I said conversationally.

"You and me both."

I took a deep breath. I did not look at the words on the wall. If I didn't look at them, they didn't matter. Words are meaningless until you read them.

Simon and I went around the room together, so close that my hip kept bumping his arm. If you didn't know better—or at least know Simon—you'd think we were an item, but I'll tell you, this was the least sexy intimacy I've ever had, and I include gynecological exams in that.

No, we just didn't dare lose track of each other for an instant because the whole world seemed hostile. And I had a thought somewhere way down, where I didn't even dare vocalize it, that if I lost sight of Simon, he might come back as something . . . other. That it would look like Simon and maybe even talk like Simon, but somehow it wouldn't *move* like Simon.

And then I'd be alone.

I don't think I've ever been so grateful for another human being's presence. Not in all the years I was married, certainly. That led to me thinking of how Mark would have handled being here, and I gave a short, choking laugh.

"Carrot?"

"Thinking how glad I am that you're here and not my ex."

He snorted. "That bad, eh?"

"He'd probably still be screaming that none of this was real. Or demanding to see a manager."

"I could try that, if you think it would help."

"That's okay." The words on the wall were behind me now. My ex had done me that much good. If I didn't look at them, I didn't need to think about them. Okay. I was okay.

Little brass tubes littered the floor on the far side of the wall.

Someone had fired a gun here. I could imagine how deafening that sound must have been in the enclosed space. You'd be deaf for an hour afterward, if not permanently.

There were stains on the wall and floor, too, but I couldn't tell you if that was blood or water or some discoloration of the concrete. There were stains *everywhere*. If they were all blood, somebody had been systematically murdering people in these bunkers for decades.

. . . Thanks, brain. That was a very helpful thought. I'm so glad I had it.

Hannibal Lecter from Dimension X! screamed my brain.

"They shot at something."

"Or killed themselves," I said gloomily.

"I don't think you need *quite* so many bullets to kill yourself."

This was an undeniably valid point.

"Through the opening, then," I said, sweeping my flashlight over toward the opening in the wall.

And stopped.

"Oh, God," I said softly.

As the light passed over the wall with the door, the one we'd entered from, it caught more letters. They were scratched in the paint, a foot and a half high, just like the other ones. We just hadn't seen them because we hadn't looked behind ourselves until now.

The same blocky shapes. If I had to guess, I'd say the same person had written them.

Pray They Are Hungry

I did not freak out again. I looked at the letters. I looked at them for quite a long time, then I looked away and Simon didn't say anything and I didn't say anything and we both did not say anything so loudly that the room rang with our silence. It felt as if we were standing on the skin of a soap bubble, and if either of us so much as breathed, the bubble would pop and I would descend into a screaming breakdown.

But neither of us broke the bubble. I turned away from the words and walked into the opening.

9

It was another hallway. I wasn't surprised. One side dead-ended about twenty feet down. The floor was an alluvial fan of debris, with a thin puddle of water against the wall. I turned my flashlight the other way, joining Simon's light, which shone against a door.

More metal, more rust. Standing ajar.

Simon and I looked at each other. I couldn't see more than the vague outline of his face and top hat, but that didn't matter. I sighed, squared my shoulders, and went forward.

Whatever was in there, I felt as if it couldn't be as bad as what might be outside.

(Looking back, I have no idea why I felt that way. They, whatever They were, could just as easily have been something that lived in a bunker and came out. The brass shells could have been from an attempt to kill Them in Their lair. Fortunately, I did not think of that at the time.)

"English," said Simon abruptly.

The non sequitur jarred me out of my thoughts, and, happily, my terror. "What?"

"The writing was in English. The school bus, too. Not Cyrillic or whatever that was."

"Oh." He was right. I gnawed on my lower lip, still staring at the half-open door. "It was, wasn't it?" Despite the strange font choice on the bus, it had definitely been English. I'd been so distracted, I hadn't thought about it.

Simon hooked his elbow through mine and we made our way down the hallway together. I suspected he had no more desire to lose track of me than I did of him.

Well, if I don't make it back, he has to report me missing, and then the cops will have some words about all that LSD. . . . No, that was unkind. I believed that Simon liked me for my own sake, and vice versa. We were neighbors and maybe even friends.

God, I hope we're friends. I'd hate to be trapped in a hellish otherworld with someone I didn't like.

Simon touched the door. Either the water hadn't made it to this side or the rust was more recent, because it actually moved. In grim silence we watched it swing inward.

After about thirty seconds when we were not attacked by brain goblins, I said, "Well . . . ," and the two of us, arms still linked, went sideways through the door.

It was a larger room than the one with the writing, although most of that was length. The entryway had been divided up into what looked like a kitchen area, with crude counters made of packing crates. I moved my flashlight over five empty cots, two made up with olive-drab blankets, two rumpled and messy, the heads pushed up against the wall. The air smelled vaguely of mildew and dust, but not of rot.

"People lived here," I said unnecessarily. I shone the flashlight under each cot in turn—*don't think about eyes looking back at you don't think about things under the bed don't think about people hiding here from the things that hear your thoughts*—but there was nothing.

"And left under their own power. At least two of them." Simon wiggled the beam of light over the unmade beds.

"Or four, and two were slobs."

"Look, I don't make my bed in the morning either. I'm just going to sleep on it again."

"I'm not judging."

We made our way down the row of cots. Each one had a footlocker, surprisingly free of rust. It all looked very military, except . . .

Simon flicked his flashlight over the wall over the head of one of the unmade beds. There was a bolt in the wall, and a rosary dangling from the bolt.

"Huh," I said.

"No matter where you go, the Jesuits got there first."

This struck me as hilarious for some reason. I shoved the side of my hand into my mouth to keep from howling with laughter. Simon chuckled.

"Right," I said after a minute. "Right, okay. I'm fine."

"That's the spirit." He highlighted the very end of the room with the beam. A curtain hung there, so stiff with age and disuse that it cracked like a board when I pushed it aside.

The cubicle behind it was perhaps four feet on a side. There was a bucket. The contents of the bucket had dried, which was probably for the best.

"Oh, look," I said, "there's a roll of toilet paper left and everything."

"How civilized."

We left the cubicle. We looked at the cots, then at each other, then back at the cots.

"What do you think?" Simon said.

"Shut the door, take a cot?"

"I guess that's the best we're going to get. Better than sitting in the room out front, anyway."

The door closed. It even had a dead bolt. We opened and closed the door several times to make sure that we could get it open again, then shot the bolt and turned back to the cots.

"I'd rather take the made-up ones," I said. "It feels less like I'm sleeping in a dead person's bed."

"Maybe they aren't dead," he said hopefully. "Maybe they went home."

"You think?"

"It's possible. Anyway, we didn't find any more skeletons."

"Yeah, that's true." I looked at the cot again. "You're not . . . um . . . getting any kind of vibe off these, are you? Like in the bus?"

Simon sighed. "I don't know *what* I got in the bus. I just saw you headed for the seats and it was like I was watching someone about to walk off a cliff."

"You probably saved my life."

The flashlight beam moved as he shrugged. "It was probably the eye, not me. Sometimes I see things in our world, too."

"What sort of things?"

He shrugged again. "Not, like, ghosts or anything. Well, I don't think I see ghosts. I can't see real people all that well either unless the light's really good, so for all I know, sometimes I do see ghosts, and they're just blurry like everybody else."

I had not previously contemplated the focal length required for ghosts, but was glad to think about that instead of the willows. "Huh. You'd think they'd be really in focus instead."

"Right? Anyway, mostly what I see are just weird colors around things. Sometimes stuff looks dark that shouldn't be, although I won't swear that's not the depth perception. But nothing like the bus."

"Tell your twin thanks for me, then."

"I'll pass that along."

I could have let it drop. I wanted to let it drop. But . . . "Nothing like the bus?"

He groaned. "Did you see the driver?"

"No. I *knew* something was there, but I didn't see it. Did you?"

"Yeah." For a minute I thought he was going to stop there. He shone the light over the door again, as if double-checking that it was closed. "I saw her."

"Her?"

"Yeah. You know those animations people do, where the cubes turn themselves inside out? They're supposed to show you the fourth dimension or some shit?"

"Right."

"It was like that. She was sitting in the chair and then she sort of moved and turned inside out, and she was *around* the spot she'd been in. But she was looking at me the whole time."

"Yikes," I said, which was the understatement of the century. "All I saw was the kids in the seats."

"She was farther away than they were." He laughed, although without any humor. "I can't tell you how far away that wall is, but I could tell you that."

"What does that mean?"

"How the hell should I know? I don't know what's going on. I don't know how any of it works. I don't even have real depth perception, my brain's learned to fake it. So that's all I've got. My brain said she was just . . . farther away."

Farther away. On the back side of reality, but not pressed against it like the kids had been? "Fuck."

"Yeah."

I sat down on the nearest cot. It creaked, but the fabric didn't seem to be rotted out. The blankets were stiff and dusty. I used my backpack as a pillow, which was lumpy but better than nothing.

"Don't go out without me," I said. "Promise me?"

"Christ, no!" Simon grabbed the second cot and dragged it so that it was touching mine. "You neither. I'm not leaving this room without you."

I slid under the blankets. Nothing bit my toes, and the blankets did not seem to be a cleverly disguised monster devouring me from the ankles up. I switched off my flashlight. I heard Simon's blankets rustling, then he switched his light off, too.

The room was pitch-black. Really, really black, mine-shaft-on-a-moonless-night black. I stared up into the darkness and then closed my eyes because I didn't want to think about something hovering above me that I couldn't see.

Pray they are hungry.

"I hate this," I said quietly.

"Me too."

"I was thinking, though . . ."

"Yeah?"

"About the English writing."

I didn't want to think about what had been written in English on the wall, but it wasn't like I wasn't going to be lying in the dark with *pray they are hungry* running through my head anyway.

"Look, you read the Narnia books, right? All of them?"

I nodded, forgetting he couldn't see me. "Yeah. Even the one where they shot the talking horses, and I was pretty pissed about that."

"Right. You remember *Magician's Nephew*? With the Wood between the Worlds?"

I laughed, although without much humor. "I've been thinking about that since we got here. It's like a weird reverse version, isn't it? Instead of grass with pools of water, it's a lot of water with little islands of grass."

"Well, what if it's like that? Lots of worlds touching this one? Not just ours. And sometimes people find ways through. So you'd get someone from a world that's a lot different from ours, and they leave graffiti in an alphabet that we don't know, and then you get people from one that's almost exactly like ours, and they write in English."

"Except the school buses are a different color and they use a serif font. . . ." I rolled over on the cot to face the sound of his voice. "Yeah. I can see it. Except we haven't found any other holes. If we're in the Wood between the Worlds, we're real short of pools."

"Maybe they don't happen all the time."

"Maybe they don't exist at all, and the Cyrillic is just people with bad handwriting from our world. Or this one." I stared at the dark. "We could be in Byricopa County right now."

"I thought of that," said Simon. "But how did the school bus get there?"

"Eh?"

"No road. It's axle deep in sand. You don't take school buses off-roading."

I had no good answer for that. He wasn't wrong. "But why a hole in the Wonder Museum, of all places?"

"Have you *seen* your uncle's museum? If a hole to another world was going to open up anywhere, it'd totally be in your back room."

I grumbled. Fine, yes. There are weirder places all over the world, but certainly none in Hog Chapel. "Okay, so now we're positing a whole bunch of . . . what, parallel universes?"

"Do you have another explanation?"

"Not unless we go back to the black mold, I guess." I mulled it over. "But who made the bunkers?"

"Dunno. We saw that guy in the boat, maybe there's a bunch more people somewhere. Or I guess if a school bus can get through, there's probably a hole big enough for a cement truck from somewhere else. Or maybe they were here already and people just hide in them because . . ."

He trailed off, which I was grateful for because I didn't want to think about the *because*.

"I suppose the people who left these cots could have made the bunkers. They're that military poured-concrete-type thing. Maybe we can find the military base they came from and get help."

Simon's silence was oddly loud.

"Are you about to tell me something I don't like?"

"Do you really want to tell a military organization from an alternate universe that there's a big hole to our reality lying around? Seems like a good way to get invaded."

". . . Shit."

I brooded about the holes and alien invasions for a bit. "We're assuming a lot here. There's no hole in this bunker. Or any of the ones we looked in. So far we've got exactly one hole and two worlds."

"What about the bus, though?"

"I'm not sure adding another universe satisfies Occam's razor."

"We saw kids stuck inside seats and a woman turning herself inside out and you want to talk about Occam's razor?"

"Fine, fine . . ." I held up my hands, even though he couldn't see them. "What if they *were* from a third universe? What would that explain?"

I heard him swallow. "Maybe they got stuck in between."

"In between worlds?"

"In between . . . something."

The skin of the world is very thin and they're behind its skin pushing out and if they push too hard they make a hole and the hole goes somewhere else. . . .

"Tomorrow," I said firmly, trying to drown out the gibbering voice of panic. "Tomorrow we will find our own hole and we'll go home and we'll patch up the wall and then we will go to the liquor store and I will max out my credit card and we will drink until we can't stand up."

"See, I knew you were my kinda people."

I closed my eyes and I must have been exhausted, because I fell asleep almost immediately.

*

I woke up in the dark. It was impossible to tell what time it was. "Simon?"

"I'm here."

"Do you think it's light out yet?"

"We can go check."

We went together, using only one flashlight. It had occurred to me that conserving batteries might be important. I hated the thought because it meant that we might be here in the dark for a long time, and I didn't think I could handle that. Sooner or later we'd run out of granola bars and laced coffee.

Pray they are hungry.

We unbolted the door and crept down the hallway. A thin gray light came from the open door at the top of the stairs. Simon turned the flashlight off and we made our way up the steps together, dropping low, the same way we had when watching the boatman.

It was not yet dawn. Maybe we'd slept a long time. Maybe nights were shorter here. Either way, I was definitely late opening the Wonder Museum, and we were going to miss a whole lot of tourist income. The Black Hen, too. If we did get back, we were going to have to come up with a good explanation for the coffee shop regulars.

I knew that it was a stupid thing to be worrying about, but if I was worrying about what to tell people when I got home, I wasn't worrying about being in a bunker in a nightmare world where children were imprisoned inside their school bus and outside reality. I'm not saying it was a good coping mechanism, just that it was what I had.

The gray light came from the horizon. The fog had lifted, or at least settled far enough that I could clearly make out a horizon line. It was dark and irregular but low against the sky. Trees, not hills. The grayness was less light than absence of dark, a cold, smudgy brightness behind the black lines of the willows.

Without leaving the shelter of the bunker entrance, I couldn't see if the moon was up. I could make out a few stars, but I'm not going to pretend that I know anything about astronomy. I can find the Big Dipper, the Little Dipper, and Orion's Belt, and that's where my knowledge ends. These could be the same stars I knew from home or be wildly different, and I wouldn't be able to tell the difference. All I knew was that the stars I could see didn't make up one of the Dippers.

All that said, I suspected that the moon must be up, because the nearest willows shone silver with it.

One of the willow islands was across from and a little to the left of our bunker, and the wind was shaking the trees, sliding through the long silver leaves, branches moving back and forth, back and forth, while they hissed and whispered and snickered to each other. I did not like the sound.

The next island farther back was laced with darker silver, and beyond that they faded into blackness. I strained my ears for the sounds of insects or night birds or frogs or anything, but there was only the hiss and chatter of willows.

Simon's hand closed over my forearm. I glanced over at him, and in the dim light I could see his expression was strained.

"Do you see it?" he whispered, so softly that it could have been mistaken for a broken breath.

I almost said *See what?* But then I saw it and didn't need to ask anymore.

Something was moving in the willows.

10

Simon and I drew together instinctively, shoulder to shoulder, watching the willows twist and sway in the wind.

My first thought was that my eyes were playing tricks on me. The willows were full of irregular shapes, their branches braiding and unbraiding, gaps forming and vanishing as they moved. But in the gaps, in the spaces made between them, I could see more.

There's a concept in graphic design called *negative space*. It's all the spaces where you haven't put something. If I draw a figure eight, for example, the negative space would be the two holes and the space around the outside of the lines. A good designer can use that to advantage. If you've ever looked at the FedEx logo, the negative space between the *E* and the *x* forms an arrow pointing forward.

It isn't always your friend. I once did a design where the negative space . . . well, let's just say it had a certain male anatomical quality to it. Sometimes when you've stared at something for too long, you miss the really obvious.

Whatever was in the willows, it was made of the negative space between the branches. I don't know if I can explain it better than that. As the branches moved and swayed and the leaves shifted, they made shapes in all the places that they weren't.

Those shapes were full of bodies. Not human bodies. Not even physical bodies as I understood it. But something there nonetheless. Silver light, though here and there I caught glimpses of bronze, patterns of light and shadow moving up through the willow branches. They rose up from the sand and slithered through the willows, huge and inhuman, shifting like smoke.

I tried to focus on one, hoping that it would resolve into just an optical illusion, just the play of wind and leaves. *Like clouds,* I thought. *Like shapes in clouds. That's all it is.*

The body I focused on was faceless. Its neck stretched out, twisting like the willow stems, and I could not tell if it had two legs or ten or a hundred, if its arms were really arms or if they were tree roots. It slipped up from the sand, squirmed eyelessly through the willows, while its shape changed as leaves fell across it.

When it reached the top of the willows, it rose up in a drift of amber light, joining dozens—hundreds—of other shapes rising from the other willows. They twisted, hardly visible, above the bushes, then they vanished.

One, I could have explained away. Dozens were harder. And the colors were not quite right and they were too clearly bodies, even if they weren't bodies of anything that I understood.

Are these Them? Should I be frightened?

The figures did not seem to notice we were watching. If they could hear us thinking, they didn't care. They were just there, twisting, streaming upward, a vision I didn't understand.

"That can't be real," I whispered to Simon. "It's an illusion. It's just the light."

"Black mold," he said, not as if he believed it. That was understandable. I didn't believe it was a trick of the light, either, yet the light seemed to be part of it, as if the light were bringing the spaces in the willows to life, animating them, giving them form and substance beyond what they had possessed.

I was not as frightened as I should have been. The things rising up through the willows did not seem to have anything to do with us. There was nothing human about them, nothing I could get a grip on to fear. Even the long, sinewy shapes looked like willow roots, not like tentacles. Everything in a Lovecraft story has tentacles. These weren't like that. They didn't look like squid or werewolves or brain goblins. They looked like the dreams of trees cast in bronze. What I felt was more like wonder than terror.

It was hypnotic to watch them, like staring into a fire as it burned. Simon and I must have lain across the steps watching for an hour at least, long enough for me to start shivering, for the concrete to leave flat red marks on my elbows and knees. The dawn light grew no brighter, but stayed a sullen gray mark on the edge of the world.

Then they vanished.

We both jerked upright, as if we had fallen asleep.

Something went through the willows. Not a ghost this time. Not a shape made of the wind and the leaves. This was solid and dark, and we saw the branches bow down as it passed.

The wonder snapped like a bone breaking, and horror rushed in. Whatever was moving was dark and solid, and the willows bent down as if they were worshipping it. We watched it move through the bushes as if it were going somewhere, rapid and businesslike.

Then it, too, was gone.

I had no problem believing that the solid thing had been one of Them, whatever They were. Every animal instinct screamed at me to get away from it, to run away and curl into the smallest ball I could and pray that it went away.

The feeling didn't lessen when it vanished. If anything, it got worse. They were somewhere and now I couldn't see Them and that meant They could be anywhere, They could be moving around behind the world, like the kids on the school bus, They could suddenly come out right on top of us. . . .

By mutual unspoken consent, Simon and I backed down

the stairs together. The silvery willowlight gave him an ashen pallor, but I'm not sure if regular light would have made him look any better.

We didn't talk until we had retreated to the far room and bolted the door. The *skreek* of the bolt made me shake with relief. I knew that was ridiculous—the things we had been watching were made of smoke and silver light, they could have slithered under the door—but the bolt divided the world into *in here* and *out there*, and as long as they were *out there*, we would be safe. Surely.

"What was that?" whispered Simon. "What did we just see?"

"The dark thing at the end or the things in the bushes?"

"The ones in the bushes can't have been real," croaked Simon. "Not *really* real."

I just looked at him.

"They can't," he said, as if I'd argued. "Look—shit—one time when I was high, I watched the clouds turn into ghost trilobites and eat the moon, okay?"

"We're not high. I mean, not unless you cut the coffee with more than whiskey."

"Black mold," he said hopelessly.

I leaned against the concrete wall, feeling the coldness against the back of my head. "But I saw it, too. If we were both high, we'd have seen different things, right?"

He fell silent. I thought for a minute that he might cry, and I didn't know what I'd do then. Instead he pinched the bridge of his nose for a bit, as if fighting back tears, then he said, "What did *you* see?"

"Shapes in the willows. In the gaps. Big shapes, going up and up. *Gods.*"

I don't know why I said that last word, but once I said it, I didn't regret it. It wasn't quite the right word, but it was closer than anything else I had. The willows had been full of gods or ghosts or spirits. Something alive.

"Not human gods," said Simon.

"No. Gods of this place, maybe. Or the willows, anyway." The bunker didn't seem to have much to do with those strange, stretching shapes.

"And the thing that came after them . . . ?"

I spread my hands helplessly. "I don't know." The sudden appearance of the shadow in the willows and the vanishing of the spirits had reminded me of when my ex-husband used to fill the bird feeder in the yard. One minute the bushes would be full of twittering activity, then he'd step outside and the birds would all rush away and fall silent, waiting for the big scary thing to leave.

Pray they are hungry.

"What did you see?" I asked. "The second thing, I mean."

He shook his head. "It was different. Bigger. Solid. Not here, but solid . . . somewhere."

I tried to explain about the birds to Simon. Probably I babbled a lot. He shook his head, frustrated. "So is *Them* the willow spirits or the big thing? Or neither of them, and they meant the guy in the boat, or the . . . whatever that was on the bus . . . or something else we haven't seen yet. How can we tell?"

I groaned. He wasn't wrong.

Simon sighed. "If I had to guess, I didn't feel like the spirits we saw were dangerous. I'm not suggesting we go roll around in the shrubbery, but I don't think they had anything to do with us, really. It was more like the light was making them alive for a bit, and then it stopped. It felt like . . . oh, like weather. Like just a thing that's here."

"Weather?" I tried to focus on that thought. Yes. I could see it. The silvery light had been like wind, except instead of making shapes in the clouds, it had brought shapes in the branches to life. Then something had come along and the light had changed.

"What about the second thing?" I asked.

"I would *not* fuck with that thing."

We sat in glum silence for a while. I wondered if dawn had progressed at all, but I didn't feel like going up to check.

The silence was broken by a loud growl. I would have panicked, except that it came from my stomach.

I rummaged in my backpack, but I'd eaten the last PowerBar hours ago. Simon came up empty, too.

"We can make it a few days without food," I said. "But we're going to have to find water."

"We're surrounded by water."

"Do *you* want to drink it?"

He grunted. After a minute he said, "Well, we might not have much choice."

"Won't we get the snail parasites?"

"Hell if I know. But I keep thinking about what they say about fairies, you know?"

"What?"

"If you eat or drink food from fairyland, you have to stay there forever."

"I thought that was only pomegranates."

"No, that's Greek myths. Jeez, what are they teaching kids in schools these days?"

"You're what, four years older than I am?"

"I'm forty-one."

"Seven years, then. Apparently they phased fairyland survival out of the curriculum before I graduated."

"Yeah, it's all just standardized-test prep now."

We both started giggling. It was hysteria, plain and simple, and it was only possible because the bolt was there. *Out there*, there were monsters, but *in here*, we were hilarious.

My stomach growled again. I wiped at my streaming eyes and sighed. "Well, if They can hear us thinking, at least They're getting quality entertainment."

"That's the spirit. Imagine if we were thinking about spreadsheets or something."

"Hey, my catalog is made of spreadsheets. Don't you insult the noble spreadsheet."

"Heaven forbid." Simon's stomach growled this time and he thumped it. "Oh, good, stereo. Do you think there's any food in here?"

"We haven't checked the footlockers, but I suspect anything in there would be spoiled by now."

Simon turned off the flashlight and took out his phone, using the light of the screen to illuminate the footlockers. He opened the one at the foot of the bed and poked through it. "A sweater." He pulled it out. "And a . . . oh my God!"

"What? What!?" I hitched back on the cot, away from him, picturing severed heads or bear traps or brain goblins lurking in the locker.

He pulled it out. By the light of the phone, I could see glossy pages and improbable skin tones. "It's a porno magazine."

"You have got to be shitting me."

"Doesn't matter what universe you're in, guys are all the same." He set it down at the foot of the bed. I leaned over and saw an improbably endowed woman covered in, for some reason, postage stamps. The headline informed me that it featured "Miss Brandy—Unwrapped!"

"And of course it's a gay man and a straight woman who find it," added Simon.

"You know, I was cold and was thinking I'd steal the sweater, but now I kinda don't want to touch it."

He went back to the footlocker. "Hmm, no cans, no . . . ha! Jackpot!" He pulled out a shiny foil pack.

"Jackpot?"

"This looks like an MRE."

"A what-what?"

"MRE. Meals Ready to Eat. The military uses 'em. They keep forever." He held it up for my inspection.

The front said FRR in large block letters, with FIELD READY RATION—INDIVIDUAL in smaller letters underneath, and MENU THREE: CHILI WITH BEANS under that. In very small print at the bottom, we were informed that the FRR was property of the UNA government and not for resale.

"UNA...," I mused. "'United Nations'? 'Ugandan National Assembly'?" Where was that? Were we in it right now? Was Byricopa in the UNA?

Simon pulled out another FRR. "I don't care if it's the Union of Nasty Anarchists, it's food. You want chili or cheese tortellini?"

"Tortellini."

There was no silverware in the footlocker. If the former inhabitants had actually been military, presumably they had some kind of mess kit that traveled with them. Simon tore open the chili and squeezed it directly into his mouth. I did pretty much the same thing, grabbing each tortellini in my teeth.

"Mmmm, heat-stabilized food. Just like Mom used to make!"

"She did not."

He grinned. "No, but it might have been an improvement. How's yours?"

"I can't decide if it's good because I'm hungry or terrible because it's terrible."

"Both."

We finished off the FRRs and then killed the last of the laced coffee. I was still thirsty—the FRR had been incredibly salty—but I didn't much want to go up top and start drinking the water.

For lack of anything better to do, I picked up the porno magazine and flipped through it, looking for clues as to where the owners had been from. All the ads looked pretty much the same as ads in our world. Apparently people were looking for penis enhancers and cheap car insurance the universe over.

The interview with Miss Brandy listed her likes: long walks on the beach, cuddling, romantic movies; and her dislikes: mean people, traffic jams, people who put their shoes on the bed. It also had her moon house, which was Hebridean, and her blood sign, Leaf. Assuming a moon house was like a horoscope, I could just about see that, but *blood sign*? Was that like blood type? I flipped back to the cover and peered at it.

"They're fake," said Simon, rummaging in another footlocker.

"Well, obviously. I'm looking at the stamps."

The stamps adorning Miss Brandy's anatomy said UNA—$4. This told me little, except that postage was expensive and apparently UNA was the name of the country.

I checked the table of contents. It would have been too much to hope for that there was an article about military spending on doors to another world. No, apparently it was going to be "Twelve Tips That Will Drive Her Wild" and "Eight Signs Your Girl Is Cheating." I sighed and dropped it. "Anything useful in that locker?"

"Three more MREs. FRRs. Whatevers. Another sweater."

"I'll take the one that hasn't been touching a porno magazine."

He passed it over. It was olive drab and too big in the shoulders, but it was warm. "Stylish," I said.

"Alternate-universe chic."

"It'd have to be an alternate universe if I'm chic."

Simon opened the footlocker at the bed with the rosary and whistled softly.

"What is it?"

"A Bible." He held it out to me. I took it and began to flip through the table of contents, trying desperately to remember what books of the Bible I'd learned in Sunday school a million years ago, and whether these were the same ones. "Was there always a book of Judith?"

"Can't remember. Didn't she stab that one general?"

"Someone did. Um . . . Amos . . . Elijah . . . I think most of these are the same. . . . Oh, hmm, there's a book of Sorrows, but I guess that's the same as Lamentations? Oh! A book of Saul!"

"Guess he didn't change his name on the road," said Simon.

"And there's like five books of Thessalonians. I guess they kept up with letters better in that world." I hefted the small

Bible in my hands, wondering how much of a stir I could make with it back home.

Probably nothing. Nobody's going to believe where you got it, and they'll just assume you made a weird forgery for your own amusement. Or worse, some people will *believe it and you'll wind up forming a cult or something.* I had enough troubles at the moment without forming a cult. I tucked the Bible into my backpack. If we ever got home, it'd be a fun addition to the Wonder Museum. "Anything else?"

"Just this." Simon brandished a clipboard at me. "It's a log, I think?" He flipped the top page of the clipboard back into place. "'Day one. Entered the vacuae with gear. Secured campsite in abandoned fortification. Transferred gear to it.'"

"Wait, what?" That didn't sound as if this was a military installation. "Do you think we're in that abandoned fortification?"

"Seems likely. There's a lot more, but it's all acronyms. What's a vacuae?"

"No idea. Something to do with vacuum, maybe?"

"Or another acronym." Simon turned the page. "'Day two. Reconnaissance of surrounding area . . . Day three. Duty Roster as follows: Steen, Petrov, Marco, Chang . . .' More acronyms. Day four is alphabet soup . . . huh."

"Huh?"

"Day five is blank. So's all the rest."

"Do you think they left after day five?"

"Or they stopped bothering to write things down."

Neither of us made the obvious suggestion, but I'm fairly sure we were both thinking it. Had something happened on day five? Something like whatever had happened to the kids on the school bus?

Had one of them written *Pray They Are Hungry* as he left?

I groaned. When you find some kind of journal in a strange alternate universe, it's supposed to have helpful information that explains what the hell is going on, and maybe how to stop it. Instead, what do we get? A bunch of military acronyms, a Bible, and a porno magazine.

Well, at least there had been food and sweaters. Probably I was being ungrateful.

"This proves it, though," said Simon.

"Proves what?"

"That there's more than two universes. I'll bet you they came through the vacu-whatever the way that we came through the hole in ours. They weren't from here either."

I grimaced. Somehow more worlds seemed worse than just one extra. I wanted to say that we didn't know the vacuae had involved another universe. Maybe they'd just gotten an airlift and *vacuae* was their word for "helicopter." But whatever Simon saw with his dead twin's eye had prompted him to guess there was more than one world here, and who was I to argue with a dead woman in my friend's head?

"Well, they definitely didn't build this place," I admitted. "Not if they're calling it an 'abandoned fortification.'"

I didn't want there to be more worlds. If there were more, then if we found a hole other than the one we entered by, we might not get home. We'd end up somewhere farther away.

You already suspect there are, though. You kept thinking of the Wood between the Worlds.

". . . Shit," I muttered. Fortunately Simon took this as a general comment, not a conversation starter.

"I'm going to try to get some more sleep," he said. He switched off his light, plunging the room into darkness.

"Sounds like the best idea." I set the porno mag down on the floor and slid back under the covers. Behind my eyelids, inhuman shapes in silver and amber flowed and joined together, like amoebas made of smoke and willow, until sleep trampled through and set them all to flight.

11

I woke to a sound of liquid hitting a bucket, which I correctly interpreted as Simon using the facilities. I waited until he was done before saying, "Is it morning?"

"Your guess is as good as mine. I've only been up a few minutes. I didn't want to check without you."

"No, of course not." I got up, yawning, and raked my fingers through my hair. My teeth felt as if things were growing on them, but there wasn't a lot that we could do about that now.

We crept up the steps, blinking in the sunlight. It was well past dawn now, which seemed odd. Had we slept that late? We couldn't have spent that long poring over the Bible and eating heat-stabilized food, could we?

Well, maybe we could. In the dark, with no sense of time, who even knew anymore? Or maybe time moved jaggedly in this world, or the sun didn't rise until the willows were ready for it.

The killdeer cried far away and light glinted on the surface of the water as it flowed past. No one was visible. I didn't see any boatmen, and the willows looked as they always looked, empty of gods or ghosts or monsters. Had it been just a phenomenon of the silver light? Like an aurora that turned things alive, then went away again?

It seemed utterly nonsensical, but at this point, what wasn't?

I turned my head quickly after we stepped out, checking for things perched on top of the bunker's doorway. I had a nebulous idea of monsters with huge claws lurking, waiting to drop on us as soon as we showed our heads, like a cat at a mousehole. Or maybe it wouldn't be anything so obvious as claws, maybe it would be a beast made of willow leaves. . . .

Nothing. The willows on top of the island hissed and rustled in the wind, but the gaps made no coherent shapes.

Simon was peering up at the willows with a puzzled expression.

"Something wrong?" I asked. "Or . . . well . . . more wrong?"

He shook his head. "I didn't remember there being willows here. I thought this was one of the grassy islands."

I frowned. "Now that you mention it . . ."

"It was dark last night," he said with a false attempt at cheer. "And we were getting pretty frazzled. We probably just didn't pay any attention."

"That's probably it." I don't think either of us believed that for a second, but if we had to face that the willows might be moving around independently, then we had to face all kinds of things, and it was too early and I was thirsty.

"I'm going to drink the water," I said.

"You sure about that?"

"No, but I don't know what other choice I have."

He looked as if he was going to argue, then nodded instead. "If you will, I will."

"Suicide pact?"

"Something like that."

We dipped our hands in the river. It was cold, and it moved like water and dripped off my fingers like water.

"*Salut*," he said, and we drank from our cupped hands.

It tasted vaguely of algae. As soon as I drank it, my thirst came roaring back. Well, if I was going to get giardia or liver snails, the first sip was probably as fatal as the last. I drank until I wasn't thirsty anymore, while the killdeer sobbed in the distance.

"Do you hear that?" asked Simon abruptly, cocking his head.

"Hear what?" I listened. I could hear the lap of water against the tiny island. The wind had died down, so the willows were not making their awful rustling chatter for once. "I don't hear . . ."

And then I stopped, because I did hear something, or I had been hearing something and now I wasn't. It was a distant, almost electronic noise, like a hum. I pulled out my phone, but it was silent and nearly out of battery in any event. "I heard something?"

We listened, heads cocked to the side like that dog in the phonograph ad. I had nearly given up when I heard it again. It sounded almost like a gong, only without the percussion of its being struck, just the humming aftermath as the note died away. Like a finger dragged over a wineglass, perhaps, but a fraction deeper.

I couldn't even begin to figure out where it was coming from. "Is it the wind?" I asked. "Maybe blowing through something?"

"There's less wind than there was. I'd think it would have been louder last night if it was blowing." He frowned. "Sounds almost like one of those Tibetan singing-bowl things. You run the little copper stick around and it makes a noise?"

I nodded. The Wonder Museum had one, of course, although I expect it was made in Mexico.

"Where's it coming from?" I turned my head to try to orient on the sound.

"I'm not sure. . . ."

All told, we must have stood there for ten minutes or more, listening and turning in place, and at the end we were no closer to figuring it out than we had been. The sound was coming from overhead, or underground, or far away, or inside our heads.

It was creepy, but when you have spent the night in a nightmare world filled with willows, merely creepy things no longer make much of a dent on you. Eventually we looked at each other and shrugged and set off to try more islands.

We were systematic this time. Assuming that the rising

waters had not actually buried some bunkers, our entry point was from the second line of islands from shore. We left a stick jammed on top of the one where we spent the night and began checking each one, in a zigzag line going upriver.

"What if we don't find it?" asked Simon.

This pissed me off because I hadn't been asking that exact question for a reason, but I swallowed it. It was my fault Simon was in this mess with me, and it was my own damn fault I hadn't marked our entry point better. "We'll try downriver."

He gave me a sidelong look that indicated that had not been what he meant. I ignored it because the only answer I had to the real question was "Eat all the FRRs, then go mad and starve in the willows." This was a bad answer.

✳

We waded to the next bunker and found a closed door. The one after that was crowned with willows, which our bunker hadn't been, but we checked it anyway. Neither of us wanted to say that the willows might be moving around at night.

There was a sandspit with ant-lion divots in it between us and the next bunker. I had an urge to dig down and see what the bug at the bottom looked like, which I squelched ruthlessly. All I needed now was for the insects to go all Wrath of Khan and burrow into our brains or something.

I also still had the awful nagging feeling that the skin of this world was terribly thin, and if I tried to dig down, I'd punch a hole in it and end up on the other side, looking up at the willows from behind. Maybe on that side the spirits would no longer be confined to negative space. Maybe they would be real and present and fall upon me hungrily.

I kept thinking that's what had happened to the kids in the school bus. They'd fallen through to the other side of the world and were now pressed up against it, trying to push their way back in.

The humming-gong sound came again, closer. At least, it seemed closer. Actually it seemed as if I was hearing it inside my chest, the way you hear the bass when you stand too close to a speaker at a concert.

"I kinda think we should go away from that noise," said Simon.

"That'd be easier if I knew where it was coming from in the first place."

Simon turned in a slow circle, listening.

I grabbed his arm. "Careful!"

He looked down, to discover his stockinged feet perilously close to one of the ant-lion nests. This was a big one, the size of a dinner plate.

"Oh, jeez . . ."

"I'd rather not have alien bugs leap out and grab your toes."

"You and me both." He scowled, then tore off a willow branch from a nearby shrub.

I winced. Even though the stem was green and flexible and

didn't snap loudly, I had a sudden intense feeling that we were going to call attention to ourselves, that the things we'd seen last night would feel the willows being harmed.

He poked the branch down into the center of the ant-lion nest and stirred.

I held my breath, waiting.

Nothing happened.

He tried another, smaller divot in the ground, then another. Nothing latched on to the branch.

"I don't think these are bug nests at all," he said. "Not doodlebugs, anyway. They should have latched on a dozen times by now." He frowned, then, to my mild horror, stuck his bare left hand into the sand.

"Simon . . . !"

"Nothing. Really, truly. Look." He stirred the sand, and if it were a horror movie, at that point a monster the size of a Buick should have leaped out of the ground, but this wasn't a movie and reality has no sense of dramatic timing. Nothing continued to happen, except that we heard the humming gong again.

I sat back on my heels. "Well, if they aren't ant lions, then what are they?"

Simon shrugged and tossed the willow branch into the water, where it slid away downstream. Something about the motion made me think of a snake swimming, not a tree limb, except that I rather like snakes.

"Dust devils, maybe," he said finally.

"Dust devils?"

"You know, little tiny tornadoes, a couple feet tall? They move around some leaves and some sand and then go away again. . . ." He trailed off as I looked around the sandspit, which was pocked like Swiss cheese everywhere there weren't willows. "Look, I didn't say it was a good theory."

"The sand's mostly wet. Or damp, anyway. It'd have to be a pretty strong dust devil."

Simon shrugged helplessly. "In this place? Who knows what the weather does at night?"

I remembered the ghostly forms rising out of the willows and stood up. I didn't want to think too much more about it.

The humming noise sounded, as if it were directly overhead. We both looked up, but there was nothing but gray sky.

Without speaking, we stepped off the side of the sandspit and began to wade toward the next bunker. Even when we found a closed door, we didn't say anything, just continued wading to the next one.

The sound came again, farther away, as if whatever it was had gone in a different direction. Relief shivered through me, although even that was probably ridiculous.

The next bunker had a cracked doorway and got our hopes up, until we realized it was mostly flooded and might be one of the ones we'd looked at last night. Two more after that, one completely without a door, and my spirits, not particularly high, began to sink.

Oh, suck it up, I told myself. *What are you going to do, sit down and cry and refuse to keep looking for a way out?*

The next bunker had a half-open door. Simon looked at the water level and shook his head. "Too deep, I think."

"Even with the rain yesterday?"

"Well . . ." He frowned. "Dammit, I can't tell. You've got depth perception, what do you think?"

He swept the flashlight beam across the far wall, almost negligently, and I fell back as if I'd been kicked in the chest. The sound I made was more like a kicked dog than a human.

"What . . . ?" Simon began, half turning, and then the image must have tripped inside his brain and he saw it, too.

The back wall had an alcove in it, made by two concrete pillars rising out of the water. Wrapped around one of them, emaciated but clearly alive, was a person.

As we watched, the figure turned their head and looked at us. Eyes shone in an angular, sunken face. They stood waist deep and had long hair that fell clear to the water. When they moved, I could see the hollowed outline of their ribs. Their arms were wrapped around the pillar, holding it tightly. The arms were so thin that they had looked like vines or tree roots.

Slowly, slowly, the person released the pillar. I saw their throat working, and finally they said, in a wet, raspy voice, "Please . . . the light hurts . . . my eyes . . ."

Simon and I scrambled backward. Simon's hand was shaking so badly on the flashlight that the person seemed to move as if they were in a strobe light.

"The light . . . please?" they said again.

Their words finally penetrated. Simon dropped the circle of light to the water. The surface was black and oily-looking. The skeletal figure was still visible at the edge of the beam.

"Move back . . . a few steps . . . please?"

It was a Southern accent. That was what killed me. This nightmarishly thin figure was in the middle of another goddamn dimension, and they had a drawl like any of the good old boys down at the hardware store. Not the genteel *Gone With the Wind* kind, with the I's drawn out until they had an extra vowel in them and the R's softened down almost to nonexistence, but the kind that drinks out of a mason jar and wouldn't know a mint julep from a hole in the ground.

". . . yes . . . ," they said. "I . . . probably can't . . . reach you . . . there . . ."

What the hell does that mean? I didn't know. I didn't want to know. I backed up another step.

Then they laughed, or something like a laugh. The sound was a swallowing click. "Gck . . . gck . . . gck!"

"Oh God," whispered Simon. "Oh fucking God."

The laughing person stood slumped in the water, hair hanging down like a shawl. The tips of their fingers were black and violet.

"No . . ." they said. "Not . . . God." They coughed, and their voice became a bit stronger. "Not God. Sturdivant. Martin

Sturdivant." They lifted their head just a little, hair clinging to their skin like algae. "Are you . . . real?"

God help me, I almost said "No."

Simon was made of stronger stuff, or maybe he'd done enough drugs that he was better at dealing with impossible visions. "Are you?" he asked.

"I am . . . I was . . . a park ranger . . ." They laughed again, but cut off quickly. "Not anymore. Obviously."

This isn't Narnia, I thought. *This is Middle-earth and we just found Gollum.* I swallowed. Surrounded by water, and my mouth was as dry as the surface of the moon. "Are you okay?" Which was a stupid goddamn question, because no one who looked like that was anything *like* okay. I tried again. "What happened?"

Sturdivant trailed his blackened fingertips over the surface of the water. "This place. This place . . . happened. *They* happened."

Part of me, the kind and decent part, the Uncle Earl part, was saying that we should pull the poor man out of the water, put a sweater on him, get some food in him, he was obviously sick and starving and near death. The other part, the part that's a lot like my mother, was saying that if Sturdivant took another step toward me, I should grab Simon and run like a rabbit.

"Are you from here?" I asked instead.

"Gck! No one is . . . *from* . . . here. Everyone comes . . . through . . . and most of us die or wish we had."

"Did you find a hole into this place, then?" asked Simon, steadying the light with the other hand.

Sturdivant kept brushing the water with his fingertips, as if stroking it. "A hole. Kudzu. Do you have that, where you come from?"

We both nodded.

"Did you come through it?"

"No," said Simon. We glanced at each other. "There was a hole in the wall. Inside a bunker."

"Inside . . . ," breathed Sturdivant. "Lucky. Very lucky. Inside is . . . safer. I was not so lucky. I came through the kudzu. It was all through the park. It had grown over trees by the water. Real tall. Cathedrals . . . we call them cathedrals. . . . Gck! Gck!"

Simon and I tried to flinch backward simultaneously and ended up sitting down hard on the steps behind us.

"Sorry," said Sturdivant. "Sorrysorrysorry. I forget. It's been so long." He shook his head, but his hair was so long and wet and clinging that it seemed to limit the distance he could turn his head. He coughed again. "The kudzu. I went into the kudzu cathedral. It's like a basket underneath. I heard something. I went toward it, and then it got darker and darker, and I tried to turn around, but I came out here. In the willows."

"And you couldn't get back?" I asked.

"No . . . I could never find it again. I was lost or it had closed already. I spent days in the willows, looking. . . ."

"I hate those things," I said.

"Yes. You should." He kneaded the water as if it were dough. "Yes. The willows are the soul of this place."

"So the holes are everywhere?" asked Simon. "Not just the bunkers?"

"Everywhere. Anywhere. You come through where you come through." Sturdivant raised his head. "Have you heard the sound yet?"

Simon and I looked at each other, then back. "There was a hum," said Simon cautiously. "Like a gong a long way away. We weren't sure if it was real."

"Yesssss. . . ." Sturdivant sank an inch or two down in the water. "Yes, that is Their sound." After a moment he added, "You'll hear it again."

"*Whose* sound?" I asked.

"Them. The ones here. You must have seen their mark already."

Simon and I looked at each other again, shrugging helplessly.

"Perhaps not. Perhaps I'm remembering wrong." Sturdivant sank even deeper in the water, still stroking the surface with his fingers. "It's been so long. How long have *you* been here?"

"Since yesterday," said Simon.

"Not long, then. No. Not yet." Was it just the water that he was touching? No, there was something else in there, something he was running through his fingers, over and over. I couldn't make it out, except that it was long and dark. Waterweed, or . . . oh, Lord, maybe his own hair, in the water. How long *was* it? "Some holes last longer, I think. Yours may be there still. Or not."

It hadn't even occurred to me to worry that the way home might have closed.

"Did you see a school bus, when you got here?" asked Simon.

"School bus? No."

Simon tried to describe it, the way the children were trapped inside. It was hard to wrap words around it. It was doubly hard when we were talking to a wet, skeletal man lurking in the dark water, stroking his floating hair.

Not that he seems hostile, exactly, but . . . what did he mean by "I probably can't reach you there"?

The first person we'd met and I wanted to get the hell away as quickly as I could. *Typical. Although if he can tell us something about this place . . . like what They are . . .*

"Yesss . . . ," said Sturdivant when Simon had finished. "That sounds like something They might do."

"*Why?*" I asked. "Why would someone do that?"

"Because . . . They weren't hungry." Sturdivant closed his eyes.

"What does that *mean*?" asked Simon. "I don't understand!"

For a long moment, I didn't think Sturdivant would answer. He was so emaciated that even talking to us must have exhausted him.

"We have some food," I said hesitantly. "If you're hungry." As skeletal as he was, I didn't see how he couldn't be hungry.

Sturdivant shook his head. He was submerged to the collarbone now, but I could see his shoulders moving, as if he were treading water. "I've been starving this long. If I eat now . . . I'd have to start over."

That made more sense than I wanted it to make. I didn't want to think about it, but there were so many things now that I didn't want to think about that they were fighting and jostling for position in the back of my head.

"What are They?" I asked.

He shook his head. "This place. They live here. Don't think too loudly. If you think about Them, it draws Them in. . . ."

I didn't want to look away from Sturdivant, but I looked over my shoulder just in case. Nothing but sunlight and willows.

"Where *is* this place?" I said. "What is it?"

Sturdivant's bony shoulders rose out of the water in a shrug. "A place. Just a place. Old. Touching many places. But eventually the willows found it and got their roots in. . . ."

"They live in the willows?"

"From them. Of them."

"We saw . . . err . . . spirits," I said. "In the willows last night. And something bigger."

"Yesss. . . ." He lifted one hand. Hair or waterweed stuck to it as he made a vague gesture, then dropped it back into the water. "The light of the willows brings things alive. Then not alive. You understand?"

We didn't. Sturdivant shook his head, the wet, sticky hair wrapping around his cheekbones. "Things come alive in the willowlight. Not Them. Just things. Then the light goes and they're not alive anymore. But the willows serve Them . . . never doubt it . . . gck!"

"Is the boatman one of Them?" asked Simon.

That was a good question, and one I hadn't thought to ask. "Oh, *him*." Sturdivant shrugged again. "Don't let him catch you. Or do let him, maybe. He's *always* hungry." He opened his eyes. "You asked what They do . . . if They aren't hungry . . ." He smiled, baring teeth in black, swollen gums. I had to look away. "Then They play with you . . . take you apart to see what makes you tick . . . *change* you . . ."

My skin was already crawling, but it crawled harder, as if it wanted to leave my body completely and go try to find the way home by itself.

"There was a woman," said Sturdivant abruptly. "I met her. She came through before me. A different way. She'd been here for days. A researcher." He tried to shake his head again, but the thick weight of wet hair prevented him. "They got her a few days later. But They weren't hungry. They came for us and we ran. . . . When I found her again, she was all twisted up and They'd stacked her bones up next to her, all very neat, from small to large . . . all the little hand bones lined up like beads." The water shivered around him. "She was still alive. It took ages to kill her. She was like jelly. . . ."

My mind had gone completely blank. It felt like the black water at our feet, each awful word falling into it and leaving ripples.

"They don't come down here . . . ," Sturdivant said wearily.

"Too much . . . concrete. The willows can't . . . get their roots in." He laughed softly. "Though that's . . . changing. Water and muck and dead leaves . . . turns to dirt in the dark . . . and then they'll start sending their roots down." He had sunk so deep into the water now that it lapped against his chin when he spoke.

"So They didn't make the bunkers, then?" said Simon. I marveled at his ability to concentrate on that. I was thinking of the school bus, of children and the driver changed in some way I could only barely comprehend because They hadn't been hungry. So They'd twisted their victims around, pulled them halfway out of reality, left them pressing against the skin of the world like hungry ghosts trying to get in.

Sturdivant shook his head, sending ripples through the water. "I don't think They could. I don't know who did. Someone . . . before . . . maybe. Before the willows. Or after. Bunkers to hide from Them. Maybe someone trying to . . . fix . . . this place." He closed his eyes. "But there's no fixing it. Gck! Gck!"

After a moment he said, "You came through here, on the river . . . yes?"

I nodded, then realized his eyes were closed. It didn't seem to matter, because he answered his own question. "Of course you did. You're alive. No one . . . lives . . . anywhere else."

"What do you mean?" Simon's voice was calm and polite, the customer-service, no-we-don't-serve-Frappuccinos-here voice, wildly out of place in this world.

Yet somehow, Sturdivant seemed to respond to it. "There

was a woman. No . . . wait. I said that . . . already? Didn't I?"

"You did."

"We tried to . . . get away. From the river. We went as far as we could. Three days." He shook his head slowly, fingers pulsing on the surface of the water, wrapping thick tendrils of his hair around his hands. "We had to turn back. There was no more water. Nothing but willows. Willows forever. The light . . . all the time, the light. All the shadows coming alive in the light. But we saw buildings . . . great concrete things. Like parking garages. That big. But you couldn't get near them. They were everywhere . . . the buzzing around the buildings . . . like . . . like wasps . . . we thought if we could get in one, it would be safe . . . but we couldn't get close. They were watching those buildings. They hated them. Wanted in. The river . . . seemed safer . . . somehow . . . gck!"

"The willows are making the light?" asked Simon carefully.

"Yes. Watch for it. Won't hurt you. Probably. But if you see the light, the willows have gotten their roots in."

I was sweating, despite the cold. I wiped the back of my neck, and it felt as clammy as a mushroom. "But we're safe in the bunkers?"

"Safe . . . ?" Sturdivant's body shook with laughter. "Safe! None of us are . . . safe. They touched me and I fell down here. It stopped Them changing me more, for all the good it did me."

"I'm sorry," I said helplessly. "Can we do anything?"

"Safe . . . ," said Sturdivant, and then he stood up in the water.

It wasn't hair.

Martin Sturdivant's skin stopped at the bottom of his ribs, and his lower half had been taken apart. His guts were black with algae and dirt and hung loose in the water, some of them floating, so that he was moving through a cloud of his own organs. I realized that when he had been stroking the surface of the water, he'd been stroking his own body dissected around him, fingers moving across intestine and bowel in a horrible, loving touch.

Simon and I let out twin screams and fled.

12

I made it to the opposite shore, among the willows, and collapsed. I couldn't seem to breathe. All I could see was Martin's lower body, spreading into the water. *It stopped Them changing me more, for all the good it did me. . . .*

I pressed my face against the sand, breathing in through my teeth, and tried to think of something else. The Wonder Museum. Prince, with his magnificent spread of antlers and benign glass gaze. Uncle Earl, speaking earnestly and kindly to tourists. His Sunflower Holiness. The taxidermied mice riding cane toads, which were also horrible but a different kind of horrible, a familiar, tacky one that I had a grip on.

The Wonder Museum existed. If I could hold on to that fact, then I didn't have to think about other things that existed. If I could get back to it, then I could shut the door and never, ever think about those other things again.

If I could get back to it.

If it was still open.

Oh, God, what if we found the right bunker and went down the hall and there was only the dead man in his room and the way home was gone?

I wondered again why he had died. Had he starved to death in the little concrete room rather than go out into the willows? What world had the poor bastard come from?

I could imagine it all too easily—someone stumbling in like we had, finding their way to what felt like safety, and barring the bunker door to the outside and the horrors that lurked among the bunker islands. Whatever he had seen in the willows had convinced him to stay in that room, even if it meant his death.

After seeing Sturdivant, I couldn't blame him.

If only the hole to our world had opened sooner, maybe we'd have found him in time. But he'd been dead for years. We had passed close in space, but separated by far too much time to make a difference.

The throbbing, gong-like note came again, from overhead or underfoot, I couldn't tell. It sounded louder or maybe just closer.

"We're going to die here, aren't we?" I said, finally sitting up.

"Yeah." Simon was sitting next to me, wet sand all across his fishnets and his shorts. "Yeah, we probably are."

He sounded so matter-of-fact and resigned that it helped. We were going to die. It was one of those things that happened.

No sense screaming about it. Maybe death was just a thing that happened, like finding that a tourist had knocked a hole in the drywall or that we were out of size XL T-shirts. *Well, damn.*

I wiped sand off my face. "God. I can't believe I spent so much time crying over my marriage. What a load of horseshit that was, when there was all this. . . ." I gestured vaguely at the willows and the water and the world that wasn't our world at all.

"Well, it's not like it would have helped at the time. If somebody showed up and said, 'Stop crying, Carrot, you're going to die horribly in an alternate dimension later this year,' would you have listened?"

I snorted. There was sand up my nose and I wiped my nostrils raw trying to get it out.

The willows were higher than our heads, a series of shifting, leafy walls. If the spirits we had seen last night were still here, only invisible, we were right in the middle of them.

Things come alive in the light, then not alive, Sturdivant had said. Which probably meant that the spirits *weren't* here, because the willows did not have that strange silver glow that he must have been referring to, the light that made things alive— but now I was thinking of Sturdivant again. I closed my eyes and concentrated on breathing.

After a few minutes, I was settled enough to actually say it. "Sturdivant . . ."

"Yeah."

"You saw it, too."

"Yeah. I thought it was hair or algae or something, but . . ." Simon shook his head.

"He said he came from somewhere else, too," I said dully. "Someplace with kudzu."

"That could be ours. Although it wouldn't surprise me if they've got kudzu everywhere."

"All right. We're here. This is one world. The hole in the museum opened into the bunker in this one world. We know there's probably at least one more world. The one the porn magazine came from." I had abandoned any hope that *vacuae* was a helicopter. "Maybe two worlds, if that's not also where Byricopa County is." It was easier to think about other worlds than it was to think about Sturdivant and what had happened to him and what might yet happen to us. "So that's a minimum of three, with ours. Maybe four."

"Maybe five hundred," said Simon, and he didn't say *So what?*, although he could have, because knowing the exact number of alternate universes didn't help us in the slightest.

So there was a chance we could fall through a hole to another world, not our own. I said as much to Simon.

"At this point, I'd take it," said Simon. "I figure they need good baristas in every world, you know?"

I sighed. I didn't want an alternate universe, I wanted to go home. Besides, if we left the hole in the wall behind us, Uncle Earl was going to find it, and then he'd die in the willows instead.

"Come on," I said, standing. I slapped more sand

off my knees. "Let's keep looking."

The sun crept overhead. The killdeer called. The mist burned off. We went to bunker after bunker, looked in the doors, and kept going.

I banged my foot on a rock under the water and gouged my big toe pretty well. We couldn't do much about it, though. If alien organisms were entering my bloodstream through the wound and beginning to devour my flesh, I couldn't feel it under the general throbbing from my damaged toenail.

"Of course I didn't bring toenail clippers," I muttered.

"Next extradimensional jaunt we take, we'll bring spares." I knew Simon was being cheerful and snarky to keep my spirits up, or maybe to keep his own spirits up, so I tried not to get annoyed. Someone had to be cheerful while the other one freaked out. That was the bargain we'd made.

Something moved in the water near the bend in the river. I caught Simon's arm and pointed. It was underwater, mostly, rolling and twisting. I caught the occasional flash of light off a dark, wet back rising out of the river.

"What the hell is that?"

"Fish?" I said a bit doubtfully. "Or . . . uh . . . otter, maybe? Do you see anything weird?"

"With the eye? No. But I've never seen a wild otter."

"Don't they have them in Florida?"

"We have gators in Florida. If there are any otters, they're very scared."

I thought of the giant otter in the case at the Wonder Museum. Somehow I suspected that it would not be particularly scared of a gator, even the big ones.

We stepped down into the river again. My throbbing toe quieted briefly in the cold water. *If They get me, I won't have to worry about my toe falling off,* I thought, and bit down on a hysterical giggle.

Don't think about Them. It draws Them, Sturdivant had said.

How the fuck do you not think about the things that are going to kill you or take you apart or pull out your bones?

I tried to get a song stuck in my head. This is a surprisingly hard thing to do. I thought of all the theme songs to TV shows and jingles from commercials and Christmas carols and tried to jam the catchiest bits into my skull, and in under a minute I was back to thinking about Sturdivant surrounded by his halo of organs unraveled in the water and *oh, Jesus, that's going to happen to us.* . . .

"We're getting too far from shore, I think," said Simon as we stepped up onto the next bunker island. "This is the third or fourth one out."

I glanced over at the opposite shore of the river. Tall grass grew along the edge, and behind it, great gray masses of willows. No buildings. That was probably for the best. If anything lived here, the willows had gotten to it by now. Sturdivant's description of the dirt and the leaves piling up until there was something inside the bunkers for their roots to get into came back to me.

How much faster could they do it with a building where the willow roots could work in from the sides?

Stop. Think of a song. Any song. "John Jacob Jingleheimer Schmidt, his name is my name, too. . . ."

"Back to the shore, then?" I said. "We'll start closer."

"We're getting near the bend."

"Yes."

I shaded my eyes and looked downstream for the bunker where we had spent the night. Could we find it again? I could just pick out the stick atop it, so hopefully yes.

There was a small bluff on the river bend, if you could call something that short a bluff. It was only about ten feet high, but I don't know what else you'd call it. Willows covered the top, but it was also the tallest point of land for a good distance. I pointed.

Simon shrugged. "It's all you. Depth perception's not my strong suit."

"Right. Well, let's see what I can see from up top."

On the far side of the bluff was . . . something. It looked like a tangle of downed trees at first, with willows growing up and through it. But some of the trees were too smooth and regular, and they had grooves and they weren't trees at all, they were boards of some sort. Then I turned my head and it seemed to resolve into a shape, like a broken house, but the shape was odd.

"It's a ship," said Simon. "An old-style one. Jesus."

As soon as he said it, I recognized it. A boat. Half of one, anyway. The prow was up in the air and partly on its side and there were gaping rents in the hull, and at least one actual uprooted tree was jammed through it. The tangle of roots had confused the shape.

We stood looking down at it. There was something written on the hull, but the uprooted tree had gone right through it and willows had overgrown the other side, so all I could read was RON MOUN and then tree roots.

"Ron Moun . . . ," I said, trying to think of a name that would fit. What did ships get called, anyway? "Aaron Mounds? Darron Moundlebrot?"

"Iron Mounties?"

"Of course that's what you came up with. I suppose you dated a Mountie once?"

"No, but I had a calendar of pinups."

"Of course you did." I shook my head. "Well, I know we didn't go past this thing." I looked south. "So let's start working our way downstream from here."

Neither of us had the slightest desire to go into the ship. For one thing, there was no way our route home was there, and for another, I think we were afraid there'd be something else inside. Something like Sturdivant, or worse.

They'd stacked her bones up next to her, all very neat, from small to large. She was like jelly. . . .

"I wonder if the ship's from here," I murmured, trying not to think about that.

"Can't be. It's too big. You couldn't get it through water this shallow, and there's all these little bunker islands here. Nobody'd bring a ship down this way."

"Oh, hmm. Yeah, I guess."

I turned to descend from the bluff—and froze.

Something that wasn't there passed us in the willows. It was not a ghost or a spirit or a trick of negative space. It wasn't there, but it still went past us, just on the other side of a line of branches, and the humming noise came so close that my ribs vibrated with it. Simon put his hand on his sternum, grimacing, and I looked past him and saw the willows bend as the thing walked by.

The spirits last night had been made up of the shapes where the willows weren't. This one forced the willows out of the way, just like the big thing we'd seen the night before. The same kind. Maybe even the same one. It was on the other side the way that the kids on the bus had been on the other side, pushing against reality hard enough to move leaves and branches out of the way.

I wanted to run, but that might attract attention. I didn't even dare cry out. I reached over and put my hand over Simon's mouth, and his eyes went as wide as mine and we stood in absolute silence while the sound rang in our chests and I tried so hard not to think of the thing I couldn't help but think about.

John Jacob Jingleheimer Schmidt . . .
His name is my name, too!
Whenever we go out!
The people always shout!
Fuck fuck, we're going to die, we're going to die
There goes John Jacob Jingleheimer Schmidt!

I could feel sweat trickling down my back. I dug my toes into the sand and concentrated hard on it, the tiny grains, the large piece of gravel digging into my toe . . .

It walked away. Simon turned his head, taking my hand with him, and we watched the willow branches bow outward from the passing, and it was invisible except that *invisible* was not the right word, because its not-there-ness hung in the air like an afterimage.

It reached the water and stepped onto it. We watched as concentric rings spread out and were immediately lost in the current. Eventually it either went away or the current was too swift to see it. The hum went with it, moving away.

"Is it gone?" I whispered finally, after long minutes had passed. I let my hand drop.

"I don't know."

"Did you see it?" I asked hoarsely.

"Yeah." He rubbed the eye that might belong to a dead woman. "Yeah, I saw it."

"What did it look like?" I didn't want to know, but I asked anyway.

"Like that thing in the willows last night. The second one. Only bigger and . . . more. Like if that one was a rat, this would be a dog. No, that's not right." He shook his head. "Like a trilobite made of skin. Like you got really high and the back of your eyelids glued itself to your eyeballs, and then that got up and walked around. No. I don't *know*."

I nodded. I didn't understand and I didn't want to understand. What else could I do?

"Let's not go in the water for a bit." His voice was raspy. "I think it's still over there. Or it . . . it went *behind* the water. Somehow. But there."

The ship was still unappealing, but at least the walls seemed as if they might offer some kind of shelter. We slid down the slope, avoiding the funnels that might or might not contain this world's equivalent of ant lions.

There was a rent in the side of the hull. The willows lined a path to it, as if they were a hedge on either side. I didn't like touching them, but that ship had sailed long ago, no pun intended. We stepped inside.

It was dim. Light slanted through holes in the boards. I could see what looked like a bar counter on one side, affixed to the wall and tilted at a forty-five-degree angle. Sand and gravel had filled in the bottom of the hold. No ant lions, though.

I lowered myself down to sit with my back against a board. It was good to sit somewhere dry, anyway. Simon sat down next to me, rubbing his hands over his face.

It went behind the water somehow. . . .

I was struck again by the intense feeling that this world was only a skin over a vast other space. Were the things in the willows moving in that other space, behind the world? Were They looking through from behind it? Was that why They hadn't been able to pinpoint us exactly yet?

Was Simon seeing, however dimly, through the skin and into that other alien space?

The humming noise chimed, coming closer again. Something moving behind the world, looking for us.

A willow was growing through a break in the corner, where a shaft of light came in. The leaves were small and stunted. I felt as if it were a spy in the room, watching us for its masters.

Still better in here, I thought. *One spy is better than a whole crowd of them out for blood.*

The noise rang out again, then again, overlapping itself. Two of Them? One getting excited? Did numbers even apply to Them? Were They a singular entity or something like a swarm of bees where the individual didn't matter?

They take you apart to see how you work . . . change you . . .

They ate us when They were hungry, took us apart when They weren't. Were we some kind of alien food animal to Them? Something tasty, and then when everyone was done with dinner, the willow equivalent of a scientist chopped you apart? Like dodos or Galapagos tortoises for early sailors, something to eat on the long voyage and then the naturalist said "Oh, hmm,

I wonder how that bit attaches . . . ?" and went after you with the knives?

I could appreciate the cosmic irony a lot more if I weren't about to be eaten by it.

I wondered how the kids in the bus fit in with that. Maybe if you were wandering around behind reality, the way They were, it was obvious. Maybe it was only alien and unknowable and horrifying because we couldn't *see*.

I pinched the bridge of my nose. No, I was pretty sure it was still horrifying. Maybe the fact that I couldn't make sense of it was the reason I wasn't a shivering wreck right now.

The humming was directly over the boat now. I looked at Simon and he was looking up, as if he could see through the hull of the boat. "Think about something else," he hissed.

"Is it—"

"Right there. Yes. *Think about something else.*"

I had been thinking about Them clearly, probably loudly. Was it like lighting a signal flare for Them? Like . . .

The gong noise seemed to descend, as if something had dropped lower and was hovering only a few yards up.

Stupid. What are you doing?!

"John Jacob Jingleheimer Schmidt . . . his name is my name, too." . . .

When I get home, I'll work on the catalog. Number one, Prince the elk. Number seventy-four, stuffed grizzly bear. A lot of them were assorted toads. We've got way too many toads.

Simon's already pale skin was nearly translucent. I could see a bead of sweat trickling down his forehead. He'd closed his eyes and his lips were moving, but I couldn't make out what he was saying. Reciting something, probably. Good thought.

. . . "*Whenever we go out, the people always shout . . . there goes John Jacob Jingleheimer Schmidt*" . . .

Something happened. My ears popped and I felt a sudden hard thrum in the center of my chest. Simon's nails dug into my wrist so hard that I nearly yelped. I sank my teeth into my lower lip to prevent it.

Sand sifted down from the tilted ceiling. It was overhead. It was here.

. . . "*Whenever we go out . . . whenever we go out . . .*" I couldn't think of the rest. I couldn't think of anything. I could hear Simon whispering to himself but I couldn't make out the words. It could have been the Lord's Prayer or the words to "Bohemian Rhapsody," for all I knew.

There were steps overhead. I wouldn't call them footsteps, exactly. More like tank tread, a sense of continuous rolling weight. The wood groaned like a dying animal.

Catalog number 126, armadillo lamp. Number 127, mounted fur-bearing trout. Number 128, Genuine Feejee Mermaid because he bought another one, goddammit, even though I snuck the first one out to the trash when I was sixteen. Catalog number . . . number . . . number infinity, a monster on the roof, waiting to take you apart and string your bones like beads. . . .

The movement stopped directly over my head. The willow was rustling almost excitedly. I would not have been surprised to see it squirm with delight, like a puppy pleasing its master.

Simon's eyes showed white all around the edges, and if I didn't stop thinking about Them, I was going to get us both killed or turned into something like Sturdivant. Sturdivant, saying, "I probably can't reach you there." Sturdivant, starving himself in the darkness, and if he could have reached us, would he have tried to eat us? Swallowed us down in bites that passed into his guts and floated in the water around him? *Hell, maybe he just has to hold us underwater and he'll start to digest us, maybe that whole room full of water is his stomach and he'd absorb us as we started to rot. . . .*

Stop. Thinking about Sturdivant was not the same as thinking about Them, but it led to it too easily. "Jingleheimer" wasn't working, it was too easy, I could still think too clearly around the edges of the words. Did I know anything else to recite? The Gettysburg Address, maybe? *"Four score and seven years ago, our fathers brought forth, upon this continent, a new nation, conceived in liberty and" . . . uh . . . something something . . . "history will not note nor long remember" . . . oh, blast, Miss Kaister in fifth grade would be so disappointed in me. . . .*

I still bore a certain degree of resentment toward Miss Kaister, who had referred to any behavior she didn't like as "fourth-grade." "Now, Kara," she'd say, looking over her glasses at me, "that's behavior I'd expect from a fourth-grader, not from a fifth-grader like you." I had been a cynical small child who remembered fourth grade fondly, and I resented what she was saying, by implication, about my younger self.

The weight shifted to one side as if it were drifting away. Sand pattered down closer to the prow of the ship.

They do hear us thinking, I thought. *And when we don't think about Them, they start to lose track of us. Or maybe it's not Them, maybe it's just fear in general that draws Th—Oh, fuck, I'm thinking the wrong thing again, fuck, "John Jacob Jingleheimer Schmidt . . ."*

It would be a supreme irony if being mad at Miss Kaister saved my life. Who else was I mad at? My ex? Yes, I was definitely still pissed at him. *How dare he? He could have suggested counseling or something, instead of just "Right, this isn't working." I would have been willing to go to counseling. But then I suppose the counselor might have decided it was someone's fault, and Mark really wanted it to be no one's fault so that we could stay friends and tell people we'd just grown apart.*

Friends. Ha. He hasn't given a shit about my interests for years. He doesn't even know the name I write fanfic under.

Not that I want him to. That would be embarrassing. The only way you can splay your id out on the page is if you know that only total strangers are going to read it. And they're right there reading it, so they're practically accomplices, unless they're one of those people who decide to leave comments telling you that shipping those two characters makes you worse than Hitler.

This was an old, well-worn outrage and I dwelt on it lovingly with my toes in the sand of an alien world and a malign intelligence moving overhead. Part of my brain was screaming that it was small and petty and utterly ridiculous but if I listened, I was lost. I wallowed in petty outrage until I was ready to burn down the internet around fandom's collective shoulders.

My ears popped again. The sense of weight began to fade. Had it gone?

When the hum came again, it was at least a dozen yards away. I started to feel relief, then caught myself and forced my brain back to its previous channels. *"How dare you ship those two together? That would be abusive and probably incestuous and definitely you are the worst."* . . . *Yeah, go ahead, leave a comment like that, I'll just ship it twice as hard with more blow jobs.*

And what about the time I wrote twelve thousand words for a fic exchange, and they never even thanked me? What about that?

The sound slowly drifted out across the river. It was probably a quarter hour before we were willing to move. Finally Simon exhaled and we looked at each other and crawled toward the exit.

The first step out of the hole took more courage than I knew I had. I waited for something to grab me, probably a tentacle, something to lash out and wrap around my neck and then unmake my body for its amusement. It didn't happen, so I looked up into the upper levels of the boat, but it looked the same as it had before. I couldn't tell if the ruined boards had been rearranged or not.

We kept low, crawling into the willows, which was stupid because the willows were obviously part of the whole mess, but the alternative was to stand out in plain sight, and that felt worse.

"Can you tell me what you saw?" I asked Simon. I was keeping my voice down, which was probably stupid when They could hear thoughts.

He made a small, pained noise. "I don't know how to describe it. They go in and out of underneath? The world sticks to them? Shit. I can't see three dimensions most days, but apparently I can see four. How fucking useless is that?"

"The world's just a skin and they're moving around under it?" I suggested.

"Better. But the skin's everywhere. You and me and the air and everything else. They could come out of one of us." He held up a hand. "Just . . . let's not. I don't want to think too loud and call something."

I nodded. We slogged down to the water and prepared to get back to work.

✳

The fifth or sixth or tenth bunker after that took us home.

We almost didn't go into it because it had willows growing on top and I distinctly remembered that there had been no willows on our island. But I had forgotten about the willows on the bunker where we spent the night, and if I was being completely and totally honest, I thought there was a chance that they were moving around when our backs were turned, but if I didn't say anything, I wouldn't have to think about that. So we slogged out to that island, feet cold and pruned with water, and I didn't mention the willows and Simon didn't mention my not mentioning them.

I wasn't expecting to get home anymore. I wasn't expecting anything. I was going down the stairs mechanically, listening to the humming sound get closer and louder. I wondered if they would open up our guts like they had Sturdivant's or pull out our bones or trap us underneath the surface of wherever they caught us, like the school bus. I wondered if one of us might get away and be able to come back and kill the other one. Then I realized I was thinking again and began singing "John Jacob Jingleheimer Schmidt" inside my head and trying not to think around the edges.

Then I stopped thinking anything because I was standing at the bottom of another set of stairs, and Simon's toolbox was right there at my feet.

"Simon," I croaked, pushing it with my foot. "Simon, look!"

He was right beside me. He fell down to his knees, grabbing at it, and said, "It's mine, it's really mine," and then I yanked him to his feet and we sprinted through that silent concrete room and into the hallway.

I didn't believe that the hole would still be there. Not really. Ever since Sturdivant had said that the holes didn't last, I had been expecting it to close. I didn't believe that we'd get out so easily, not after everything I'd seen. But there it was, a hole in the world, and on the other side was the fluorescent light of the Wonder Museum.

We were both crying. We skidded the last few yards down the corridor and half climbed, half fell through the hole, and then we were there, we were in the Wonder Museum again and the real world, our world, the world with Chinese takeout and coffee shops and sunflower pictures of the pope, a world where willows were only willows.

I reached out and touched the cabinet that held up the case with the stuffed raccoons. It was cheap fiberboard and it was real and I didn't feel like there was a whole nightmare world just on the other side of reality. Simon was rubbing his hands over the floorboards.

"It's real," I said, choking on tears. "It's real. We're back. We made it."

Home.

13

The phone was ringing downstairs. Simon and I couldn't get far enough from the hole. We rushed for the stairs. The phone stopped ringing.

Part of me was simply astonished that there was still a world with phones and I was in it and I could pick up that phone and maybe talk to someone on the other end and that was *normal*. Had I really always been able to do that? Was I really part of this utterly normal world?

Before I'd gotten very far into this musing at all, the phone started ringing again. I grabbed it off the cradle, and my mother started talking before I even got through "Hello."

For a minute I was too stunned with relief to speak. I hadn't expected to ever hear her voice again. This had the happy knock-on effect of her wearing out her first outraged demands while I was still getting my composure back and was able to wonder why she was calling the museum in the middle of the night. *Was* it the middle of the night? Had time moved differently? If you go to fairyland, time goes differently. Oh, God, what if it was next week? What if Beau had starved to death in the bathroom?

Panicking about this caused me to lose another couple of sentences, but that was fine because my mother doesn't actually want to talk at first, she wants to yell so that she gets it all out of the way up front. I looked for the clock over the front desk, which is made from the taxidermied body of a cuckoo and resembles a dad joke given flesh. It was 1:27 A.M.

". . . and on a Saturday, too! You know that's his busy day! Where *were* you? I've been calling you all day! I thought you were dead!"

Saturday. We'd been gone for all of Saturday, just as I thought. Time hadn't done anything strange. I sagged against the counter in relief. "Mom, it's the middle of the night."

"I know that! I was about to drive over there! Mr. Bryce called your uncle to ask why the museum was closed, and he tried to call you four times! And you weren't answering your phone or the store phone!"

Of course it would be Mr. Bryce. He was a coffee shop regular and a friend of Uncle Earl's. It took someone with the patience of Uncle Earl to deal with Mr. Bryce, who had been thrown off the neighborhood watch committee for being a geriatric jackbooted thug. I could just imagine how the whole thing had snowballed—Uncle Earl trying to call, then asking Mom if she'd heard from me, and then once Mom got it into her head that I had been AWOL all day, the wheels of anxiety had started turning. I could almost hear Uncle Earl trying to talk her down, but once Mom had the bit between her teeth . . .

"I'm sorry, Mom, I—"

"I thought you were dead in a ditch!"

My cell phone, which had not gotten any signal in the other world, suddenly dinged to let me know that I had seventeen new missed calls.

"Mom, I had no choice. It was Simon from the coffee shop. I . . . uh . . . had to take him to the ER."

Simon raised both eyebrows, but inspiration had struck and I was off and running. "Yeah, I went over for coffee and found him on the ground. He had a seizure. . . . No, he's fine now. They think it was an allergic reaction to . . . uh . . ."

"The flavored syrups," said Simon, lips twitching. "Those things are full of chemicals."

"The flavored syrups," I said gratefully. "Yeah, he was mixing up a new latte or something and had a reaction, and then the bottle broke when he fell down, so he was covered in it. . . . Uh, I'm not sure. I think it was the maple-bacon flavor. . . . No, I don't know who wants bacon-flavored coffee. . . . Right. So I ran him to the ER and then I had to stay with him because he was really woozy and I didn't feel right leaving him. . . . No, I know. I would have called, but the hospital is all cinder blocks, I couldn't get any signal at all. . . . Yes, I know. I should have gone out and called but I didn't want to leave him. I'm so sorry I worried you. I . . . Yes, I know. I'm sorry. . . . Thanks. . . . No, he's fine. He's got a friend coming over to sleep on the couch in case something else happens. . . . Uh-huh. . . . Uh-huh. . . . I'll open up on Monday to make up for it. Right. Love you, too, Mom. All my love to Uncle Earl. Bye." I dropped the phone and sagged against the front counter.

"I see why you didn't want to move back home," said Simon.

"Oh my God. I survive a hideous otherworld and then I had to talk to my mother. I could sleep for a week."

"So could I. But we have to get that hole closed, or I don't think I'll ever sleep again."

*

Neither of us wanted to go back in the willow world, even just into the corridor to close the bunker door, but if we didn't . . . well, whatever came out would probably be worse. We went back through the hole together. Maybe it would have made more sense for only one of us to go through. That way if the hole closed in the next two minutes, at least one of us would survive. But we'd come this far together, and neither of us wanted to be alone.

The door closed with a metallic screech. Simon threw the bolt. We scurried back to the hole and came through, and I didn't kiss the ground, although I thought about it.

Simon got his drywall kit. I fed Beau, who was angry about his incarceration and had scored dozens of claw marks in the bottom of the door. I shut the door on his angry yowls and went to help Simon.

I didn't want to put my arms into the corridor—what if the hole snapped closed and I wound up with a pair of stumps?—but the drywall patch didn't have a stud to anchor itself on, so I had to reach in and brace part of it. My hand touched something that rolled and I pulled back, startled, but it was only the stupid corpse-otter carving. I'd meant to pick it up and put it away a few days earlier, but there had been a lot on my mind. I fished it out of the corridor and set it on top of the nearby raccoon case.

In the end, Simon had to screw the patch into the existing wallboard, and the patch was huge and ugly. I didn't care. I'd have welded steel plates over the hole if I could have.

We hung a batik sheet over it, then each took an end and moved the raccoon case to partly cover it. If anything came through, at least we'd be alerted by the sound of crashing taxidermy.

"God, this feels flimsy," I muttered.

"I don't know how to fill it with concrete," Simon admitted. "We'd have to flood the whole corridor, wouldn't we? That'd be a lot of concrete. A couple of trucks' worth, at least."

I couldn't see how we'd get a truck to the second floor of the museum anyway. The patch and the batik would have to do for now.

And that was that. We stood looking at each other, and I said, "Well . . . I think I'm going to take a shower and go to bed."

"Yeah, okay."

Our society doesn't teach us a graceful way to handle the aftermath of incredibly stressful events. If he'd been straight and I'd been interested, we'd probably have fallen into each other's arms and had poorly considered sex, but, thank God, he wasn't and I wasn't, so we hugged fiercely and then he went off to the coffee shop and I went off to my shower.

I won't say that I didn't cry for about twenty minutes, standing in the hot water, because I did. But it was okay. I was home. I could cry if I wanted to. Nothing was going to hear me and come and turn me inside out.

Beau was in a mood and not inclined to cuddle. I hugged Prince awkwardly instead. Taxidermy isn't terribly huggable, but I needed to hug something. I put my forehead against his carefully painted muzzle and said, "I'm home. I made it back," and let out a dry sob of horror and joy and frustration.

Just a girl and her giant stuffed elk head. Nothing weird going on here.

Maybe if I were less weird, I would have had nightmares and screaming horrors, but in fact I fell down and slept without so much as a dream.

*

I woke up with ten minutes to spare before the Wonder Museum opened. I almost went back to bed, but the irrational guilt that I hadn't opened yesterday—despite a truly extraordinary reason!—nagged at me. I got up, ran a brush through my hair, threw on fresh clothes, and staggered out to flip the sign.

One of the regulars at the coffee shop came by to ask why we'd been closed yesterday. Kay was a wiry woman with short hair and an angular face. In a fanciful moment, I once compared her to one of those puzzles where you stare at the brightly colored lines and move your head around and suddenly it's a spaceship or a cheetah or something. At the exact right angle, Kay is stunningly beautiful; then she turns her head or you blink and she goes back to being like the rest of us. It's a neat trick.

(I mentioned this to Simon a while back, and he said those puzzles don't work for him because of his eye and also he's not into women, but he'd take my word for it.)

"You okay?" Kay asked. "Both you and the Hen were closed up yesterday. Bryce was convinced you'd both been murdered."

"Had to run Simon to the ER. He had an allergic reaction to one of the flavored syrups, and I know that sounds just too stupid for words, but I went over to get my morning coffee and he'd keeled over behind the counter."

"My God!"

"I know, right?" I paused. "Um . . . this is going to sound horribly insensitive, but I slept later than I should have. Could

I beg you to grab me a cup from next door and bring it back?"

"Of course," said Kay, as somberly as if I were entrusting her to throw a magic ring into a volcano.

She came back with coffee before I woke up enough to worry that Simon wouldn't remember the absurd cover story we'd come up with, but nothing in Kay's manner indicated that he'd told her I was lying. Instead she set the coffee down and said, "He looks pretty ragged."

"Simon?" I raised my eyebrows. "Well, he was pretty knocked down by the allergies, but he's probably still better dressed than I'll ever be."

Kay laughed. "How's your uncle?"

"Oh, you know. Just out of surgery. Mom says it went well, but it's early yet."

Kay nodded. I thanked her for the coffee and she went back next door to drink her own coffee and work.

It was a slow morning, thank God. Mr. Bryce came in and told me that next time I had to leave, he'd be happy to run the museum. I smiled and thanked him and silently vowed to do so over my dead body. The UPS guy had left a box yesterday, which, upon opening, was nothing but birdhouse gourds and dried cane toads. I didn't even bother to catalog them individually, just noted them as *toads, lot of 8* and *gourds, lot of 4*. My spreadsheet was getting lengthy.

Narnia, hole to. Willows, lot of ten million. Them, number unknown.

There were no customers, so I didn't feel bad at all about sliding off the chair and down behind the counter and wrapping my arms around my knees and letting tears slide down my cheeks.

This is normal, I told myself. *This is totally normal. The world completely turned upside down and you were scared and you had to be competent and not freak out. Now you can freak out again and it's just taking a while to all break loose. You're fine. This is normal.*

Beau came by to see why I was on the floor. He head-butted my hand, which was rather like being affectionately punched. I rubbed his ears and he purred his gravelly purr at me.

"At least I'm not crying over my marriage," I told him, and started laughing.

14

After the museum closed, I went next door to check on Simon. He looked hollow eyed and tired, but he was still there. He raised his coffee mug in salute and I leaned against the counter. There were customers, so I couldn't say *Oh my God, did that really happen?*

Besides, I knew it had really happened. The olive sweater from the bunker was still lying across the chair in my bedroom. I could have hallucinated a lot of things, but that sweater was *real*.

He slid my coffee across the counter and I fist-bumped him awkwardly, which was the best I could do. He nodded. So did I.

"After . . . uh . . . you close up . . . ?" I raised my eyebrows. The customers probably thought I was propositioning him.

"Yeah."

I'd brought my laptop over and stared at the screen. My

cursor hovered over the search bar, but what the hell was I going to search for? *People visiting other worlds?*

I tried it, on a whim, and got three ads for the Church of Latter-day Saints and a whole bunch of videos about alien cover-ups. *Alien willow trees* got me a list of invasive species taking over Australia.

I searched for *Byricopa County*. The search engine decided that I must mean *Maricopa County* and began showing me school districts in Arizona.

I looked up *vacuae*.

It was Latin, to no one's surprise. The feminine form of *vacuus*, which was the plural of *vacuum*. I scrolled through the various definitions: *empty space. An empty space, one practically exhausted of gas or air. A vacant space. See also* emptiness, *see also* vacant, *see also, see also, see also.*

One definition far down the list caught my eye: *space unfilled or unoccupied, or apparently unoccupied.*

Apparently unoccupied.

The willow world had been full of apparently unoccupied spaces that were nevertheless full of . . . something. The bus driver. The children. The thing that had walked past us.

I lifted my head from the wall and dropped it back with a slight *thunk*. A customer glanced around to see what the noise was, then pointedly looked away from the weird woman beating her head on the wall.

Knowing the definition didn't do me any good unless I could

get an internet connection to the other world and see how they use it. Maybe it was something like *blood sign*, where they were using the same words but it presumably meant something else over there.

Shit, for all I knew, the military people really had meant a helicopter.

The customer finished her coffee and left. Simon squinted at his wristwatch, said, "I give up," and went and flipped the sign to CLOSED.

"So . . ." I trailed off because what the hell was there to say?

Simon held up both hands. "Not yet. Drinking first. I've got microwave popcorn and tequila."

"You are the brother I never had." I followed him up the narrow staircase

Simon's apartment had huge posters for the Cocteau Twins, Nick Cave, and the Cure, which did not surprise me in the least. The carpet was the vague stained beige of student apartments the world over. That was what it most reminded me of, a college apartment, down to the bright orange linoleum and the secondhand furniture.

"You should make Uncle Earl renovate this place," I said, sitting down on a couch that might predate the Wonder Museum itself.

"He's offered. But he doesn't really have the money, and I don't have anywhere to live while they're doing it, so I'm not too worried about it."

Simon went into the kitchen. I heard beeping noises and then the familiar fireworks of microwave popcorn. It was so strange that I was in a world with microwave popcorn in it. I couldn't seem to hold it in my head, that there could be willows and Sturdivant and microwave popcorn, all at the same time in the same place.

But there isn't, I thought. *They aren't in the same world. That's over in the other world, on the other side of the Wonder Museum wall.*

I just wished that the wall between us was more solid than drywall and a batik-printed sheet.

Simon came out with the bowl of popcorn and a bottle of something called Dragones. He poured an inch into two juice glasses and handed one over.

"We're not going to mix it with something?"

"This is a sipping tequila," he informed me. "None of your cheap-ass bottom-shelf stuff."

I took a sip, expecting agony. Instead it tasted like desert sunlight sliding over my tongue. "Tastes expensive."

"When you've been to hell, you get to break out the good liquor."

I took a handful of popcorn and stared at it. "So it really happened, then."

It wasn't a question, but Simon answered it like one anyway. "Oh, hell yeah, it happened."

"Not black mold?"

"I'm not creative enough to have hallucinated some of that shit, no matter how much mold I huffed." He leaned back and nudged his backpack with his boot. "And there's one of those FRR things in here. I don't think black mold can make MREs from another universe."

I groaned, remembered the Bible I'd stashed in my own backpack. "Yeah, me too. What do we do?"

He poured out more tequila. "You're asking me? It's your family's museum."

"You're from Florida. There's got to be more holes to hell in Florida than any other state."

"Touché." He clicked his glass against mine, presumably for the honor of Florida's hellmouths.

We ate popcorn. I drank more distilled sunlight. "There's something that's bothering me, though," said Simon finally.

"What, only one thing?"

"Heh. No, but, Carrot—what the hell kind of tourist knocks a hole in the wall that just happens to lead to another universe?"

I opened my mouth and closed it again and finally just drained my tequila because I realized that I didn't have an answer.

*

That night I dreamed I was in the concrete corridors again. Bits of grit rolled under my bare feet. It was dark, but there was a silvery willowlight coming from the open doorway. *Oh God*, I thought, *I'm back here*.

Had I ever left? Had I only dreamed that Simon and I had gotten home safely?

My fingertips ached. I'd been clawing at the walls with them, hadn't I? Trying to get out. Or back out. Or back in, depending on which side the willow world was on.

In my dream, though, I was back in that world. I walked forward, step by step. It was incredibly cold, but whether I was shivering from cold or horror, I couldn't tell you.

This is a dream, I told myself. *Please, God, let this be just a dream.*

I walked up the concrete steps. Sturdivant stood in the water just outside. I could see his organs spreading around him, like a drop of ink in water.

This is a dream.

"Did I get out?" I asked him.

He shook his head sadly and opened his mouth to say something, but only willow leaves came out.

*

I woke up, sucking in air in hard, choking gasps. They turned into coughs and I sat up, hacking my lungs out. "Shit," I wheezed in between gasps. "Shit. Shit."

Beau looked at me as if I were an idiot. From his point of view, I probably was. I'd been lying there in bed and suddenly woke up choking on my own spit.

I fell back against the pillows. The sheets were cold with

sweat. I'd been having quite a nightmare.

"Well, no surprise there," I told the cat. "If I get out of this with nothing more than nightmares, I'll be astonished. I've probably got PTSD. I mean, how could I not?"

I was not looking forward to finding a therapist to explain that I had PTSD from something that I absolutely could not tell a therapist about. How would I ever try to explain that? Claim I'd been high and had an unbelievably detailed hallucination that was so scary I had actual issues afterward? Was that a thing that happened? What would I even say I'd been on?

"Two pounds of LSD," I said to Beau, and snickered. "Yeah, right."

I got up to go to the bathroom. In the harsh light, my face looked puffy and I had dark circles under my eyes.

"Yeah, well, who wouldn't?" I splashed water on my face. Just a dream. It had just been a dream. I was out. I was safe.

I climbed the stairs to the upper floor and looked over at the batik. It hadn't moved. The raccoon case in front of it was undisturbed.

Just a dream.

What kind of tourist knocks a hole in the wall that happens to lead to another universe?

I went back to bed.

✳

My fingertips were raw the next morning. I stared at them

blankly, as if they belonged to someone else. There were gray half-moons under my nails, as if I'd been digging in dirt, and the skin was red and sore, with tiny blisters.

"Now how the hell did I do that . . . ?" I said aloud. Beau, passing by, gave me the good-natured but contemptuous look that cats reserve for humans they like.

In my dream, I had had bloody fingertips from clawing at the walls, trying to escape.

It was a dream it was just a dream it didn't really happen I wasn't really there. . . .

Well. One of the things that doesn't really come up if you don't work with a lot of stuffed moose heads is that taxidermy is a nasty business. A lot of the older skins are preserved with chemicals that are so banned now that you can't even say their names without a permit. I had been digging around in boxes for the catalog and handling a lot of taxidermy. Something could have reacted with something else and left my fingertips looking god-awful.

"And that would explain the dream," I told Beau. "I had sore fingers, so my brain added that into the dream."

The only three universal home remedies in the South are Epsom salts, Vicks VapoRub, and whiskey. This did not seem like a Vicks VapoRub situation, and it was a little too early in the day for whiskey. My head was surprisingly clear after the tequila, but I didn't want to tempt fate. I found some Epsom salts under the bathroom counter and filled the sink.

My fingertips stung. I rubbed them gingerly with a washcloth and dug up Band-Aids. Uncle Earl being the sort of person he was, the Band-Aids had little angels on them and a Bible verse on each backing paper. I wrapped Jeremiah 17:14 around my left thumb, shaking my head.

Typing on the spreadsheet didn't seem like a good idea this morning. I went next door to the Black Hen for a muffin and coffee. No one was in yet, thankfully.

"You doing okay?" I asked Simon.

"Nightmares," he said tersely. He had dark circles under his eyes, but had managed to hide it nicely by applying so much black eyeliner that he looked very Undead Chic.

"Me too," I sighed.

He forced a smile. "Given . . . everything . . . it'd be amazing if we didn't have them. But I'll be glad when things . . ." He waved his hand near his temples, as if unsure what word he wanted. I got the gist. After a minute he said, "Have you checked the patch?"

I nodded. "All the stuff we put in front of it is still there."

"Good." He stared down into his coffee. "I keep feeling it there. Like knowing there's a wasp in the room, except in the next building over. Whenever it slows down in here, I can just . . . feel it."

"The hole is closed. Isn't it?"

Simon gave me a long, unreadable look. "What do you think would happen if we pried that patch off?"

"I don't know," I admitted. I was hoping that the other side of the wall was just concrete now, that it had turned solid by whatever extradimensional magic let it be plaster on one side and six inches of concrete on the other. "I guess we could try to make a better patch. . . . It'd take us weeks to move enough concrete to fill the hallway, though. Uncle Earl would be back by then."

"I'll see if I can't figure something out." Simon frowned into his coffee.

"Maybe it's fixed and the way's closed," I said hopefully. And then, rather less hopefully: "Maybe it's still right there on the other side of the wall and always will be."

"That'll make it fun the next time we need to work on the HVAC system."

"If we were smart, we'd probably start running and never come back here."

"Somebody's gotta watch the coffee shop."

"Yeah." I sighed. "And I can't bail on Uncle Earl. Even if I told him, he'd never leave the museum. It's his whole life."

That was what it came down to. I couldn't afford to go anywhere, and even if I'd had all the money in the world, I couldn't leave Uncle Earl to the mercy of the willows. How long can you really live in a building without having to get inside one of the walls? How long before a tourist bashed into something again, or the pipes needed work, or Earl tried to hang something too heavy on a nail and tore it out of the wall and suddenly there's a pinhole leak from our world into the next? He'd go in and find the skeleton and he really would call the cops and then everything would get very weird, very quick, and the *best* scenario was that Uncle Earl would lose the museum and the FBI or the military or somebody would take it over and also Simon would wind up going to jail for two pounds of LSD.

Hell, even if we pulled the skeleton out and barricaded the metal door, Uncle Earl was bound to find the door eventually, and he wouldn't even have a token conversation about its being a horror movie, he'd take a jackhammer to that thing in hopes Bigfoot was behind it.

"If only we knew why it had opened, or how far it goes . . . ," I said, digging my nails into my scalp. Simon had been right. I couldn't really believe that a careless tourist had knocked a hole in reality with their elbow.

So what had happened? How had it opened up? Accident? Fate? Had some nefarious being come to the museum disguised as a tourist and tried to open a way to another world?

I had a sudden image of a willow wearing a trench coat and dark sunglasses saying, "How do you do, fellow humans?"— and I fought down the urge to giggle hysterically and then start screaming and never, ever stop.

"Heads up," murmured Simon, looking past me. A moment later the front door banged open and a couple of tourists came in, hunting for coffee.

"What time does that place next door open?" one asked. "It looks wild!"

"It looks like a junk heap," grumbled her companion.

I took my coffee, gave them both a bright smile, and said, "I'm just about to open up!"—and left Junk Heap Guy turning red in the middle of the coffee shop.

✳

Junk Heap Guy and his girlfriend were the first two customers, although Junk Heap couldn't meet my eyes. She bought two T-shirts and a souvenir mug, possibly by way of apology.

Brief flash of pettiness aside, I truly didn't care. I had bigger fish to fry. World-size fish. I'd joggled my own brain, talking about how far the hole went, because we didn't know, did we? We'd cut the hole bigger, right where it was, but we were enlarging the existing hole, not making a new one.

What would happen if we went six inches over? Would we cut a hole into the corridor, six inches farther on, or would we find ourselves looking at insulation and studs?

Did I dare to experiment?

I gulped.

"It can't be every wall," I muttered to myself. I was supposed to be working on my spreadsheet, but I'd been staring off into space for ten minutes. "Can it?"

The two customers had left. I grabbed a screwdriver from the junk drawer behind the counter and tried to think of a chunk of wall that no one would miss. Not my bedroom . . . if it did make a hole to the willows, the last thing I wanted was that in my room.

Not the bathroom, either. I'd never crap peacefully again.

Behind the grizzly bear. There's a space there, if you hold your breath and wiggle through, and while it shared the same wall as the original hole, it was a story down and a dozen yards away.

The bear's glass stare looked over my shoulder, one paw raised in salute. I patted his flank absently as I passed. Uncle Earl used to give him a high five every morning when opening the museum. The bear was old and the fur mostly hid that one of his legs wasn't attached as well as it could be. Uncle Earl had said that he related to that more and more, the older he got. I got down on my hands and knees and punched the screwdriver through the wallboard behind the bear.

I had to wiggle it a bit to make the hole large enough to press my cell phone up against the gap and get the flash as well. "I'll spackle this later, I promise," I muttered to the bear, or possibly to the absent Uncle Earl.

I pulled the phone back out and pulled up the photo. My heart was pounding, and not just because crawling around behind the bear took some effort.

The photo was of a narrow space a couple inches deep, with a layer of fluffy, mouse-eaten insulation. The flash had washed out everything, but it definitely was the inside of a wall, not a concrete corridor in a world made of willows.

I sagged back against the bear and wiped away tears of unexpected relief.

15

Over the course of the day, in between being cheerful at tourists, I poked test holes in three more places in the Wonder Museum. None of them led to the willows. One had been in the wall directly under the room with the patch, and the only thing I encountered was a piece of pipe that, thankfully, I didn't damage with my inexpert probing.

I was not brave enough—not yet—to test the patch behind the batik. Like Simon, I imagined I could feel it there, the wasp in the room, the hole to something else. But now I knew that not every wall in the building led to it.

I closed up the shop, nuked the last of my leftover takeout, and sat on the bed, staring into space and trying to make sense of things.

If the willow world and my world were touching in the wall

of the Wonder Museum, was it just in that one single place? I
put the tips of my chopsticks together and stared at them. Was it
a limited space within the wall, the tips just touching? Or were
they lying alongside each other, with something between them
like . . . like . . .

I picked up the red paper sleeve the chopsticks came in and
sandwiched it between the two lengths of bamboo. Beau, who
had wandered in looking for treats, watched me do this as if I
had completely lost my marbles.

"Look," I said to him. "Say this one's our world and this
one's the willows, and the paper between them is . . . uh . . . a
barrier of some kind. Whatever keeps one world from bleeding
into another one. Like a cell membrane." (I had a feeling that I
was completely butchering high school biology, but it sounded
good when I said it to the cat.)

Beau blinked to indicate that he was with me so far.

"But there's a hole in the paper, right? And the little hole in
the paper is where the worlds touch. And . . . um . . ."

I stared at the chopsticks for several minutes. But they were
just chopsticks and the red paper sleeve was just paper and
whatever breakthrough I was trying to make, I wasn't making it.

Beau reached out and delicately attempted to tease a cube
of pork loose from the pork fried rice. I dropped my model of
the multiverse and fended him off.

Worlds running alongside each other . . . did that mean
that there could be many holes? People could wander into the

willows from anywhere? Sturdivant had gone through a kudzu cathedral and into the willows. Had that been a hole somewhere else in the South?

Maybe it wasn't alongside. Maybe worlds wrapped around and passed through each other, and then . . . I don't know, something something hyperspace and black holes and probably string theory or quantum.

Maybe I couldn't get my brain around that many dimensions.

Maybe all I had was a couple of chopsticks.

Beau went for the pork again.

I was reminded of the feeling I'd had in the willows, that the reality I could see was only a skin over vast emptiness. But I couldn't figure out how to make that fit with my chopsticks and the paper.

I finished off my meal, still struggling with concepts that were too big for me, trying to find a metaphor that would snap it all into focus.

Maybe the willows surrounded my world, or maybe my world surrounded it, like a tumor in my world's flesh.

Maybe the place of willows was bigger. Maybe it was a lot smaller. There was no way to tell, short of going back with surveying gear, and there wasn't enough money on earth to get me to go back there. Not after seeing Sturdivant.

"No, tumor's not the right metaphor," I said. Beau, perched on the end of the bed, glanced up at me to see if I was saying any important food-related words. "It touched other worlds, didn't it? Like . . . uh . . ."

I'd dropped my bag in the corner earlier. Now I dug inside. Two FRRs in foil, and a small, rectangular book with onionskin pages.

I picked up the Bible and stared at the soft, pebbled cover.

What a profound, astonishing discovery. Another world. Another universe. And here was physical proof, held in the palm of my hand.

And it was so profoundly, utterly useless.

Hell, for all I knew, it was profoundly inimical, not just useless. There might be a disease on the cover, something slow incubating that I had picked up from touching it, and in a few days it would wake and destroy my entire species because none of us had the antibodies for it.

"Well, if not this, then the porn magazine," I said to Beau. "That's way more likely to have been covered in diseases." Beau, untroubled by human depravity or the potential for human eradication, purred.

"It's not like I could do anything about it anyway. I'm sure they'd love me at the CDC. 'Pardon, but I went to another world and I think I'm maybe infected with a superbug that will kill us all.' I bet they've heard *that* one before."

Beau closed his eyes, presumably agreeing that the CDC was unlikely to be helpful.

"Anyway, if people made it back before, then . . . then . . . what?" We couldn't be the first, could we? Simon and I were much too incompetent for that. And the soldiers must have had some ability to go through because they'd been sent on a reconnaissance mission with full kit and supplies. You don't carry cots and blankets and buckets if you're just poking your head into a weird hole in the world.

The *vacuae*.

I grabbed my phone and padded out into the dark museum. There was a thump and a disgruntled noise behind me as Beau jumped down from the bed to accompany the human.

The sunflower visage of His Holiness smiled benevolently down at me as I sat down and leaned against the wall. Beau, never a lap cat, sat close enough that I could reach him if I suddenly realized that I needed to scratch a cat behind the ears.

My phone picked up the Wi-Fi from the Black Hen and I looked up holes to another dimension. I got a whole lot of stuff about black holes, Stephen Hawking, and CERN. One website that looked fairly respectable and devoid of aliens suggested that I think of the universe as a sheet and a wormhole as a "throat" connecting our sheet to another one.

"I could really have done without that image," I told Beau. "Since I think Simon and I very nearly got swallowed."

Beau blinked solemnly.

It worked, though, image aside. The big hole in the wall was a throat to another world. The other holes I'd punched with my screwdriver were just holes.

Say that all the universes out there were a pile of sheets, and more than one had wormhole-throats leading to the willows. Was it some kind of hub? Or was it just easier to break into the willows somehow? Maybe wormholes were drawn to it.

Hell, maybe it had been a perfectly ordinary world once upon a time, and then the willows got their roots in. . . .

"And then the people there built bunkers to try to hold them off," I said, "but the willows ate everything anyway."

That was one possibility. The other was that the bunkers were leftovers from something like a nuclear war and there wasn't anyone to fight back when the willows showed up. There was no way to know. You'd need an archaeologist to go digging around to find out, and what's the average life span of an archaeologist in hell?

Still, the idea of a nuclear war made me add radiation poisoning to the list of things I should be worried about. I tried to chew on my thumbnail and got a mouthful of bandage instead. Jeremiah 17:14. I wondered what the otherworld version was.

I opened the Bible, held my phone up so the light fell over the page, and ran my bandaged finger down the list of books. I flipped through to Jeremiah . . . and stopped.

I hadn't seen it before, since I hadn't been going through and actually reading the text, but someone had written on the margins in blue ink. It was a combination of print and cursive and reminded me vaguely of the way my mother wrote when she was in a hurry.

It would start on one side of the page, at the top, then go down the side and around the bottom. The writer could only fit in one line or so, and the title of the book would still be at the top in midsentence, so the first line I read said, "If Marco doesn't stop talking every goddamn minute, I'm going to put a slug in his JEREMIAH head and throw him in the river. If we're all going to die anyway, at least let us have a little bit of quiet."

I stared at the page for quite a long time.

Something about the handwriting reached out across worlds and grabbed me. This was a *person*. Until then, the contents of the bunker had felt vaguely like movie props, real but impersonal. Suddenly this Bible belonged to a real person who had written in the margins in blue ink and who had really wanted Marco to shut up.

My cell phone screen went off and left me sitting in the gloom under His Sunflower Holiness.

I picked up the Bible and went back to my room, trailed by Beau. I am sure he was starting to think that the occasional cube of illicit pork was not worth all this back and forth. Still, he jumped up on the bed, punched my arm with his fist of a skull, and flopped down beside me.

The writing started at the beginning of First Chronicles, partway through the Old Testament. It was slightly larger then, and the author had drawn a little box around the title of the book.

I left my journal back home in case I didn't come back. I thought I could probably go a few days without writing but it's the second day and I'm already itchy. The problem with taking up a journal to quit smoking is that I want to write every time I want a cigarette and I really really want a cigarette. So I'm writing in the Bible from Mom (sorry Mom) and it feels super weird like I'm drawing on the pews at church and the deacon's going to come smack me.

Starting in Chronicles because it's a chronicle, right? If we make it back home I'll transfer it over or maybe tear out the pages and glue them into my journal (really sorry Mom) but I don't know if it'll even matter. It'll probably all get classified anyway and they'll take this away and anybody who talks about the vacuae gets thrown in the stockade.

Fuck I hate FRRs.

Going through the vacuae was also super weird. It didn't feel like anything. All that buildup and the lectures and the big shiny membrane and enough razor wire to shred a buffalo and decontamination and then we just walked through some plastic sheeting and we were here. All that buildup and it didn't even make a noise. I don't know what noise I wanted it to make. Glorp or some kinda theremin shit.

The landscape on the other side of the vacuae looks a little like the bends around the Rio Grande. Gravel spits and bushes and water. Lots more fog though. Marco says it's like some river up north in Pennsylvania. Marco hasn't shut up since we got here and he talks in his sleep.

It's pretty, anyway, just weird and quiet. (Except for Marco.) You figure you go to another planet and stuff would look different, but no. There's some birds and some bugs. Steen got super excited over that, taking tons of photos. I wouldn't mind doing some fishing, but we don't get to eat it if we catch it. Supply gave us FRRs and we better be grateful! Tax dollars at work!

Fuck I want a cigarette.

There was a gap and some doodles, just abstract stuff in blue ballpoint. I set the unexpectedly talkative Bible down and went to get a cup of tea. Uncle Earl started drinking tea in the afternoon because he says that coffee gives him palpitations that late in the day, and then some of his correspondents figured out that he liked tea, so the tiny break room has about fifty boxes of the stuff. The only problem is that they send tea the way they send artifacts. Most of them are old and some of them aren't labeled except for somebody scribbling TEA on the envelope.

Hell, for all I know, the owner of a rival museum somewhere sent him poison and has been waiting for years for him to finally reach the critical tea bag and expire. Except I'm not sure if there are any rival museums, and it's hard to imagine anyone wanting to poison Uncle Earl.

I pulled out a tea bag, sniffed it, put it back, rejected two more that smelled more like silage than tea, and finally found a box of elderly Lipton in the back of the cupboard.

✱

When I returned to the bedroom, Beau had moved to the warm spot on the bed that I had been sitting on. I attempted to pick him up, whereupon he became extremely heavy in that way that cats have, and I gave up. He graciously allowed me half an inch of space on the edge of the bed, so I perched there, armed with my tea and the Bible from another world.

"Their military sent them," I said to Beau. "I mean, we knew that, right?"

Beau blinked slowly. He had indeed known that.

"But it sounds like they found a hole and then quarantined it off with razor wire and stuff. . . ." Which, I had to admit, was probably sensible. *Decontamination*, the Bible writer had said. Decontamination, so they didn't track any foreign diseases into the vacuae? And presumably they'd decontaminate the soldiers again on the way out, so that they didn't carry diseases back.

Hell, I'd been thinking about the CDC, but maybe Simon and I had carried diseases into the willows and they'd all get . . . I don't know, Dutch elm disease, or whatever the willow equivalent was.

I had a hard time summoning much grief over this. I love nature and all, but if every one of those willows rotted and died, I'd have considered it a good day's work, after what they did to Sturdivant.

"And what they did to you, my friend," I said to the Bible writer. He hadn't made it back, had he? He and the other three had left their gear and a pile of spent brass behind and vanished.

"Unless they knew where an opening back to their world was, and something spooked them back into it," I said thoughtfully. Lord knows there was enough in the willows to spook anyone. They could have found that school bus and just turned tail and run.

This was a more pleasant thought than holding a book by a dead man.

Speaking of dead men . . .

I set the Bible down for a moment, went out to the Wi-Fi spot, and looked up *Martin Sturdivant*.

Five pages of search results later, I gave up. Apparently this was not an uncommon name, and also there was somebody in the Civil War who had led a cavalry unit. Entering *park ranger* and *missing* into the search engine didn't give me anything useful. If Sturdivant had been from our world, he was buried deep. Then again, it wasn't as if thousands of people didn't go missing all the time. His name could be in some police report that nobody had bothered to put online. *And what am I going to do, even if I do find it? Call them up and say that he's alive, sitting in another universe in a pool of his own intestines?*

I didn't see that going well. I tried *willow world* and got a whole bunch of links about geishas, which were apparently called the "flower and willow world." This was fascinating from an anthropological standpoint, but absolutely destroyed any chance of finding useful information. Adding more keywords about visiting a willow world got me an even split of travelogues and fetishes, which was depressing in a way that had nothing to do with missing park rangers.

I picked up the Bible again.

Something weird going on out there. Petrov was on watch and he came down and woke us up. Weird shit in the trees. Everything's moving, and it looks full of aliens. I don't know. Marco says it's not real, but he can fuck off because I know that's not wind.

"You tell him," I muttered to the book. "Fuck Marco, anyway. What does he know?"

There were some disturbing squiggles in the margins, possibly the writer's attempt to draw the things in the trees. I turned the page in a hurry.

The commander's gone. We were going through the bushes and he was right behind me, but he didn't come out. We looked for him for hours. Marco thinks it's a sinkhole but we would have seen a sinkhole.

Petrov says something in this place got him. Marco wants to go back to the drop point right now but it's not open so I don't know what good that's gonna do. He says

*they'll have to open it for us but that's bullshit. They
won't open it until a week's gone by, and there isn't a
door for us to hammer on.*

"Now, that's interesting . . . ," I muttered. Did Bible writer
come from a place where they could open and close the way to
the vacuae? It sure sounded like it.

Which meant . . . which meant what? That they had
invented some kind of technology that opened wormholes to
other worlds? Or had they found one of the throats to another
universe and figured out how to open and close it, then sent
Bible writer and his squad through to see what the hell they
were looking at?

Maybe it wasn't even some high tech. Maybe they'd found
a hole the same way we had and were covering it in spackle and
drywall, same as we were. When it was time for the soldiers to
come home, they'd pull aside their version of the batik sheet
and open it up again. Here I was picturing something with
lasers zapping portals in reality, and for all I knew, they were
just like Simon and me, muddling through as best we could.

*Come on, Bible, casually mention the details of how you
close up the hole, come on, that would be really helpful. . . .*

Bible writer did not see fit to include this in his journal.
Instead he detailed Marco's freak-out and how Steen thought
the commander might come back, but that was stupid because
the commander was definitely a goner. We got out of Chronicles

and clear to Nehemiah on this subject alone.

I hate this place, I hate this place, I hate this place, the author wrote, and underlined it so fiercely that the scar from the pen left an indentation on the next dozen pages.

"I feel you, brother," I muttered.

It was two in the morning, and tomorrow was a busy tourist day. The after-church crowd on a Sunday was reliably busy, as everybody came into town for brunch and then wandered around looking for something to do. I wanted to keep reading, but it wasn't as if we were under a deadline. The owner of the Bible wasn't going to come looking for it. The hole was closed. It was all just morbid curiosity now.

I shut the book, stuck my foot under Beau, and went to sleep.

*

In my dreams, I walked down the steps of a bunker. Sturdivant looked up at me, surrounded by a pool of water and viscera, long hair hanging like tree roots.

"Don't come any closer," he warned me.

"I have to get out of the willows," I said. "There are things in the willows."

He shook his head. "They're not in the willows. They *are* the willows."

I wanted to explain to him that the distinction was meaningless, that I still had to get away from the willows, but I heard rustling behind me. I turned and the doorway was full of leaves, and something without eyes looked out at me from within them.

I woke, sitting up in bed, with my throat aching as if I'd been yelling. My heart was hammering and my tongue tasted like metal.

"Shit. Shit." I staggered to the bathroom because I couldn't think of anything else to do. My shirt had hitched up and was twisted around my armpits, and when I hauled it back down, it was clammy with sweat. "Shit."

I was moving on autopilot, and when I turned on the tap, it soaked the Band-Aids over my fingertips. They stung angrily. Christ, had I not gotten whatever was on them off?

"It's otherworldly flesh-eating bacteria," I muttered, peeling them off and wincing. "I'm being devoured from the nails up."

There was more white goop under my nails. "Please let it not be pus," I muttered to myself. I'd mostly been joking about the flesh-eating bacteria. Really.

It came out powdery, like talc. Well, I usually throw baby powder under my boobs at night, so it's possible that it had gotten down into the Band-Aids. Had I done it last night? I didn't know anymore. I didn't know anything. My head hurt.

I took some aspirin and went to open up the museum. It was a dull morning, busy but boring. I took money, I sold T-shirts. An artist came in and got permission to sketch some of the taxidermy. That happens sometimes, and I'm happy to give the artists permission.

On a whim, I went to the Wi-Fi spot and searched the internet for *how to close a portal to another world*. The results said a lot about humanity, but nothing directly useful for my situation. A bunch of links were to spiritual warfare, which Uncle Earl had told me about once, where people think they're off fighting demons. I suppose that's one way to make church more interesting, but it all sounded like Jesus LARP to me. (I told Uncle Earl that, which forced me to explain LARPing. If you've never tried to describe hitting other people dressed as orcs with foam weapons, particularly to an elderly relative, you haven't really lived.)

My phone rang while I was holding it. I didn't recognize the number, but I usually answer the phone anyway, since you never know when it's going to be the highway patrol telling you they've found a family member wrapped around a tree. (This probably says a lot more about me than I'm comfortable with.)

"Hello?"

"Kara?" said a vaguely familiar male voice.

"Speaking."

"Kara, it's me."

"Sorry, who is this?"

The man on the other end made an exasperated noise, and *that* was what I recognized, not his voice. "Kara, don't be like that."

"Mark! Sorry, is this a new number? You didn't come up on the caller ID."

"Oh. Yes." My ex coughed, embarrassed. "Yes, once I didn't

need a family plan, it turned out to be cheaper to just cancel the plan and get a new one than to sort out the switch. Sorry, I didn't realize I hadn't . . ."

He hadn't needed a family plan anymore because I wasn't on it. Right. I watched the front door while he rambled on about his new phone. A small knot of tourists ambled by, then Kay on her way to the Black Hen. "Yeah, it's fine. What do you need?"

"I don't need anything." He sounded nonplussed. He was the magnanimous one in the relationship, the one who'd supported me without complaining, who had given so much in the divorce, had offered me the house, everything. We had our assigned roles in the drama, and I wasn't playing mine correctly. "I wanted you to know that I'm selling the house."

"Okay."

Kay came back out of the Black Hen and opened the door to the Wonder Museum. I pointed at my phone and then at my coffee cup and made pleading gestures. She smiled, took the cup, and went to get me a refill. Goddamn, I liked Kay.

"I just thought you'd want to know."

"I mean, it's your house. You can sell it if you want to." We'd refinanced to take my name off the mortgage as soon as the divorce proceedings started. Thanks to a rather shady initial mortgage, there was maybe a thousand dollars' worth of equity in the place, tops, and I'd already used my share to pay down my credit cards.

"Yes, but . . ." He was getting frustrated now. One of Mark's great character flaws was that he'd have an idea in his head about how a conversation would go, then get upset when it didn't go that way. "You loved that house."

"Yeah?" I tried to remember. Had I? Probably. It seemed like a very long time ago now.

Jesus Christ, there was a portal to hell in the wall and this asshole was expecting me to have performative emotions over the phone for him. I didn't have time, and I certainly didn't have energy. "I'm sure somebody else will love it, too. It's fine."

"Kara . . ."

What did he want from me? Was I supposed to burst into tears and tell him to keep it as a shrine to our failed marriage? "Do I need to sign anything?"

"No, but . . . look, is this about Riley?"

Riley? My brain tried to sort out who the hell Riley was, and all I could come up with was the dog that belonged to the neighbors two doors down. "The chocolate Lab? What about him?"

A long, long silence. I was pretty good at reading Mark's silences, even now, and this was the I-don't-know-if-I-should-be-mad-or-not one. "Is that a joke?" he said finally.

"One of us is very confused. I'm not sure which one."

"Riley," he said in clipped tones, "the woman I've been seeing."

Oh. Huh. I'd been right. *How 'bout that?*

I did a quick inventory of my soul and realized I didn't even feel righteous indignation. He was in another state. He would have been awful at pretty much everything about the current situation. I realized, with sudden intense relief, that I did not need to explain it to him. He never had to know. He could go hang out with Riley.

Ladies, get you a man who can handle a portal to hell without freaking out.

"Kara?"

"Didn't know. Good for you."

Another throat-clearing noise, the defensive one he used when he realized he had just put his foot in it. "Oh. I thought, since I'd said something online, and you're always . . ." He trailed off.

I decided I was not here for the implied criticism. "Only Wi-Fi in this place is at the coffee shop. Look, I've got some customers here, I gotta go. It's fine about the house. If I need to sign any extra papers or something, just mail them to the museum. Bye."

I hung up. Kay returned to find me glaring at the phone.

"Trouble?" She handed me my newly warmed-up coffee.

"You are a saint. No, just my ex."

"Do you need an alibi for the next few hours?"

"Ha! No. He'll make some nice woman very miserable someday. Today, apparently." I slugged back the coffee. "How are you doing?"

She launched into a saga about her extended family's legal battles, which were almost Medici-like in their complexity and malice. I listened, fascinated, to the tale of an estranged aunt storing cats in the house vacated by her late grandfather, when said house was supposed to be on the market, and the Realtor opened the door and ten feral cats bolted out. "A litter box in every room. None of them changed in months."

"Jesus." I had a strong urge to go scoop Beau's litter box, even though I had just done it that morning.

By the time more tourists arrived and Kay excused herself, I had been cheered into a better mood. Other people's horrible relatives are remarkably soothing. You can be comfortably appalled without having to deal with them yourself.

I closed up the museum, went next door to mooch Wi-Fi, and worked on logos. I had a client who didn't know what she wanted but would know it when she saw it. This phrase fills every designer with intense dread. On the other hand, I was billing by the hour and she paid the invoices on time, so there was that.

I waited until a gap in the tourists and told Simon about the Bible.

"Creepy," he said.

"Do you want to read it?"

He rubbed the back of his neck. "Show me?"

I opened to a relevant page. He took one look at it and snorted. "Yeah, no. I'll go even blinder if I try to read that handwriting. I gotta use the giant font on my ebooks already. Give me the highlights."

"They're stuck in the willows and the commander vanished."

". . . We have a different definition of highlights."

I glanced around to make sure that there wasn't a customer lurking unseen in the corners. "They saw a lot of the same stuff we did."

Simon was silent for a moment. "Yeah," he said finally. "I mean, that doesn't surprise me, really, but I'm glad it wasn't just us. Except I wish it hadn't happened to anybody else, you know?"

I did indeed. After the Black Hen closed, I opened up the Bible again. "All right, bud," I muttered. "Let's see what happens to you now. . . ."

We found the commander today. Something got him. It was the same thing that left all the holes all over the islands. Big funnel shapes in the sand, except they were all over him instead. No blood, just these cones scooped out of him and the edges all red. There was one through the side of his head and you could see his brain and skull all neat lined up layers like a sandwich.

Marco puked. Petrov thought it was some kind of weapon, but Steen pointed out it was the same as the ones in the sand. Fuck fuck fuck I want a cigarette!! I want out!

I set the Bible down and walked to the bathroom, and then, much like the absent Marco, I heaved my guts up.

Big funnel shapes in the sand . . .

They hadn't been ant lions.

They'd been *everywhere*.

The marks had been on every sandspit. They'd been on practically every surface that wasn't concrete or stone. We'd been walking through Their footprints with every step.

I went back to my room and shoved the Bible under my bed. Two pages and I couldn't take any more. I was out. Reading it felt like watching a snuff film in slow motion. I knew they were dead. Somewhere in there, the writer had written the last entry in the Bible, set it down, left the bunker, and gone out into the willows. I didn't want to go back there. I wanted my time in the willows to be over and done and not a thing that was still happening to me every time I closed my eyes.

*

There was an ancient VCR in one of the back rooms, and some home videos. I shoved one in. In another place, I might worry that I was going to locate Uncle Earl's porn stash, but here . . .

Tinny music played and I watched the famous footage of a guy in a Bigfoot suit walking across the forest. Then I watched it again, slowed down, while a guy in a lab coat pointed to various things and explained that absolutely nothing we were seeing could be explained by someone wearing a rubber suit. This bit here was definitely a muscle, not a suit. This was not a seam. He pointed to the seam several times while telling me how clearly it was not a seam.

When that video was done, I watched *The Search for Bigfoot*, *Behind the Red Eyes* (that was a Mothman video), *Bigfoot Unveiled*, *Loch Ness: Home of Mystery*, and a documentary on the phenomenon of phantom kangaroos. (People in America see kangaroos a lot, often in areas completely devoid of kangaroos. I don't know if this says more about kangaroos or Americans.)

I fell asleep sitting in the back room with Beau on my lap. When I woke up, the tape had played all the way through and the screen was a soft blue. I staggered to my bedroom and slept for the next few hours, fitfully, dreaming of Bigfoot walking through the willows and turning away, while things hummed and buzzed and screamed overhead.

I woke with a dreadful crick in my neck, probably from sleeping in the chair, and slammed down some coffee and aspirin. I did my quick walk-through of the museum before opening, partly to make sure the cat hadn't barfed anywhere, mostly, if I was being honest, to make sure that the hole was still closed.

The upper floor was quiet.

"Nothing to see here," I muttered, and turned to go, then I saw a flicker of movement.

The batik sheet belled out as if a breeze moved behind it.

It was the most innocent thing in the world. I stared at it for upward of a minute, watching the pattern of blue spirals ripple gently. The sheet went out to the edge of the raccoon taxidermy case, and there it stopped, but without a doubt air was coming in behind it.

It's an air vent overhead, I told myself, not believing it even as I thought it. If there had been a vent, it would have been blowing the last dozen times I'd come back through here.

I picked my way across the room as carefully as if it were a minefield. It seemed very important to set each foot just so, very precisely, as if I might stumble and fall through the world.

You fell through the world once already. . . .

The giant river otter bared his fangs in the case. I trailed my bandaged fingertips along the cold glass and it hurt a little, but I didn't stop.

As slowly as I walked, though, I could not stop myself from finally reaching the other side. I stared at the wall, at the batik moving softly in the unseen breeze.

You have to look.

You have to look.

It's not like Medusa, looking won't kill you. But you have to look.

I reached out and pulled the batik aside.

There were huge gouges in the wall patch. It looked as if someone had tried to dig it out with his or her nails. I stared at it for a long time, then down at my own bandaged fingertips.

The stuff under my nails hadn't been dirt. It had been plaster dust.

I am still amazed at how calm I was. I felt as if ice had glazed over my mind and my nerves, six inches thick, and all my emotions and most of my thoughts were on the other side.

Calmly, very calmly, I studied the gouges. Part of the board had been ripped down. Was it large enough to fit through? Had I actually gone through into the corridor, in those dreams where I was sleepwalking?

No. No human could have fit through that. Even Beau would have had a difficult time.

I let the batik drop back down over the hole. I pushed the raccoon case back into position. Something rattled on the floor as I moved the case, and I reached down mechanically to pick up the stupid otter carving. How many times had I had to pick it up? It seemed like it was always rolling off something. It didn't want to lie flat.

The top of my mind was able to think about the difficulty of cylindrical carvings. Under the ice, I was screaming, but that was fine. That was miles away.

I went downstairs. I picked up Beau, who was puzzled, but draped his paws over my shoulder to see what happened next. I picked up my car keys in my free hand. I had no thought anywhere in my mind except to get in the car and drive away until I ran out of gas and to never, ever, *ever* come back.

The only thing that stopped me was the phone ringing.

I set down my keys, picked up the receiver, and said mechanically, "This is the Wonder Museum."

"Carrot? It's Uncle Earl."

The ice began to crack. If I left, Uncle Earl would come back and there would be no one here to warn him. I knew that. I knew it. He would go into the willows and They would get him. I couldn't just start driving.

"Carrot? Are you there?"

And I had to tell Simon. I couldn't leave him to deal with this alone. I was briefly appalled at my own selfishness, for even thinking about leaving without telling him, or offering him a spot in the passenger seat.

"I'm here, Uncle Earl. How are you feeling?"

"Oh, I'm fine. . . . How are you?"

"I'm fine," I said automatically. I was not fine. Possibly I would never be fine again. I could not say any of that to Uncle Earl. "Are you sure you're okay? How was the surgery?"

"Well, I'm pretty sore, and they want me to take all these pills. But your mom's taking real good care of me."

"Driving you nuts, I bet." I was on autopilot. It was bizarre how much of a normal conversation I could have while I was screaming internally.

He laughed, which was as close as he'd get to an admission that, yes, her hovering was making him nuts.

Beau decided that he was not interested in being carried any longer and launched himself off my shoulder. I squawked.

"Carrot?"

"It's fine." I fumbled with the phone. "Just Beau."

"He's a terror. Heard you had some excitement the other day."

This was the sort of understatement that should have been accompanied by a crack of thunder. For a second I couldn't think what he was talking about, then I remembered the story I told my mother. "Yeah. I'm sorry, I had to close the museum for a day to take Simon to the hospital."

"You did exactly right. Don't you worry about it for one minute. Is Simon okay?"

"He's still a little shook up," I said, which wasn't a lie at all. "But he's getting better, I think." Unlike me, who was apparently sleepwalking and trying to claw my way into a different universe.

"Keep an eye on him, Carrot. He's a real nice fella and he works too much."

"I will. And you should take it easy, too! Don't strain anything, after they did all that surgery to get you fixed up!"

"Doubt your mom will let me. Everything else okay at the museum?"

I am not sure how I did not burst into tears or hysterical laughter. "Tourist knocked a hole in the drywall," I said. "Simon patched it up, though."

"It's always something."

We said our goodbyes and he hung up and I didn't get in the car and drive away and three tourists came in at that exact moment, so I didn't start screaming, either.

Instead I stood at the front counter, clicking the end of a ballpoint pen, while my brain raced in frantic little circles.

I'd been trying to get back to the willows in my sleep.

Why?

Was my sleeping brain suicidal? Was something deep in my

psyche trying to fling itself into the void? I wasn't the sort of person who looked over cliffs and heard a voice telling them to jump. I looked over a cliff and went "Damn, that's a long drop," and then stepped back to a sensible distance, possibly behind a guardrail.

Maybe it's not you, whispered the voice that didn't ever tell me to jump. *Maybe it's the willows. Maybe they got their roots into* you *and they're dragging you back.*

That did not seem any better.

Well, there was only one thing to do. I was going to have to wait until the tourists left, then go next door and tell Simon that I had lost my sleeping mind.

16

"That . . . is a problem," said Simon.

"Little bit," I said. "Little bit of a problem." I had tried to stay light and sarcastic, and I knew I wasn't quite pulling it off, but if I stopped being sarcastic, I was going to burst into tears. "I don't suppose you've been sleepwalking?"

He shook his head. I could feel myself turning red. There is something horribly embarrassing about going mad. I'd had no idea how humiliating it would be.

"Look, I'm mostly telling you this so that when I vanish, you'll know where I went and you can maybe make sure the tourists don't bang on the door too much. Put up a little sign or something." I leaned against one of the tables. I could feel the sob lurking deep in my chest, but damned if I was going to let it out.

"You don't want that," said Simon. "My handwriting is

terrible. Come on, let's go see what the hole is like."

We put up the BACK IN 5 MINUTES sign and tromped to the museum. I shoved aside the batik and turned my head away. I didn't want to look at it. The long gouges looked like badges of shame.

You've lost the plot, I told myself. *You've gone around the bend. All this time, you thought you were pretty solid, but your sleeping brain is completely gone and you don't have the money for meds or therapy and what would you even tell a therapist anyway?*

"Pretty impressive." Simon reached out and touched the patch, where a big chunk had been pulled back and had fallen to the floor in a spatter of powder. It had been behind the raccoon case, and I hadn't noticed it.

I looked down at my hands, at the fresh bandages. "Yeah. I've been doing this for a few days, I think. My fingers were raw the first day, but I didn't realize anything was wrong. It wasn't until I noticed that there was air coming through . . ." I gestured.

"Hmm." He glanced over at the raccoon case. "It's all up at the top. You weren't moving the display case, just hauling the fabric out of the way, I think."

I shrugged. As consolations went, it wasn't much.

"We could put something else heavy in front of it."

"And I'll probably yank it down on my own head," I said bitterly.

"I mean, it's possible."

I put my head in my hands, trying to think of solutions. Concrete was too slow. "What if we burn the building down?"

Simon gave me a startled look. "Hard-core. It'd kill your uncle to lose the museum."

"Yes, but he'd still be alive for it to kill him." I grimaced. I hated the thought. I probably couldn't light the match. But given the choice between Uncle Earl losing the museum, and losing him to the willows . . .

"I doubt it would work," said Simon. "Buildings are harder to burn than you think. And if you go to jail for arson, it'd still kill him, and the hole will still be there."

"Okay, but—"

"And"—Simon held up a finger—"what if it doesn't close the hole?"

I blinked at him.

"When we cut at the sides of the hole, the hole got bigger. What happens if it burns?"

I had a sudden vision of a burned-out building, and the opening to the willow world hanging in midair above it, no longer small but huge and jagged and smoking at the edges, while firefighters stood underneath, scratching their heads.

The description written in the Bible came back to me, about the razor wire and the plastic sheeting. The military would take control of it, wouldn't they?

They damn well ought to. The willows are no place for normal people.

. . . And look how well the other military fared there. You think ours would do any better?

They'd close it off, anyway, I argued to myself. *And make sure no one got in.*

And a bunch of soldiers would die in the process. And downtown Hog Chapel would turn into an armed camp and you'd put Uncle Earl and Simon's sister and everybody else out of business. The town would be done.

"If I ever find the bastard that knocked that first hole in the wall," I said through gritted teeth, "I'm going to kill him."

"I'll hold him down for you. Assuming that it was a person, which I am increasingly skeptical about. But I don't think we're going to get anywhere good burning the building down."

I sagged against the otter display case. "Why am I doing this?" I asked hopelessly. "Did they get in my head? Did I drink the water and now they're trying to drag me back?"

"I drank the water, too."

I groaned. Simon shrugged. "Maybe you're nuts."

"I didn't think I was."

"Yeah, that's always a bitch when you figure it out, isn't it?" He leaned next to me and thumped an elbow into my arm in a companionable way. "But, I mean, maybe you aren't trying to get back. Maybe you're just really, really pissed off and trying to attack the other world, by way of the drywall."

For some reason, that struck me as hilarious. I started laughing and nearly fell over. The giant otter gazed past me as

I howled. "Oh, God! Oh, God, I'm trying to pick a fight with another universe!"

"Could happen." Simon grinned. "I mean, it'd be better if you just shouted Yo Mama jokes at it, but, hey . . ."

I dashed hysterical tears from my eyes. Something in my chest felt a little looser. "Yeah, okay. That would be better. So what are we going to do?"

Simon held up a finger. "First we're going to go fix the drywall patch. Then we're going to tie you to the bed."

". . . Kinky."

"Yes, but you're not my type, hon. It's for sleepwalking. You tie your wrist to the bed, and then when you hit the end of the tether, you either wake up or stop sleepwalking, anyway." He paused. "I'd offer to let you crash on my couch, but there's a lot of stairs, and I don't want you sleepwalking down them and breaking your neck. Also I've never had a woman tied up in my apartment, and I'd rather not set a precedent."

"Won't the rope get, like, wrapped around my neck and then my head will fall off?"

He grinned. "Not the way I'm gonna do it, no."

❉

"Pink leopard-print handcuffs?"

I stared at the items in question for a good half minute, dumbfounded. "Pink. Leopard-print. Handcuffs."

"They're not handcuffs," said Simon. "They're Velcro

wrist restraints. Easier on the nerve endings."

He applied the wrist restraint, which was indeed on Velcro. I stared at it, then at him. "You're kinda playing to stereotype here, Simon."

He laughed. "I would be, except these are from a Halloween costume."

I gave him a skeptical look.

"High camp is one thing, tacky is another. Hold out your hand."

"Dear diary . . . ," I said as Simon secured my left wrist to the bedpost.

"Not too tight? Circulation okay?"

"Yeah, seems to be. What stops me from taking it off in the middle of the night?"

"You'd have to stop and think about it. It's not an automatic movement. You can work a doorknob in your sleep without thinking about it, but getting yourself loose from a bedpost is another thing. So if you're sleepwalking and tearing at the drywall patch, this'll stop you."

"Great." It was a lot of faith to place in a pink leopard-print handcuff, but at this point, I was running low on options. "Shut the door on your way out."

Simon patted my shoulder, turned off the light, and let himself out of my room. "Nighty night, Carrot. Sleep tight."

"And don't let the willows bite," I said as the door closed behind him.

*

Sunlight blazed over the willows. The boatman stood at the edge of the island, beckoning.

It didn't work, I thought, despairing. *I'm still having the dream.*

No, wait. That wasn't right. The dream wasn't the problem, it was the sleepwalking. As long as I was having the dream in bed, it wasn't . . . well, it was a crappy dream, but at least I wasn't trying to shred the patch on the wall and get into the willows.

"This is a dream," I told the boatman. I was standing on the steps gazing out, a little below his eye level. "I should wake up."

He said nothing. The sun was behind him and his face was in shadow. He beckoned again.

I stepped up onto the next stair. I didn't want to, but my feet were moving without me. Can you sleepwalk in a dream?

Apparently you could, because I took another step.

The boatman held a long pole in one hand. His boat was small, a raft only a few feet wide. I didn't know how he could balance in it, let alone keep it upright.

Don't let him catch you, Sturdivant had said.

"Go away," I told the boatman. "Go away."

He beckoned again, impatient. The killdeer cried somewhere on the sandbanks.

"I shouldn't be here. I shouldn't." I took another reluctant step. Why weren't my legs obeying me?

I lifted my hand to push hair out of my eyes, and that worked fine. Was it just my legs?

I bent down and grabbed my own knee, picked it up in both hands, and tried to walk myself back down a step. This didn't work well at all, but I lost my balance and fell sideways, hitting my shoulder on the wall.

The pain cleared my head a little. For a dream, this was extraordinarily vivid. I could see cracks in the walls and the tiny bits of sand and grit inside those cracks. And I hadn't woken up, the way I usually do when I'm in a dream and realize I'm dreaming.

Am I absolutely sure this is a dream?

"I'm tied to the bed!" I told myself. "Look, I'm . . ."

I look down at my left wrist. The garish pink restraint was still there with the long Velcro ties dangling behind it.

"Oh, shit," I whispered. "Oh, shit. This is bad."

I could hear the willows rustling behind the boatman, and the soft hiss of the current against the island.

Whatever force inhabited my legs got me to my feet. The boatman watched me, impassive, or maybe I just thought he was impassive because I couldn't see his face clearly.

I reached the top step and stood there. The boatman was a little below me now, a dozen feet away. His boat didn't move in the water at all, even with the river moving around it. He didn't have to pole against the current to stay in place.

Stop! I screamed at my body. *Stupidawfulgoddamn-bitchfeetstop!*

The gong noise sounded, very close now. I lifted my foot to step down.

Something hit me from behind, grabbing me around the waist and hauling me backward. I yelped, slapping at the arms around me, and Simon yelled in my ear, "Carrot, *wake up!*"

"I'm not asleep!" I screamed, and something snapped in my head. My feet stopped obeying an alien master. I let out a sob and the high alien noise came again, but shrill, like a hunting bird seeing prey.

Simon and I clutched at each other on the top step. The boatman lifted his head and shrieked.

It wasn't a human noise. It wasn't a human face. His jaw opened wide, wide, far wider than any human's could, and his lips pulled back from impossibly long gums, like a baboon screaming.

The shriek he made harmonized with the shrill alien sound and also with the willows. He jammed the pole down into the water, and the end of the raft lifted up onto the tiny island as he tried furiously to reach us.

It was then that I noticed that he didn't have any feet. His legs were rooted to the raft like willow trunks growing out of the ground. When the end of the raft came up, I saw white, wormlike roots coming from underneath.

He shrieked again. I saw the flash of teeth.

The pole came up. Simon and I fell backward into the bunker, skinning elbows and knuckles and God knows what else as we went, but the end of the pole hit the metal door, not us. My knee hit the edge of a step right under the kneecap, and pain exploded up my leg. The pole made a harsh metallic clang that cut across the humming and the rustle of willows, but I barely heard it.

For a long second, all I could think of was the pain in my knee, not that we were all going to get eaten by Them. Simon and I hunched together while I clutched my knee and he clutched his elbow, and the sound of our harsh breathing echoed off the bunker walls.

The boatman hit the door with the pole again, in evident frustration. I rocked back and forth, hands locked around my knee, tears streaming down my face. A minute earlier, I would have sworn that nothing could cut through my terror, but some pains were so extraordinary that they made terror seem positively quaint.

The humming call came again, but farther away, as if whatever had sought us had lost track and moved off. The boatman, however, had not.

I rolled sideways, deeper into the bunker. The pole hit the steps, not the door. Something whipped against the concrete steps.

It's the roots it's the white roots oh shit oh my knee oh shit oh shit

Darkness filled the bunker as the boatman blocked the doorway. I could see the roots backlit, squirming against the wall.

Getting his roots in.

"Get back!" Simon rasped, hauling on my arm. "Get back!"

The pole hit the door again. Metal squealed. Dear God,

could he get down the steps? Would he be pushing himself on those wriggling roots and the metal pole, down the corridor to the museum?

"We've got to get the door closed," I gasped. I must have unbolted it in my sleep. Shit. Why hadn't we sealed it with a torch or something? Why did my knee hurt so badly? What had I done to it?

The boatman tilted forward . . . and stopped. He was too large to fit through the doorway, rooted to the planks as he was. He couldn't fit.

Another scream filled the room, echoing off the walls, as the boatman shrieked his frustration. He slammed the pole against the door, over and over, wailing in rage and thwarted hunger.

And then I heard the worst noise I could imagine hearing, worse even than Their humming.

The hinges began to give.

"Oh no," said Simon.

In the moment, what I remember is how resigned he sounded. It was the "oh no" of the toilet backing up or the car getting towed, one of life's small but consuming annoyances. In another place, I might have laughed.

The top of the door loosened from the hinges. I could not imagine how shattering the power in the boatman's blows must be, to move that heavy metal door, but he kept pounding and screaming and the weight began to twist the lower hinge off as well.

"We have to get out of here," said Simon hoarsely. "Can you walk?"

"I don't care," I said, which wasn't very coherent but was absolutely true. I did not care if my legs weren't working. I would crawl back to the Wonder Museum if I had to.

We staggered down the hall together. My knee throbbed, and every throb was more pain than I'd ever felt in my life and it didn't matter. It was pitch-black in the hall, so Simon pulled out his phone and held it up and we had enough light to get to the hole, while behind us the pounding and the screaming went on and on and on.

The hole was jagged and even larger than it had been. Apparently I'd pulled the entire drywall patch off, and the only things left were screws stuck to studs that didn't exist on this side, and I was in so much pain that I didn't even care how any of that worked. I hauled myself through the hole and started to cry, partly because of the pain in my knee, mostly because I hadn't gotten out and I'd never get out and I needed to run and keep running but I couldn't because then Uncle Earl would be left alone with a hole to a willow-filled hell and partly because there was a monster on the other side of a no-longer bolted door.

I couldn't hear the boatman. He couldn't get through, not without tearing bits of himself off to fit, but I couldn't swear that he wouldn't do that, either. *Oh, gods and saints and angels, let him not get through.*

He can't. Surely he can't. He'd have gotten Sturdivant,

wouldn't he? That door was open. Oh, please, God . . .

"How did you know?" I asked Simon as we yanked cabinets in front of the hole. The raccoon case wasn't going to do it anymore. I wanted anvils and filing cabinets and bags of concrete. "How did you know I was there?" My knee was killing me, but the sheer horror of having sleepwalked back into a nightmare was starting to overtake the pain. Under that, somewhere, was humiliation. How stupid was I, to have gone back *there*?

Simon grimaced and jammed his shoulder against the big case with the stuffed puma and the teapot that might have been used by the Duke of Wellington, walking it carefully toward the hole. "I didn't."

"What?"

"I was sleepwalking, too, I think. At least at first. I thought I was dreaming, but then I got this pain like somebody was shoving a railroad spike in my eye. I couldn't sleep through that. But then I was awake, and I was really there." He shook his head. "I was about to run back, but I saw you up at the top of the steps."

"It got you, too . . . ," I breathed.

"It?"

"Whatever made me sleepwalk." Despite the awfulness, I felt a sudden urge to laugh. It wasn't *me*. I hadn't been trying to get back to the willows in my sleep.

It's not a good thing to have a hellish otherworld trying

to drag you back into it, but it's somehow worse to think that you're trying to get back to it yourself out of some bizarre self-destructive madness.

"Well, that's a happy thought. But, yeah, I guess. I must have come out of my room and through the back door."

"If we get in the car, I can have us halfway to Virginia before sunrise." I had no idea what I was going to do about Uncle Earl. Kidnap him and take him to Virginia, too, maybe. Nothing in Virginia was going to help, but maybe extradimensional horrors couldn't cross state lines. *If they do, they get tried in federal court. . . .* I had a strong urge to giggle and squelched it.

Simon looked as if he was thinking about it, then shook his head. "I can't. I owe my sister. And Earl." Simon gestured to himself. "Plus I'm not really dressed for it, you might notice."

This was the first time I'd registered that he was wearing an oversize T-shirt with Eeyore the donkey on it and a pair of boxer shorts.

I looked down at myself. I was wearing the same T-shirt I'd gone to bed in and a pair of granny panties that would have embarrassed any self-respecting granny of my acquaintance.

"I'm really glad you're not a straight man right now."

"Carrot, I mean this in the nicest way possible, but even if I was, that outfit would not do it for me. Also, your knee's a wreck."

I looked down at my knee. It was red, with that peculiar puffy shade that means purple is not far off.

"You better wrap that sucker," said Simon. "It's gonna swell like a grapefruit. Do you have health insurance?"

"Ha ha ha."

"That's what I thought."

My knee was a raw red agony. If this was what Uncle Earl had been dealing with, he wasn't just a saint, he was a martyr. Fortunately, the one thing the back room had in spades was knee braces, medicated heated kneepads, and all manner of other treatments. I hobbled into the bathroom, opened the cabinet under the sink, and pulled out something that promised lidocaine and knee support, then tossed down a couple of aspirin.

The knee was indeed swelling, but if I could keep it wrapped, maybe it'd just hurt and look ugly. I'd have to call Uncle Earl and tell him that now we matched.

I heard grating sounds from upstairs. Simon was moving more cases around to block the hole. We'd tried that before and it hadn't worked, but maybe we hadn't tried hard enough. And we couldn't just leave it open.

I leaned my forehead against the mirror, feeling dizzy. It had happened. The boatman had been there. The roots coming out of the bottom of the boat and the way it melted together . . .

But it's not me. It got Simon, too. That means I'm not trying to kill myself by going back into the willow world. I may be crazy and I probably am—who wouldn't be, after all this shit?— but it was the willows grabbing my brain, not my brain trying to kill itself.

Was that better? Maybe a little. At least this meant that it wasn't my fault. We were just possessed or mind controlled or something, that's all. We'd drunk the water and breathed the air, and now the willows had their roots into our heads.

Comforting thought.

I must have spent longer in the bathroom than I thought, because Simon eventually appeared in the doorway. "I've done what I can. Once the hardware store is open, we'll put something heavy-duty in place."

"Will that work?" I asked. In the mirror, I looked dreadful. My hair hung down in limp strings and my skin was blotchy. On the other hand, for having just survived an unexpected trip to hell, I was looking fantastic. I turned away.

"Dunno," he admitted. "But it's all I can think to do. Come on, grab some pants and let's go."

"Where are we going?" I wasn't arguing, just curious.

"You got money for a motel?"

"No."

"Then back to my place."

"We shouldn't sleep until we get the hole patched." I limped toward my bedroom. Beau made a cranky noise from the bed. Apparently the . . . mind control, whatever it was . . . didn't work on cats. Or maybe it would have if Beau had been to the willows, but he hadn't been, so it didn't.

I preferred that theory. Otherwise everyone in the neighborhood could potentially start trying to break into the Wonder Museum in their sleep.

"Hell no. But the adrenaline is gonna wear off in a bit, and then we'll both go down like a ton of bricks," said Simon. "We'll have to keep each other awake."

I was still trying to shake the image of a crowd of people staggering zombie-like through the streets, headed into the willows like lambs to slaughter, and it took me a minute to parse what he was saying. "Oh. Yeah." I shoved myself into a pair of sweatpants and dragged my fingers through my hair. "Yeah, okay. Let's go."

*

The steps up to his apartment were murder on my knee, but I wasn't about to suggest that we stay in the museum until sunrise. Simon went into the kitchen and I heard the microwave, followed by a familiar *glug glug glug*.

"Hot instant lemonade," he said, bringing two mugs out. "Cure for what ails you."

I sniffed this peculiar concoction. "Seems kind of high proof."

"That's the vodka."

I sipped it. It was surprisingly good. "Does it cure sleepwalking into portals to hell?"

"It might."

I took another sip.

Simon collapsed into a chair across from me. We stared into our respective mugs. Neither of us wanted to be the one to say something, I expect, but I finally had to break the silence before I started screaming or sobbing or both.

"They reached out to us, didn't They? To get us to open the way back up."

"Maybe," said Simon. "Something did, anyway. We can't both have decided to sleepwalk at the same time. I never sleepwalk."

"So They're in our heads."

He looked up sharply. "We don't know that."

"What? What else can it be?"

"Lots of things. They could just be calling us somehow. Like silent dog whistles, and we're the only ones who can hear it because we've been over there. It doesn't mean the dogs are mind controlled, it just means they're sensitive to a frequency we're not."

This was much more comforting than mind control. I sagged on the couch. *Not* in my head. Just calling. A dog doesn't have to answer a dog whistle. Hell, my dogs growing up wouldn't answer anything but the dinner bell.

"Do you think the boatman was calling us?" I asked.

Simon frowned. "I can't be sure. But I doubt it. He didn't look like . . . like . . ."

"Them."

"Figure They are the things in the willows. Not the ones from the light show. The ones making those humming calls."

"Okay." I wrapped my hands around the mug, trying to warm them. I felt so cold that I didn't know if I'd ever be warm again. "And the boatman?"

"He wasn't one of Them. He was like Sturdivant, I bet. Or the kids on the bus. They got him and did something. Did you see his feet?"

I nodded. "He was part of the boat. And there was stuff underneath, too. Like willow roots. Okay. That makes sense to me. Maybe he came through somehow on the boat . . . an opening on the river, maybe . . . and They got him. And then They called us and he was there."

" 'He's always hungry,' Sturdivant said. But also, 'Oh, him.' Like he wasn't very impressed with him."

"I imagine when you're soaking in a pool of your own guts, you're pretty hard to impress," I muttered. Was I joking about this? Yes, apparently I was. It was that or run screaming into the night, and my knee didn't feel up to that.

I tried to remember the whole horrible experience of waking up from the nightmare to discover that I was really on the far side of the wall. "I heard the call, though," I said abruptly. "Their call. The humming."

Simon nodded. "I did, too. Close. Maybe it was . . . oh, I don't know. Like the boatman was a dog flushing a rabbit so that They could shoot it."

"Making us the rabbit?"

"Yeah. I don't think They see us real well, do you? We were right out in the open a bunch and They couldn't quite find us. Like They knew we were there, but They were groping around in the dark. And we kept moving so They couldn't find us. And when we were under the boat, one of Them was right there, but it couldn't quite grab us."

"You think They can see the boatman?"

Simon sighed, draining his vodka and lemonade. "I don't know. I don't know if any of this makes any sense. But it fits, a little. Sturdivant said something about the willows getting their roots in. Maybe They're not really in the willow world completely. They're just close to it, and They can get through where the willows are."

"And the boatman was full of willow roots." I took another sip. "You think that's it? They're from yet another world but the willow world is closer than we are?" I remembered my chopsticks and paper, attempting to work it out. Maybe Simon was on the right track after all.

Simon shrugged. "Maybe the willows growing there makes it closer. I don't know. The willows could be . . . like . . . symbiotic with them. Or maybe they're some kind of invasive murder willows from dimension X."

"I don't see that one tearing up the box office anytime soon."

"I dunno, they've made movies about killer everything else. Might be worth a try." Simon rubbed his hand over his face. I hadn't realized until that moment that he was wearing eyeliner, and only then because it was smudged. Goddammit, did the man have to be prettier than me *all* the time?

I pointed out the smudge. He grumbled. "No, I don't wear makeup to bed. I just didn't get it all off, I guess." He inspected his fingers. "Twenty-four-hour waterproof, my ass."

"Well, it wasn't designed to go to other dimensions."

Simon yawned. "Neither was I. Okay. I think I'm crashing. Talk to me about something."

"What if we both fall asleep and wind up sleepwalking back over there?"

Simon considered this for a moment, then went to a closet. A minute later, he emerged with a large wind chime.

"My aunt sent me this," he said, by way of explanation. "She means well."

"You don't have a balcony. Or a deck."

"*And* I hate direct sunlight!" He waved the wind chime, which clashed and jangled, then opened the door and hung it on the outside doorknob. "There is no way we won't hear that, and no way to take it off from in here."

"Clever."

"I have my moments."

Simon's couch was not comfortable, but it also was firmly in this world. I didn't think I could possibly sleep anyway. How could I? I was still listening for dog whistles. No, there was no possible way that I was going to sleep.

I told myself this firmly and then yawned jaw-crackingly wide.

"Fuck," I muttered. "Maybe we *should* drive somewhere and sleep in the car."

"Sleepwalking around town dressed like this will get us picked up by cops at best. Talk to me, Carrot. What are you working on?"

"A bunch of logos for a chicken hatchery. They sell day-old chicks. They want fancy button designs for all the various stuff they offer."

"Cute." He fiddled with the stereo, putting on something with a pounding bass line and a lot of screaming. "Suddenly I regret never getting into speed metal."

"Heh." I ran my hands through my hair. "What are you working on?"

"I'm writing a memoir about being raised by religious party clowns."

"That seems like it would sell."

"You'd think. Do you want coffee?"

"Do you have any?"

He gave me a look.

I remembered that we were, in fact, located above a coffee shop. "That was a stupid question. Yes. Coffee would be good."

"Come with me."

We slunk down to the coffee shop and he poured out cold brew into cups, not turning the lights on in case a customer showed up at three in the morning. The bitter taste shocked my tongue. I wanted drugs or to cry or something. I leaned against the counter, drinking cold black coffee, and tried to explain to Simon about wormholes and sheets and throats. I don't know how much sense it made, but he nodded a lot.

Six hours later, I opened the Wonder Museum. I was so tired that the shadows were starting to get twitchy in the corners

of my vision. I am sure the tourists thought that I was on drugs.
I only wished that I were.

Twelve hours later, Simon arrived on the doorstep of the
Wonder Museum with his solution to the sleepwalking issue.

"Sheet metal?" I said blankly. "We're going to fight another
world with sheet metal?"

"I'm open to other suggestions." Simon turned sideways to
fit his burden through the door. "Grab this bag, will you?"

The bag was full of heavy-duty screws and a power drill.
"This is nuts," I said, following him up the stairs.

"More or less nuts than having a portal to Really Bad Narnia
in your attic?"

"The tourists are going to notice!"

"We'll hang more batik over it."

"We cannot save the world with sheet metal and batik!"

"Why not?" He climbed the stairs and I rushed past him to
save one of the fur-bearing-trout mounts from being banged by
the corner of the metal. "Sorry, depth perception . . ."

"It's fine," I said, and then I whacked my knee on the wall
under the trout and it was not fine at all. "Gaaah!"

"You got that wrapped?"

"This is utterly mad." Nevertheless, I seemed to be carrying
the bag and helping to haul the cases out of the way.

"We're all mad here. I'm mad. You're mad."

"Why couldn't it have been Wonderland on the other side
of the hole?" I asked hopelessly.

"The way things are going, we'd have giant stoner caterpillars crawling out and eating everyone. What's that on the floor?"

"Goddamn carving," I muttered. The stupid corpse-otter had fallen off the raccoon case, yet again.

#93 - Corpse-otter carving, circa 1900, from Danube . . .

"It's wobbly. Probably rolls off every time the door slams." I was tired of dealing with it. I unlocked the display case and shoved the otter inside, next to the albino raccoon and a rather moth-eaten ermine. If it fell over again, big deal, the ermine wasn't going to get any more dead.

"All right," said Simon. "Help me hold this up."

I flattened my hands over the metal while he set about patching a hole in the universe.

We put the sheet metal over the hole, and he bolted it or riveted it or did something to hold it in place. I tested the edges. They weren't sharpened, but if I tried to haul it back with my bare hands, I was going to tear my nails off or slice my fingertips to ribbons long before I got through the patch.

This would have worried me a little, given that apparently sleepwalking me was getting through the patches anyway, but after my encounter with the boatman, I didn't care if I lost all my fingernails. What were fingernails, really? So I couldn't tear open plastic packaging quite as easily, big deal.

My tentative experiments had already proved that there was something about this particular spot that made it a portal to evil Narnia, and I couldn't just gnaw through the drywall somewhere else in the museum. Probably. So this was as safe as we were going to get. Probably.

"I hate this," I said out loud. Simon didn't reply, probably because it was such an obvious statement and there wasn't anything that anyone could say to make it better anyway.

I tacked up the faithful batik sheet over the steel patch. We stared at it for a bit.

"I don't think piling up display cases is gonna work this time," I said. "I'm afraid I'll pull them down on myself. It has to be something I can't move."

"I know just the thing," said Simon. "But moving it is gonna be a real pain in the ass."

*

He wasn't wrong. By the time we got the Bigfoot statue into position, my knee felt like the inside of Chernobyl, and my back was asking if I really wanted to continue down this road. But the carved wooden Bigfoot was in position, and there was no world where I could pull it over. The base was so wide that I could have climbed on the thing and not even rocked it. If I could move that out of the way while sleepwalking, I had superstrength on top of everything else.

"I'm just glad this is over a support post," I muttered. "A couple yards over, on that sort of mushy spot, and it'd only be a matter of time before it plummeted through the floor and crushed a tourist."

"Earl would feel terrible, but he'd still probably put a sign on it that says SEE THE STATUE THAT KILLS."

I laughed, a weary, near-hysterical laughter of the sort that I was getting all too familiar with. But it was still a laugh.

"All right." Simon stepped back from Bigfoot and picked up his tools. "You gonna be okay tonight? My couch is still open."

It was tempting. It was very tempting. But the Wonder Museum and I were stuck with each other . . . and more realistically, I couldn't face the idea of going up all those steps to his apartment on my knee. If it didn't start to get better, I might have to knuckle under and go see a doctor, and that was money I didn't have and wasn't going to have anytime soon.

"No. But if you get any premonitions or whatever, call me."

"I was planning on getting falling-down drunk so I can't walk, but that works, too."

He waved, and a minute later I heard the back door bang as he left. I dithered for a minute, then limped down the hall to make sure it was locked. Beau informed me that he wanted the litter box changed, immediately if not sooner, and I begged him to forgive me but it was not happening today. I could close a portal to hell or scoop the cat litter, but both in one day was asking too much.

I went to bed, dragging the nightstand in front of the door just in case, and tied myself to the bed frame. I anticipated that it would be a real pain in the ass when I had to get up and pee in the middle of the night, but I didn't find out because I slept straight through until morning.

17

My knee stiffened up overnight again. I was starting to really sympathize with Uncle Earl. I hadn't ever thought he wasn't in pain, but the amount of pain he must have been in was being driven home like a railroad spike through my leg.

I hobbled to the bathroom and brushed my teeth and changed—not without a lot of wincing—into new jeans. My knee had swollen, but as long as I didn't take off the brace, I could stay in denial for a bit longer.

There was no way that I could have gotten up the steps to the second floor to tear down the sheet metal and climb through the hole, but just in case, I staggered up the stairs until my head poked over the top of the landing. The batik lay quiet and the Bigfoot statue was undisturbed.

A sense of profound relief settled over me. *Okay. Made*

it through a night. We're good. It was pathetic that one night without sleepwalking into an otherworldly hellscape was such a triumph, but dammit, sometimes we take what we can get.

I threw down a couple of aspirin, flipped the sign to OPEN, and went to sit behind the counter and try to flex my aching knee.

It was a slow morning. I worked on my spreadsheet, somewhat hampered by my inability to walk very far. Everything within an arm's length of the counter got cataloged, and then I started writing in entries for all of the big pieces on the walls that I couldn't take down.

One moose head . . . one cowhide shield . . . one picture made from cut pieces of palm fronds . . . (Astonishingly, that last was not by the same artist who did His Sunflower Holiness.) *One giraffe skull . . . one cross made out of saguaro ribs . . .*

A group of three came in, an older couple and their adult daughter by the look of it. They gazed around with horrified amusement, then immediately tried to school their faces into polite interest, just in case I was taking the Wonder Museum seriously.

"Isn't it wild?" I smiled a customer-service smile. "My uncle collects all this stuff. . . ."

The trio relaxed. "This must be a fun place to work," said the mom. Somehow I did not burst into braying, hysterical laughter. I said something. It must have been the right thing, because they went off to wander the museum and I heard the usual tourist calls receding into the building: "Omigosh, did you

see this?" "Honey, come look at this one!" "Ha!" "Oh, Lord . . ."
"My granddad had one of those. . . ."

I flexed my knee again and drank a little more of my cold
coffee.

A few minutes later, the daughter came down, looking
apologetic. "Excuse me, I'm sorry—there's some broken
glass upstairs."

"What?" I slid off the chair and winced as pain jolted
through my knee.

"It looks like one of the display cases broke."

"I'll get a broom," I said. "Thank you for telling me.
Sometimes the cat knocks things over . . ." This was absolutely
a lie and vile slander against Beau besides, but I couldn't very
well say, *Oh, I probably smashed open a display case trying to get
back to Narnia through a hole in the wall there.*

*How the hell did I do that? I can't have done that. I can't even
get up the damn stairs!*

I grabbed the dustpan and whisk broom from the back and
limped up the stairs. The daughter hovered nearby, clearly
worried. "Can I take that for you?"

"No, no," I said. "I'm fine. Just messed up my knee the other
day. I'm slow, but I get there." Uncle Earl used to say that when
he had a hard time getting around: "I'm slow, but I get there."

I got up to the second floor, and the parents were standing
off to one side, looking nervous, as if afraid I might blame them.
"It's just there," they said, pointing.

Glass glittered on the carpet. It had come from the raccoon display case. The front was smashed open, half of it gone, the rest a jagged spiderweb of cracks.

The batik was undisturbed. I didn't want to check on the patch with the tourists there. *Why do you have a giant sheet of metal bolted to the wall? Oh, no reason.*

It didn't make any sense, though. The raccoon case hadn't been in front of the hole. We'd moved it back to its original spot. And Bigfoot looked just fine, exactly where we'd put him.

If I were trying to break back through the hole—assuming I climbed up the stairs in a dream and wasn't feeling my knee— wouldn't I have gone for Bigfoot? Why would I have punched out the raccoon case?

"Oh, dear," I said to the tourists. "Well, these things happen. Why don't you guys head down, and I'll take care of the glass? I'd hate for you to cut yourself."

They filed down obediently. "I hope you can repair it," said the mother over her shoulder.

"Not a problem," I said cheerfully. I couldn't repair it, but I'd figure something out. I swept the glass up into the dustpan, picked a few bits out with my bandaged fingers, then studied the case. Downstairs, I heard the door jingle as the tourists left.

I couldn't have done it. I looked at my knuckles, then at the case. I tried to think of every possible scenario, and . . . no. No way could I have punched out the glass without breaking my hand. Hell, I'm not sure I could have punched out the glass even if I *did* break my hand. I am not a glass-punching person. I design logos. Those are two very different skill sets.

Well, we're used to this sort of thing at the Wonder Museum. We drape a nice blanket over the top—possibly another batik, heh—then stack some random objects on top, put up a sign about them, and suddenly it's a whole new display. Eventually somebody donates a new display case or Uncle Earl finds a used one for twenty bucks and we replace it.

I opened the top of the raccoon display . . . and stopped.

There was no raccoon in it.

The ermine was still in there, and the sign about albinism in animals and the toad wearing the sheriff's badge. But the centerpiece of the display was gone.

For once, I can honestly say that I was not thinking about the hole in the wall or the willows or anything else. I stared at the case. I stared at the glass. I stared at the floor. I looked around the room, as if somebody might have picked up a stuffed albino raccoon and put it somewhere else. I even opened the doors under the otter case, as if the raccoon would have wandered in there by mistake.

Nothing changed. We were still short an albino raccoon.

Did someone break in and steal a raccoon? And if you were going to do that, why *that* raccoon, of all things? It wasn't even good taxidermy, for God's sake; it had the cheap plastic whiskers and its tail was all ragged.

I did another sweep of the room, to no avail.

Finally, completely stumped, I limped back downstairs—
going down hurt almost as much as going up, with the jarring
on the knee joint—and found a piece of moth-eaten brown
velvet. I picked up a couple more cane toads and the lynx skull,
went back up the stairs with my teeth fastened in my lower lip,
and arranged the toads in a circle around the skull, with the
sheriff toad presiding.

"This meeting of the Amphibious Skull Worshippers will
come to order," I said out loud, and started giggling because
the world was completely batshit and there were holes in the
universe and people who went around stealing albino raccoons.

I spent the rest of the afternoon trying to figure out if
anything else was missing. Nobody had touched the till. If
they'd taken a T-shirt or fudge, I'd never know.

I checked my catalog twice. It said there had been a stuffed
fisher in the case, which was gone too, assuming that Uncle
Earl hadn't moved it to another display at some point after I'd
written things down. I tried to remember what a fisher was.
Some kind of weaselly thing. I looked it up online. Yup, some
kind of weaselly thing.

If my catalog had been better, I could have cross-referenced
everything, but it wasn't, so I couldn't, and anyway, going back
through the damn thing checking off each box was so daunting
that I shuddered.

Would it sound strange to say that I felt better? Here was a
mystery, and an obnoxious one, but I wasn't dead or sleepwalking

into mortal danger. Nobody was going to die of a missing raccoon. And my brain, which had been trying to drift back to the horrors of the willows at every opportunity, found itself gnawing over where the devil the raccoon had gone instead.

I grabbed one of Uncle Earl's canes and limped next door. He was the wrong height, so it wasn't quite comfortable, but it did have a lacquered alligator head on it, which had to count for something.

"Simon, did you borrow an albino raccoon?"

Simon, consummate professional, did not stop pouring steamed milk into the drink in front of him. "Say that again, but slowly, because I think I'm hallucinating again."

"Did you borrow an albino raccoon from the museum?"

"Yeah, that's what I thought you said." He wiped his hands on his apron. "No?"

I sighed. "I didn't think you did. You'd have asked first, and you sure wouldn't have broken the case. But you have a key and the lock's fine and nothing else is missing. I'm completely stumped." I briefly outlined the Case of the Missing Taxidermy.

"Cultists," said Simon.

"*What?*"

"I mean, they're the sort of people who would think a white raccoon was super-spooky."

"Yes, but we live in *Hog Chapel*. There aren't any cultists here. The closest we've got are snake handlers, and Jesus never told anybody to handle raccoons for the glory of the Lord."

"Can you watch the coffee shop a minute? I need to go found a religion."

"Simon!"

"Fine, fine . . ." He held up both hands. "Okay, so a tourist did a smash-and-grab on you."

"I'd have noticed," I said darkly.

"Would you? Do you watch them all when they go out the door?"

I opened my mouth, then shut it again. The trio of tourists from this morning had left without any observation. They could have stashed the raccoon somewhere, told me about the glass, and then walked out carrying it and I'd have had no idea.

Simon made me a coffee. I knew he paid his rent in coffee, but I was drinking so much that it was possible he was losing money on the deal by now. I stared at the internet for a while, wondering what the hell to do next, and eventually composed an amusing post for social media about someone having stolen the albino raccoon, probably for a cult. (I hadn't updated the museum's website for ages and was starting to feel guilty, but I couldn't very well tell people about the willows. When there is a portal to hell or Narnia lurking upstairs, you tend to fall behind on blogging.)

The internet thought the raccoon cult was funny. A few people expressed gratitude that whoever had stolen the raccoon hadn't attacked me as well.

I tied myself to the bed, just in case, and went to sleep.

Nothing terrible happened and I woke up still tied to the bed, with my hand starting to fall asleep.

It wasn't until much later that I'd realized that something else had been missing, because I'd already forgotten about putting it in the display case in the first place.

✳

The UPS guy delivered another load of skulls, mostly pigs'. I wrote them up as *Lot of Pig Skulls* and didn't bother with tags. If somebody stole a pig skull, I don't think we'd notice. A few more boxes and I might just put a sign out front that said PIG SKULL — FREE TO GOOD HOME.

It was a normal day. Just . . . normal. Nothing weird. Nothing horrible. Nothing broken. The worst that happened was that something went scurrying along the baseboard on the other side of the museum. Beau's head snapped up and he descended upon the culprit like the angel of death. I heard loud scuffling, a thump, and then Beau settled down in front of a gap under the staircase, paws folded under his chest, with the air of a cat willing to wait until the end of the world if need be.

Normal.

The next day was Monday, my day off, and I hardly knew how to act. I locked up the museum and drove away. Thankfully my left knee had been the one to take the beating, so I could still work the pedals okay. By the time I got over to Southern Pines and the bookstore there, my knee was stiff enough that I had to haul the cane out of the back seat and limp in with it. (Incidentally, if you've never had to use one, there's a skill to using a cane, and it doesn't come naturally. I switched hands like four times trying to figure out the most comfortable way to walk, where to grip the cane, and sundry other irritations. Bipedalism is just the *worst*.)

I bought a book, then I wandered around the town for a while, looking at the tiny quaint everything and the boutiques with the scented candles, then I had a crepe at the crepe shop and thought, *This is normal. I am normal. Normal life is going on.* I read my book for a while and had coffee that wasn't as good as Simon's. When I had finished the coffee, I couldn't justify spending the money on another one, so I went home.

Bigfoot was still standing guard. The batik wasn't billowing. Beau was still at his mousehole, although he was showing signs of getting bored. When I scooped him up and took him into the bedroom, he didn't protest.

The book only lasted me another hour. I should probably have just stuck to fanfic, given my budget, but the book was one of a series, and even though I didn't much care about the series anymore, the characters were familiar and seeing them in their little world, doing their little thing, was comforting.

I sat up and put my book on the nightstand, and my heel hit something under the bed.

"What the devil . . . ?"

I groped under the bed and my fingers closed on another book.

It was the Bible from another world. I'd almost forgotten it was there, which is a helluva thing to forget. I'd taken a break because it had gotten too intense, and then there'd been sleepwalking and patching and . . . Lord, had it only been a couple of days? I felt as if I was floundering around in time, unmoored from the calendar beyond "the museum is open today" and "the museum is not open today."

It looked so innocuous in its black fake-leather cover, with the little gilt words HOLY BIBLE. I wondered if they had a Gideons of America over there. *Although I guess it would be Gideons of the UNA.*

I didn't want to know. I didn't want to know what happened next. Or rather, I knew what happened next: everybody died. I just didn't want to watch through the Bible's eyes as they did.

But I opened the book anyway. I was well past Second Chronicles. And it felt somehow like if I didn't keep reading, Bible would be stuck on the other side of the pages where I'd left him, stranded in the willows forever.

"That's stupid," I said to Beau. "I'm being stupid."

Beau didn't open his eyes. He had spent most of the day in front of the hole under the stairs, and now he was exhausted from the effort of sitting in one place not catching anything.

A woman showed up today. Walked right into the bunker. Marco nearly shot her, but Petrov knocked him out of the way and he fired into the ceiling. We all went deaf for about a minute, but she put her hands up.

Says her name's Singer. She speaks like five lan-guages, which is good because she started with one we didn't know. Took a couple tries before we found one, and the first thing she said was "I'm not one of them."

She means the ones who killed the commander. She's not from here. Nobody's from here. She doesn't think the people who built the bunkers were even from here. The bunkers are pretty safe, but as soon as you step outside, things start trying to find you.

This whole fucking place is a trap.

Singer's been here five weeks. She was with a squad like ours, but civilian. Except not like ours because she's from another fucking planet. They opened a way to the vacuae and went through and wound up here too.

If we make it home, the eggheads are going to go nuts. Not one but two worlds. Except there's probably no way we're going to make it home. Singer's squad had ten people. She lost eight in the first week. Had a drop-off point same as we did and she missed it, said they were all over the rendezvous point and they got the other survivor.

Five weeks . . . I shook my head. Bible's squad hadn't lasted that long, if the logbook had been any indication. And Sturdivant . . . he knew a woman who lived two weeks, he said? Singer had been lucky or tough or just plain smarter than everybody else.

I couldn't imagine lasting over a month in the willows. *Lucky*, Sturdivant had said. Lucky that we'd come through in a bunker, not somewhere else, such as the middle of the willows. I was starting to realize just how lucky we'd been. Coming through in the bunker had let us find our feet and look around for a little bit before They noticed us. But five weeks?

Maybe if we'd crouched down in the bunker until we ran out of MREs, Simon and I might have lasted a week. I wonder what Singer had eaten for all those weeks.

She says the fish are safe, if you can catch them.

Well, that answers that, I thought.

She traded us some fish for FRRs. I'd rather have fish than heat-stabilized potatoes. She doesn't have any cigarettes.

We let her take the commander's bed. He's sure not gonna use it. She slept for like twelve hours straight. Not like we're going anywhere anyway. Marco's all for going out, trying to shoot one of these things, says maybe they won't be so invisible if we put some bullets in them. Petrov told him to shut up, we're staying put until the way back opens up. I'm going to bed so I don't have to listen to fucking Marco whine.

Woke up and Steen and Singer were talking about the things. Steen says maybe they're extradimensional.

Singer went off into some kind of jargon I didn't get, a whole lot of stuff. Steen seemed to understand half of it, but their theories have different names, so we got a whole lot of "Oh, you call it that? We call it this!" Pretty sure it's at least half bullshit. Nice that someone's having fun, even if we're all about to get eaten by monsters.

Singer says we can't shoot them, or maybe that we can, but only if they want to be shot. Otherwise they'd just step out of the way, but on an axis we can't get to, whatever the fuck that means. Marco did some dick-waving about how he'd shoot them anyway, until Petrov told him to shut up again.

I was starting to come around to Bible's opinion of Marco.

We got four days until the way out of the vacuae opens. Petrov told Singer she could come with us. The boys back at decontamination will lose their shit, but she doesn't care. Says that life in quarantine is better than here. For one thing, it'll probably be a lot longer.

If we all just stay put for four days, we might make it. Petrov wants to scout the way out day after tomorrow, says we'll have a better chance that way, instead of just charging blindly toward the exit. He figures there's a good chance that the way opening will stir up the critters and they'll try to pick us off as we go. I mean, he's probably not wrong.

Singer said a weird thing though, she said, "Maybe. Or maybe they won't even notice. Just don't think too loud. I think they hear you thinking." What the fuck??

They can hear you thinking. . . . The graffiti warning must not have been on the walls when Bible was there. Or maybe he was the one who scratched it, in the end.

It was too depressing. I couldn't keep going. I put the Bible down. We were nearly to the New Testament, and I knew I wouldn't be able to stop reading it, but not tonight.

I turned off the light, checked that I was indeed tied to the bed, and went to sleep.

＊

I woke up to a noise so horrible that for a minute I thought I was having a nightmare. I sat up, yanked against the restraint, cussed, and then the sound of my voice against the noise made me realize that it was really happening, and furthermore that I knew what it was.

Beau was making the goblin wail of a cat in the throes of extreme rage. His tail lashed against my blanket-covered legs and his ears were flat against his skull.

"Beau? What the hell?"

He hunkered down against the sheets and gave out another long, furious vowel. He wasn't looking at me, but at the door.

My first thought was that the raccoon thieves had returned,

perhaps for another piece of taxidermy, and that Beau was pissed about the intruders. Which made no sense because he was a cat, not a watchdog, and also he hadn't cared at all the first time they were here.

Then he paused for a breath and I heard it.

Scratching.

Something was scratching at the door of my bedroom.

Skritch . . . skritch . . . skritch . . .

It was a loud scratch, at about knee height. My first reaction was one of relief—*Oh, thank God, it's not intruders, it's some kind of animal*—followed by *What the hell? We're a museum, not an animal park!*

Hog Chapel has a couple options as far as medium-size animals go. It was just barely possible that one had broken in, I guess. I might have left the back door unlocked and something came to the trash and just kept going. Possum? Raccoon? Rat? Skunk?

Skritch . . . skritchchch . . .

Oh, sweet mother of God, please let it not be a skunk. I didn't particularly want to fend off a rabid raccoon, but a rabies shot seemed minor compared with having to hose down half the museum with tomato juice.

Could it be another cat?

The scratching came again. Beau's tail lashed so hard that I was surprised he didn't become airborne.

No, Beau didn't get that worked up about other cats. He

had the kind of lazy confidence that came from knowing he could take anything up to and possibly including a small bear.

It had to be a rat. I would have had to leave the back door not just unlocked but ajar, and I wouldn't have done that. In fact, I remembered checking the door twice. It had to be something already in the museum, and since all our possums and raccoons are stuffed, that meant it was a rat. A big rat, by the sound, but a rat.

Well, I had the solution to that. "Time to earn your keep, buddy." I untied myself from the bedpost. I walked to the door, grabbed the knob, and yanked it open, careful to step out of the way as I did.

Beau shot across the room so fast that I was surprised I didn't hear a sonic boom as he went. I caught a glimpse of something pale, and then Beau was on it and he and the rat rolled ass over teakettle down the hallway.

Christ, it was huge! Maybe it was a possum after all. I couldn't make out any details, just the rolling melee down the hall. Beau was yowling with rage. Whatever he was fighting didn't make any sound. Possums hiss when they're cornered, so it could have just been a giant goddamn rat.

Beau and his victim rolled out of my line of sight. I hurried after them, not sure if I should grab a broom or just let the professional do his job. I hadn't realized it would be so big. Was this going to require a trip to the emergency vet?

I limped down the hall toward the museum proper, already

wracked with guilt. I should never have opened the door. Beau was going to get bit to hell, and it would be all my fault.

Silence fell so suddenly that it rang in my ears like sound. I sucked in my breath. Oh, God, had it killed him? No, surely not. Beau had a skull like a fist and claws like box cutters. I don't think he'd ever lost a fight in his life.

I snatched up the nearest thing I could find, a didgeridoo (which I happened to know had a MADE IN CHINA stamp on the bottom), and brandished it, stepping into the moonlit museum. Where was Beau? If I had to beat the rat to death with a fake didgeridoo to save the cat, so be it.

Nothing. No movement. No sound. I looked from shadow to shadow. Glass eyes glinted back at me. Where had they gone?

And then, casual as if he did this every day, Beau sauntered out from behind a case, into a pool of moonlight, sat down, and began to groom his paw.

I swept Beau up in my arms and sobbed an apology into his fur. Beau bore this patiently, purring his rusty-engine purr. When I tried to check him over for injuries, though, he put a paw on my arm and extended the claws just slightly.

"Sorry. I don't want you to get an abscess or something."

Beau blinked his vast green eyes at me, possibly indicating that while he appreciated the sentiment, he was not in the mood to be examined by a hysterical primate at this hour of the night.

From a cursory examination, it looked as if he had lost a patch of fur and maybe gotten clawed a bit along the flank, but was otherwise uninjured. There wasn't any blood, just a raw pink line. A few other tufts of fur were missing, that was all.

"Okay. You get until tomorrow morning. Then I'm checking."

I'd have to find the dead rat in the morning, too. Nothing freaks out the tourists like dead vermin in the exhibits. I knew which case it had to be behind, but there wasn't enough room for me to squeak back there, so I'd have to pull it out in the morning.

Beau went back to cleaning his fur, which was now mussed by both combat and a human snuffling on him. I vowed to order fried rice tomorrow night and give him every piece of pork in it.

It was so late that it was probably early. I didn't see myself getting back to sleep after that.

Nerves jangling, I limped upstairs and poked my cane at the sheet-metal patch on the wall. It went *clonk* in exactly the way you'd expect sheet metal with fabric over it to do. There was no plaster dust on the floor or weird billowing to the batik. Bigfoot gazed at me from under his heavy brow ridges.

I exhaled.

It was just a rat. A big goddamn rat. Nothing to do with the willows at all.

It may sound strange, but it was hard to think that something weird could happen that didn't have anything to do with the willows. As if every awful horror had to be linked somehow.

I went back to the bedroom, stared at the bed, and said, "Yeah, that's not gonna happen."

Reading the Bible *really* didn't appeal to me. I went and made a cup of tea, grabbed my phone, and spent until dawn tucked under His Sunflower Holiness, reading about ships that had gone missing at sea and increasingly elaborate conspiracy theories about what had happened to their crews. (It was cannibalism. The answer is always cannibalism.) It was creepy, but I was also hundreds of miles from the ocean, so it was a creepy that I didn't have to worry about.

When dawn finally came, I yawned my way to bed and set my alarm an hour early so I could find the damn dead rat.

I slept surprisingly well. I did nearly jump out of my skin when I heard a scratch at the door, but it was Beau deciding it was time to patrol and use the litter box. I got up with him, turned on the Wonder Museum lights, and began Dead Rat Quest.

Naturally Beau had chased his opponent under a case where I couldn't possibly fit, and naturally it was one that was too damn heavy to lift. I had to haul the giraffe skull—a replica, but don't tell anyone—down, then walk the end of the case inch by inch out from the wall.

Bingo. There was definitely a shaggy lump back there. I gritted my teeth against the pain in my knee and kept wiggling the end. A carving of the Squash Kachina rattled against a bobblehead of Elvis, and a string of rosary beads rolled off the shelf and lodged against the glass. "Dammit," I muttered, but I kept going until I had space to get behind the case. "All right, you bugger, let's see how badly Beau beat you up."

I stopped.

I looked down at the body while the ramifications slowly worked through my head, all of them utterly impossible, all of them bad.

The creature in front of me had long gashes along its sides, and its belly had been ripped out. Straw dripped from the wounds.

Beau had gutted his opponent, but he hadn't killed it, because it was already dead.

He'd been fighting the albino raccoon.

18

I stared down at the long-dead raccoon and thought, *That isn't straw, it's wood-wool.*

I was quite correct. Taxidermied animals are stuffed with a product called excelsior, or wood-wool. It was also possibly the most useless thing I've ever thought in my life, but if I thought about anything else, like the fact that a *stuffed fucking raccoon had been clawing at my door*, I would begin screaming and I wouldn't stop until my voice gave out or they called someone to take me away.

The raccoon looked deflated. Most of the wood-wool had been yanked out. I rolled it over with my cane, feeling the skin flex over the armature. The legs were hard and dry, sticking up in the air when it rolled.

It couldn't have been clawing at my door. It wasn't possible.

But the thing that you saw was big and pale and it was dark and it could have been it could have been it could have been—

This is nuts, I told myself firmly. *You can't know that was what Beau was fighting. Taxidermy doesn't walk around. A tourist tried to do a smash-and-grab, then panicked and dropped the raccoon back there. The rats got into it and hollowed out the wood-wool for a nest. It was a rat. He fought a rat. He just chased it back here, to the nest. That's all.*

"Yes, of course," I said out loud. I rolled the raccoon back. There was a hole under its chin the size of my fist. A rat could certainly have burrowed into that. It made perfect sense. And then Beau would have chased it and the rat ran into the stuffed raccoon to hide and Beau tore at it. Yes. Absolutely logical. No one has zombie raccoons roaming around their museum. That would just be silly.

I went and got gloves because I didn't want to handle a raccoon with rats in it, then stumped back on my cane and picked the thing up. Even through the heavy-duty dishwashing gloves we use to handle ancient taxidermy that might have formaldehyde in it, it felt horrible. The furry skin rolled between my fingers and gummed itself together. More wood-wool slid out onto the floor.

"I declare this raccoon a loss," I announced to the museum. "Um. Sorry, bud."

It occurred to me that there might be a dead rat in there, and I should probably check, because if there wasn't, that meant there was a dead rat somewhere in the museum, and I needed to get to it before it started to smell. Grimacing, I flopped the head back and peered into the opening.

This is where the zombie rat lunges out and latches onto my face . . .

There was a hollowed-out tunnel as thick as my forearm inside the raccoon, but no dead rat. No live rat either, thank God. The last thing I wanted was to be carrying a live, pissed-off rat in what amounted to a white coonskin purse.

Of course, that still meant that there was a dead rat somewhere in the Wonder Museum. (Okay, there were like five, but all the others had been dead for decades and were wearing little hats.) Which meant that I got to play the world's least fun party game, Where Is That Smell Coming From?, for the next few days, and to buy enough air freshener to sweeten a battleship.

I carried the dead raccoon to the trash and pitched it. The wooden base was nowhere in sight, but presumably I'd find that stashed somewhere one of these days, too. I wondered why the thief had panicked and ditched the raccoon. It seemed like the sort of stupid prank you'd pull for a fraternity hazing, but we've got about as many fraternities in Hog Chapel as we do cultists.

Beau was not interested in being checked for injuries, but I offered him some wet cat food and poked and prodded while he was eating. All I could find were the scratches. One was deep enough that I dug out some antibiotic goo from the last time he'd gotten out of the museum and picked a fight with another cat and slathered it on. He gave me a disgruntled look.

"Don't lick that off or you'll get the cone."

Beau did not actually roll his eyes, but it was strongly implied.

"You're lucky you didn't get any bites, or we'd be going to the vet right now."

Of course he didn't get any bites, the raccoon's mouth was sewn shut.

I jammed that thought down into the subbasement of my brain and refused to think of it again.

"Jesus, what a morning," I muttered, and went next door to get coffee and update Simon on the details.

"Oh, that is fucked-up," said Simon. "It was living in the taxidermy?"

"Yeah."

"You know what that means, right?"

"Eh?"

He leaned forward. "There could be rats living in other pieces, too. Like the grizzly bear could just be full of them."

"No, they couldn't," I said with false bravado. "Some of them are resin mounts and half of them are in cases. And anyway, that's why we've got a museum cat."

"I'm just saying . . ."

I scowled. "I already checked the grizzly bear."

"And?"

"And there was a hole in the back leg, but you can't really see it from the front and there's no poop, so it's fine."

"Uh-huh."

"How's your nightmares?" I asked, determined to change the subject.

"I had the one where your teeth fall out and you can't find a dentist. But nothing to do with . . . uh . . . yeah."

"That's good." I stared into the coffee. "Yeah, that's good. Maybe we're getting over it."

"Not much choice, really. How's the knee?"

"Hurts like the devil. I've had two tourists recommend acupuncture, and one told me to rub it with hemp oil."

"Bless their little hearts." Simon rubbed the eye that may or may not have belonged to his dead twin. "Steel patch is fine?"

"It was at about four in the morning when I went and checked."

"Good, good."

The bell over the door chimed as it opened, and two tourists came in. You could tell they were tourists because the first words they spoke were "Isn't this place *cute*?"

One does not talk about rat infestations in front of the customers. One woman had a T-shirt that said WORLD'S GREATEST GRANDMA, and the other was wearing a red hat. They cooed over the charming decor and the charming barista, who they appeared to think was part of the decor. Simon, who can be much more pleasant under pressure than I can, responded appropriately. World's Greatest Grandma ordered a half-caf latte with sugar-free hazelnut syrup. Red Hat ordered a black coffee.

I checked the time, sighed, and got to my feet with the help of my cane. World's Greatest Grandma saw me, and I braced myself for suggestions of hemp oil and/or acupressure.

"Honey, you're too young to need a cane!"

One does not yell at tourists. One does not. It is economically counterproductive. Even when they start giving you their opinions about things that are none of their goddamn business. But I had been under a lot of pressure lately, and something in the back of my brain went *ping!* and I opened my mouth and said, "That's not what the guy with the baseball bat thought."

From behind the latte machine, I heard Simon choke.

World's Greatest Grandma stared at me, her mouth falling open so wide that I could admire her dental work. Red Hat put a hand over her eyes.

Simon, God love him, had my back. "Did they ever catch that guy?" he asked.

"Nope. I was lucky, though. They think he might be the guy who killed those women and cut off their"—*Shit, what could he have cut off?*—"ears. I was just in the wrong street at the wrong time."

"Was . . . was this in Hog Chapel?" breathed World's Greatest Grandma.

Even at my most malicious, I couldn't do that to the other small businesses. "Nah, it was over in Raleigh." I picked up my coffee, waved to Simon, and hobbled out of the café with my head held high.

*

It was a slow day. I found no further rats. I made a TV dinner
in the microwave, the same kind I'd made for lunch. (I'd found
a sale on Swedish meatballs, five for $5. I was going to live on
Swedish meatballs until I got scurvy.) I decided maybe it was time
to read more of the Bible. I picked it up and propped it open in
front of me, and then the phone rang. An unfamiliar number, but
just in case someone was dead in a ditch . . . "Hello?"

"Kara?"

Oh. Right. My ex and his new number. Joy. "Oh, hey.
What's up?" *Please don't say we need to talk, please don't say we
need to talk. . . .*

"I thought maybe we should talk."

Goddammit.

"I called back after hours since I know you have customers."

"Yeah?" What did he want, a medal for respecting business
hours?

He sighed. "Kara, I know you're mad."

"I am?"

Fumbling at the other end of the line. He was taking his
glasses off. "Don't be like that. You have every right to be mad,
okay? I just wanted to clear the air."

"What are we clearing the air about?"

"Kara . . ."

I had not previously realized how much I hated it when

he said my name with that inflection. Well, live and learn, as Uncle Earl would say.

"Mark, once again, I've got no idea what you're talking about. It's late, I'm tired, it was a long day. I don't want to play Twenty Questions about why you think I'm mad at you. Just get to the point already."

"Uh . . ." He sounded startled. I was going off script again, apparently. "The Halloween party?"

The words were utterly nonsensical. I had a book in my hands written by a guy in an alternate-universe hell-world full of willows, there were rats in the taxidermy, and my ex wanted to talk about a *Halloween party*?

"*What* Halloween party? Halloween was six months ago."

He swallowed audibly. "You didn't see the photos?"

"I told you, my Wi-Fi here is terrible."

"Uh. Ah. Your mom saw them and commented, so I thought she'd have told you. Uh . . . apparently I was wrong. I'm sorry to bother you."

I leaned my head against the wall, feeling the slick paper of the Mothman poster against my cheek. "Maybe she left a message."

"Yeah, uh, maybe."

"Mark, in all the years we were married, did I *ever* rush to answer the phone when she called? You *know* I don't talk to her that often if I can help it."

"No, you didn't, I just . . ." We were way off script now. He'd be pissed about it in the morning and figure out how it had been my fault, but for the moment, he was completely at sea. "I'm sorry."

Sweet, blithering Christ, why had I married this guy to begin with? I was starting to think that half of the angst of a divorce wasn't the loss of stability, it was coming to terms with just how lousy your judgment had been.

"So what's the big deal? Why am I mad?"

"There . . . um . . . there were photos of me and Riley at the party. I uploaded a bunch and forgot they were in there."

Halloween was a month before I'd been informed we were getting a divorce. Well. So much for two people drifting apart. I could see why my mom had commented. I hoped it was marvelously sarcastic. Mom definitely had her moments.

"Say something," said Mark.

I said the first thing that came into my head, which was "Right, okay." I stretched my knee. My knee that I'd banged up *in another fucking dimension.* Running from a monster that might have been a human, only warped and twisted into some kind of monster with teeth like a baboon. And I was supposed to get worked up about my ex making out with some chick at a party before he dumped me?

"Kara, I'm sorry. I should have been straight with you to begin with. I—we—didn't mean it to happen. You deserved to know and I'm a piece of shit for not telling you, and . . ."

I took the phone away from my ear so I could check the time, then looked at my voice mail. Yeah, my mom had left a five-minute message the night before. Huh.

Mark was still talking. I wondered how long the call was going to take, then realized I didn't actually have to deal with it. *We're divorced! I don't have to fix this! Hot damn, it's not my problem anymore!*

"Mark," I said, returning the phone to my ear and cutting him off in mid-guilt, "I really truly do not give a shit right now. Tell me what you want me to say so that we can end this call and I can get back to my dinner."

Silence. Then, with a flash of the humor that I really had loved, once upon a time, "I was kind of hoping you'd yell at me."

"Fine," I said wearily. "You're a cad, how dare you, my heart is forever broken, woe is me. Will that tide you over for now?"

He snorted. After a minute of awkwardness, he said, "I hope we can still be friends."

"Yeah, keep hoping," I said, and hung up. Then I erased my mother's voice mail, unheard, and picked up my fork.

My Swedish meatballs had gone tepid. I found I was genuinely annoyed about that. So my ex had left me for another woman. Just another cold Swedish meatball in the TV dinner of life.

*

I opened the Bible, which was well into Ecclesiastes by now.

Fuck it's been a night. Something tried to get in. It

busted through the doorway and Marco emptied a clip in it. We're all deaf, but it's dead.

Didn't know what it was at first. Looked like a cross between a deer and a chimp, like on all fours. Lower legs just like toothpicks. Marco said it went around the room screaming like a kid but the only thing I heard was Marco screaming before the shots started. Steen got real excited, said it was the first "native fauna" we'd found and pulled its mouth open and then he started freaking out because it had fucking fillings and then Singer looked it over and started losing her shit and yelling for a razor.

I gave her mine because if she's gonna slit her wrists she'll need a lot more than a safety razor but she started shaving its arm and it had a fucking tattoo on the biceps. A mermaid, the real old-school Sailor Tommy kind. Real distorted, but still there. Then she threw the razor down and started crying and we all stood around real awkward until Petrov finally went and hugged her and told her it was okay.

It was one of her team, I guess, although he didn't look like that when he went in. Obviously. He was the first one to vanish, she said, and she thought he was dead but apparently something happened. Marco was yelling that it was a virus and we were all going to turn into that and I'm about to hit him over the head to shut him up but Steen said not to be stupid, Singer would have it too, *and she doesn't look anything like a chimp on stilts.*

"It's not a virus, Marco," I said. "It's Them. They changed the poor bastard." I wondered what he'd thought in his last minutes, if he'd been hoping that other people would help him, or if They'd done something to his brain and he was like the boatman, only more mobile.

Singer wants to bury him but we can't. Petrov told Steen and Marco to take him to one of the other bunkers and put him in. Singer's crying mad, but she says she knows he's right.

I don't want to go out there but I kind of wish I had because Singer's crying and I hate it. I'm not good at that. Do I go do something? Fuck.

I went over and hugged her like she was one of the guys and told her it was all fucked up but she'd get through. She didn't hit me so I guess it worked. I don't know. I asked her about her friend and she told me. She was crying for part of it, but his name was Van Verth and his hobby was singing and she kept saying he was just a really good guy.

Fuck, I'm sorry.

I tried to say the right things but I just kept thinking that in another month, that's gonna be me and I'm gonna be telling some stranger that Marco was a good guy but he wouldn't shut up and Marco'll be a piece of cooling meat in the next room.

We have to get out of here.

"Yeah, you do," I told him. I knew that he was probably going to die, but I still wanted to see it through. There wasn't much left, and I needed to know what had happened to my profane, overwhelmed friend in the pages. If nothing else, I'd promised to tell Simon what it said.

Fuck, I don't know where to start. Fuck. I can't. Fuck.

Singer and I are the only ones left. They got the other three right in front of us.

We were going back to the vacuae. We did the route yesterday, everybody knew what we were doing. I was bringing up the rear because we thought that'd be the dangerous spot. Ha.

Ha was underlined so violently it had torn the page.

We drew straws. Singer was second to last and she started out and then she stopped right in the water and jumped back and grabbed me. She said she heard the noise and that meant the things were there.

And they got them. Marco was in the water and he just unraveled. These threads came off him and I thought it was his clothes and it was at first but then it was his skin, like something just grabbed a thread and pulled and he was standing in this sort of haze but it was all made out of bits of him. It didn't happen nearly fast enough. He just kept walking forward with the threads falling off and I hope to fuck he didn't feel it and then he fell down into the water.

I wanted to go to him, I was trying to, but Singer was holding on to me and I tried to fight her off but she had hold of my gun and kept saying "It's over, you can't fix it." I kept trying and then she grabbed my ear and pulled. I think she nearly yanked the damn thing off. I decked her and I'd feel like shit about that but she says that's the only reason we lived.

Steen went down the same way, I think. I only saw the tail end of it. Petrov came running back, trying to grab Steen and hold him together with his bare hands, and then it got him too. Not the same way. The unraveling started and then there was another noise and a bunch of holes appeared, like on the captain. Singer dragged me back to the bunker by then.

Singer thinks that means there was more than one of the things out there, maybe different kinds. She says they hear us thinking and the pain was what saved us. We were right out there not three yards away but when she yanked my ear half off, my brain went blank of every-

thing else and then I punched her and that made her
brain blank and the things lost us and we got away.
  I can't. I can't. Fuck.
  Fuck everything.

I got up from bed, even though my knee was stiff again, and
went to the kitchen. There was a tiny airplane bottle of rum
that I'm pretty sure Uncle Earl kept for medicinal purposes. I
decided this counted and slammed the whole thing back.

Poor Bible. Poor Singer. Poor soldiers up against something
too big and too awful to deal with.

I could guess what it was, of course. One of Them had been
hungry and the other one hadn't. That one had been taking
the people apart for . . . for whatever reason. I hoped they were
dead. *Christ, please, let them be dead, not like Sturdivant, not
alive and feeling and lying in long tangled skeins under the
water. . . . Christ!*

My skin crawled. I tossed the empty airplane bottle in the
trash and dug through the cupboard looking for another one.
No luck.

Poor bastards. Their vacuae must have been out in the
open somewhere. If it had been inside a bunker, they might still
be alive. I licked the last stinging drops of rum off my lips. Of
course, if their military was just opening a hole at random into
the willows, they couldn't have known.

There wasn't much left in the Bible. I didn't want to read

it, but I couldn't leave the author there. I leaned against the counter, in the harsh fluorescent lights, and read the end.

The vacuae will open again tomorrow. That was the plan, if we couldn't get through the first time for some reason. Singer and I are hunkered down. Tomorrow I guess we run for it. If pain makes us harder to spot, I'll bite my own damn fingers off if I have to.

We promised not to go back for each other, if one of us goes down. I don't know if I'm lying or not. I would have run out there for Marco. I couldn't think.

I'm leaving this here. If something happens, when they send the next squad through to figure out what got us, maybe they'll find it and know to get the fuck out. This whole place is a great big feeding ground for . . . for whatever the fuck these things are. Nothing but death and willows and monsters. Whoever built the bunkers here must have known, for all the good it did them. You don't see them around here either.

If I get back, I'll tell them to close up the vacuae. They won't listen, but I'll try. And then I'm going somewhere else, someplace real cold, maybe, where willows don't grow at all.

If you're reading this, just get out. Bug out as fast as you can.

Good luck.

I turned the page and that was all.

Had he made it? Had he and Singer gotten out? I didn't know. Seemed unlikely that I would ever know. The vacuae he spoke of must not have been terribly far from the bunker where Simon and I had found the Bible, but if it had closed up, how would we know where it had been? It's not like he was going to stop in headlong flight to write *I made it!* on a rock or something.

I chose to believe he'd made it. There had only been the one bunker with their gear. If there had been a second mission sent, surely they'd have found the first one's and cleaned it up or disrupted it or taken their personal effects, or something. That argued that somebody had gotten back and told them not to send any more people, didn't it?

"You made it, buddy," I told the Bible. "You and Singer both. You probably got married afterward and had ten kids. Or at least lived down the street from each other and babysat the other one's ten kids."

I closed up the book and stared at the cover. A genuine artifact from another universe, where they had Sailor Tommy tattoos instead of Sailor Jerry, and blood signs instead of horoscopes.

If I tried to tell anyone, they'd think I was completely out of my head.

It made me wonder just how many artifacts like this were out there. How many people had stumbled into another dimension and come back knowing that if they told anyone, they'd get thrown in an institution? Was the world full of random objects from the next world over? Not the kind of curios that ended up in the Wonder Museum, but banal things that no one would ever notice or pay attention to?

I sighed and tucked the otherworldly Bible into a drawer in the kitchen. It could sit next to the rubber bands and the manual for the old microwave and a couple of salt packets from a fast-food restaurant. Any one of which might, presumably, also be from the next universe over. How would I ever know?

I closed the drawer and went to bed.

✻

"How you doing?" asked Simon, sliding my coffee across the counter. It was early, and the only other person in the Black Hen was wearing headphones and had their music turned up so loud that I could hear every lyric about the rise and fall of Ziggy Stardust.

"Found out that my ex left me for another woman," I said, prodding the wound to see if it was going to hurt. It didn't, although it felt like it should.

"Oh, that sucks!"

I shrugged. "I mean, I guess? Honestly, at this point, it's just so . . . I dunno. *Banal.*"

He rubbed his twin's eye. "Yeah, I can see that." He was silent while I dumped cream into my coffee, then said, "Hey, look at it this way?"

"Huh?"

"Bet *she* couldn't survive five minutes in another world."

I laughed. It hurt a little in my chest, but in a good way, as if bits of a clot were breaking loose. Was it possible for emotions to clot? Did I have some kind of weird horror scab in my lungs?

"God." I took a swallow of coffee. "Are we gonna be doing this in ten years? Like we'll be 'Hey, remember the time we accidentally went to hell?' "

"Beats the alternative." He grabbed a muffin out of the day-old bin and tossed it to me. Men with no depth perception do not throw well, and I couldn't move fast with my knee, so the muffin hit me in the chest, bounced, and we eventually located it somewhere under one of the chairs. It was in plastic wrap, so I didn't care. A slightly squashed muffin was nothing. A wrecked knee was . . . well, something significantly more, but at least I was here on earth and the portal to hell was closed and I wasn't married to some idiot who didn't know when to stop wailing on the phone.

I told Simon about how the Bible ended. "I hope they made it," I said finally.

"Hey, we made it, and look at us." Which was either a comforting thought or a vaguely insulting one, depending on what direction you looked.

I limped back home to the Wonder Museum and spent the time until we opened redesigning our logo.

Beau was in a mood. He couldn't find any more rats and suspected me of keeping them from him. I tried to pet him and he set his teeth on my hand in that I-could-bite-down-but-choose-not-to fashion. I left him to it.

"The tourists come, the tourists go . . . ," I muttered as the door closed behind another set. "'Talking of Michelangelo.'" I tried to remember the rest of "Prufrock" so I could butcher it, but all I could come up with was "'Till human voices wake us, and we drown,'" and that was a little too close to the bone, given the other night's events.

Uncle Earl called. I assured him that everything was fine, except that a display case had gotten broken and the albino raccoon had gotten mauled by the cat. He sighed. "Well, Carrot, that's how it goes sometimes. . . ."

Even though it was completely and totally the truth, I felt like I was lying to him. But what could I possibly say?

"Have you ever thought about relocating the Wonder Museum?" I asked finally. I groped for a reason and came up with "Someplace without stairs?"

"Couldn't do that, Carrot. It's a fixture of downtown. And I couldn't afford another place anyway, not without selling the building, and I won't do that to the Hen."

"No. No, I suppose not." Anyway, how would he sell the building? *Early twentieth-century brick commercial space, large metal patch on wall covering hole to hell. Hole does not convey any value.*

I sat that night under the sunflower pope, poking at my phone. It was late but I wasn't sleepy yet, and the throb from my knee was going to keep me awake unless I was really tired. It felt weird not to be reading the Bible. I kept thinking I needed to finish it and see how it ended, except that it was over and I would never really know how it ended.

Instead I was reading somebody's rant about mislabeling fanfic, which involved the word *consentacles*, which made me giggle hysterically, and then I heard a scratching noise.

I lifted my head from the tiny screen, just as a car passed and the headlights splashed light across the Wonder Museum. In the aftermath, the light faded . . . except where it didn't.

It took me a little time to realize that I wasn't just seeing an afterimage but an actual glow. I stared at it, blinking, but it didn't go away. If anything, it grew stronger.

It's not completely out of the ordinary for something to glow in the Wonder Museum. A couple of displays have glow-in-the-dark paint on them, and you'll see that faint green-white luminescence at night. This wasn't that.

It was silvery light, shading to amber at the upper edge, and it was familiar.

It was the color of the light in the willows.

My mind went blank. I didn't think anything. Maybe that saved me, I don't know. My skull felt hollow, as if any thought in it would ring like a bell.

It wasn't coming from upstairs. Later, when I could think again, that seemed important.

It came from behind one of the display cases on the ground

floor, a fox-fire glow that seemed to move from behind the case, along the wall. It crossed the lower floor at an unhurried pace, waking sparks in the glass eyes of the animals.

My skin was trying to crawl off my body, but I didn't move. It was moving away from me, and if I made so much as a sound, it might turn around and come back.

I didn't know where Beau was. I hoped he was asleep on my bed, somewhere safe, if anywhere in the museum could be considered safe.

It passed out of my vision from where I sat behind the counter. I saw the edges of the glow along the wall and finally under the stairs. It shrank down to nothing, and then I sat there while my phone turned itself off and another car drove by and the song "John Jacob Jingleheimer Schmidt" began to play through my head, and then I was sitting on the floor in the dark with my heart jackhammering in my chest because, God help me, the willows had come here.

I have to get out of here.

I have to get Beau and get out of here.

I have to get Beau and wake Simon up and get us all out of here.

It didn't matter about the museum anymore. When Uncle Earl could walk, I'd bring him here and I'd show him the hole and we could go in it a little way if we had to but not into the willows and then he'd know I wasn't crazy and we'd shut down the museum and get the hell out forever.

unless we open the hole and it's nothing but willows on the
other side

they get their roots in, Sturdivant said

oh fuck oh shit oh please God no

I got onto my knees, which hurt like hell, and crawled to the edge of the counter, looking into the museum proper. Dozens of glass eyes watched me. I hated that the willowlight had been in them because it meant that they were stranger eyes, not the ones I'd grown up with, not the silent, benevolent shapes that had watched over me since I was small.

Something rattled in the dark.

My heart stopped and then slammed against my ribs so hard that I thought I might have a heart attack and save the willows the trouble. *Can't get to me, suckers, I'm gonna die first!*

I wanted it to be the cat. It could almost be a cat-brushing-against-something noise. But then it came again, then another, and it was a blind, groping footfall noise, something blundering its way through the darkened museum, something alive.

the light makes things come alive then not alive

Beau would never make a noise like that unless he was wounded and dying.

It sounded slow. If I got to my feet and grabbed my cane, I could hobble away, and then we would have the slowest chase scene ever. But if it was Beau, if the willows had gotten to him—

oh God what if they got him what if they changed him what if
he's like Sturdivant now or the kids in the bus and I destroyed him

because I didn't take him and run right away oh God

Maybe it didn't know I was here. Maybe I could stay low and it wouldn't find out and I could get away. . . .

My phone rang.

I flinched so hard I nearly threw it across the room. Then I almost lifted it to my ear because reflexes are reflexes and then I caught myself and fumbled for the button to silence the call. Too late, of course. The footfalls began to scrabble toward me, fast and irregular, like a wounded animal.

It was my ex's number.

For a second, the outrage at him made a clear space in my head. I wasn't scared. I was just pissed that it wasn't enough he'd left me for another woman at a Halloween party, it wasn't enough that he kept calling asking for absolution, now he had to get me killed by a goddamn willow monster because he just could not leave well enough alone.

The anger was useful. I came unfrozen and grabbed for my cane and then the noise was directly in front of the counter.

fuck fuck fuck fuck

I turned my head. The top of the counter is glass and the front is glass and one of the opaque sliding panels in back doesn't close all the way, so I had a narrow sliver of visibility. I saw only dimness and the back of one of the bits of Jewelry by Local Artist boxes from inside the case.

Just as I craned my neck to look, there was a sudden, horrible scrabble—not from the front of the case, but from the *top*—and something landed on my back.

It had claws like Beau and it was about the right size, but it wasn't. I knew it wasn't the moment that it sank its teeth into me. Its mouth was cold and dry and gritty. It felt like a pointed clamp more than a bite, but something flapped against my skin inside the ring of teeth.

I dropped my phone and heard the crack of glass. My shoulder burned but it didn't hurt as bad as my knee had. I reached up and grabbed for the thing, and my fingers closed over cool, dry hair and I wrenched it loose and threw it as hard as I could.

Also I was screaming at the top of my lungs, but that probably goes without saying.

It was surprisingly lightweight. It hit the floor and rolled and then it got up, but not easily.

It was the stuffed fisher from the raccoon display case.

Dark fur, weaselly body. Should have had dark eyes to go with it, but they were glowing with silver willowlight. Light oozed out of its mouth and leaked from a hole in its chest, but it wasn't like a beam of light, it was dripping like liquid.

It swayed on its feet and it didn't look alive but it was moving.

It was the raccoon at the door, I thought. *It was. They're walking. The willowlight made them alive and now they're walking.*

The fisher opened and closed its mouth. I couldn't remember how it had looked before, when it was one of dozens of displays, but the mouth looked as if it had been wired to only open halfway.

That's why the bite wasn't very big. That's why it didn't tear a huge chunk out of me. Its jaw can't open that far.

The dry plastic tongue moved in its mouth and I realized what that flapping thing against my skin had been.

It began to shuffle toward me. It didn't move right. Weasels all have that sinuous humpbacked lope, and this wasn't it. Its back was stiff as if it couldn't bend, and it wobbled from leg to leg like a stool that couldn't get all four feet on the floor.

When it was close enough, I rose up and smashed it in the face with my cane. My knee screamed and my shoulder throbbed, but it fell over.

I struck it again. The silvery glow got brighter, as if something had slipped loose. I hit it with the cane, over and over, and it felt like hitting a sack or a lumpy cushion, not anything alive. Its legs paddled against the air, ratcheting and mechanical, like a spider curling up on its back.

My breath came in great choking sobs while I tried to beat the dead thing to death a second time.

The last blow shoved it a dozen feet across the floor. It rolled and lay on its side. Its feet were still moving, but the hide had split in a half dozen places and silver light spilled out as if it were burning from inside.

I tried to stand up and my knee buckled. My shoulder was hot and sticky and I could maybe have dealt with that, but my leg was white agony. Every smash of the cane had pushed my knees into the concrete floor and now it felt like I'd shoved a crowbar under the kneecap and tried to pry it off.

I had a thought of calling Simon, who had two working legs, but my phone was a dark spiderweb of glass. *Shit.*

If I can stand up, it'll be better, I told myself. *If I can just get up. Kneeling is what's killing me.* I tried to get the cane under me and my muscles flatly refused to obey.

The dead fisher began to rock back and forth. I hauled on the cane with both hands, trying to pull myself up far enough that I could grab the edge of the counter. We were locked in a horrible, slow-motion race, injured woman and possessed corpse, trying to see which one of us could get to our feet first.

It won.

Its head lolled to one side, no longer functional. I'd say I had broken its neck, except that it didn't have one, it was just an armature, the only bones left were the skull and the feet and the end of the tail. I'd broken something. The hole in its chest gaped open like a mouth.

Something moved inside the hole.

I clung to my cane, all thought of getting up forgotten. Inside the fisher's chest, outlined in silver light, the corpse-otter carving turned its head to look at me.

Everything snapped into place.

#93 - Corpse-otter carving, circa 1900, from Danube.

"It was you," I said. "It was you *the whole time.*"

19

It was here. It was in my museum. It was the source of everything.

It was *here*.

How *dare* it come here? This was *home*. This was what I had been trying to get back to. I had survived the whole stupid divorce and the hellscape on the other side of the wall, and I kept coming back here and it was safe, the museum was the safe place where Uncle Earl kept a little corner of the world weird and ridiculous and kind.

It wasn't allowed to be here. It felt like a betrayal, the way my ex cheating on me hadn't. He was just a person. This was the museum.

The corpse-otter carving twitched in the hole.

The hole in the wall. Of course it hadn't been a tourist.

Simon had said as much. I'd left the corpse-otter on the shelf and it had managed to knock a hole in the drywall and fall into the other side. Then I kept putting it back, thinking it was rolling off the case. Was it trying to get to the willows?

Trying to get *back* to the willows?

Jesus. *Jesus.* If I'd just left it there, if I hadn't kept absentmindedly picking it up and putting it back where I thought it belonged . . .

Oh, God. I wanted to howl with laughter or throw up or wail. Both of us had been on the wrong sides of our respective walls, trying to get home.

When we sealed the hole, had it realized that it wasn't getting home under its own power? Had it been responsible for the sleepwalking? What the hell even *was* it?

#93 - Corpse-otter carving, circa 1900, from willow-infested hell . . .

The fisher backed away and began to limp up the stairs. One of its hind legs couldn't quite make it, so it would climb two stairs, then do a lurching hop to the next. Its body was stiff and grotesque from the weight of the carving inside it.

I tried to get up again and my body would *not* do it. I screamed in frustration at myself and my leg for turning traitor. My arms shook with strain trying to pull myself up, and something twitched in my back that made the edges of my vision go red.

Fuck fuck fuck gotta move gotta get up fuck . . .

The fisher vanished over the top step, onto the second floor.

Light flared on the second floor of the museum. Silver willowlight again, another world's madness bleeding over and infecting my own. I abandoned my attempt to get up and ducked down behind the counter.

It knew where I was, I *knew* it knew, but clearly the carving couldn't kill me by itself. I'd been picking it up carelessly for weeks. But what might it be calling with that light?

the light makes things alive

The light didn't fade. It grew stronger and began to pulse and flicker. It crawled down the walls, and the shadows of the animal heads grew and elongated like the shapes in the willows at night.

"Oh God," I whispered. "Oh God."

What was it calling up? What was it doing to the Wonder Museum? Could it call one of Them into this world, to hunt and feast and change us at Their pleasure? How was it calling the light? Was there some essence of the willows in it? Was it carved of willow wood?

And why hadn't it done any of this before?

Maybe it just wasn't frustrated enough, I thought. Well. I guessed between Beau and me, we'd gotten it plenty frustrated now.

I closed my eyes against the light, which didn't help. On the backs of my eyelids, I could picture my friends and neighbors running down the street while some unseen thing overhead hummed and chimed and unraveled their flesh until they fell down in their tracks, not alive but not nearly dead enough.

On the wall behind the counter, shadows moved. I turned my head.

The wildebeest stretched as if the animal had just woken up, then turned its head. Its skin shivered in the light, as if a fly had landed on it.

"You can't be here," I told the light miserably. "You're not allowed. Not here. This is a *good* place."

Was.

Was a good place.

Now it was alien. An outpost of the willows. Not my home. Not Uncle Earl's home.

The wildebeest looked at me. I saw silver light reflected in its eyes.

I scuttled backward on my hands and one knee, bad leg stretched out awkwardly in front of me. All around me I heard crashing, groaning, the sounds of movement.

The wildebeest snorted. I heard it breathe and it couldn't be inhaling, it didn't have *lungs*, there was no *place* for the air to go—but still it breathed.

I looked at the phone on the counter and realized that I had no idea what Simon's phone number was. He was a name in my contacts list, a button I pushed. I could no more have dialed him on the ancient antique rotary than I could fly.

Call 911? Yeah, that would be terribly helpful. They'd think I was on drugs and probably hit me with a Taser. Or they'd start shooting the taxidermy. God knew I couldn't explain what was happening in less than two hours.

I reached the corner of the counter and looked around it again.

The grizzly bear leaned back, scratching its back against the wall. The kudu's ears swept up, alert to danger. In the cases, bones rattled and articulated themselves together. A bone snake reared up and struck the glass, and I heard the shadow of a hiss leak through.

"Stop," I said hopelessly. "Stop. Please."

They did not stop.

I have to stop it. I have to get rid of whatever it is. If I can get the carving and destroy it . . . throw it out . . . smash it . . .

I had no real idea how I could destroy it. Putting it out at the curb in the trash probably wasn't going to cut it. Would it burn? I didn't have an axe.

It can't move much, can it? Or it would have been wandering around by now. It can only move a little bit, surely. I remembered it in the hallway, always falling on the floor.

The bone snake struck again, hissing.

That was before. Now that the willowlight is here, now that it's got a host, what can it do?

I did not want to leave the questionable safety of the counter, but I had no choice.

I got my legs under me. "Come on . . . ," I hissed, jamming the cane into my armpit. "Come on, just let me get up."

My knee screamed, but it held. That was fine. If I needed

surgery like Uncle Earl after this, fine. I'd declare medical bankruptcy. Or they could just take it off at the hip. I didn't care. The only thing that mattered now was stopping the carving before the museum's beasts tore themselves off the walls.

The wildebeest snorted again, loudly, and I heard the scrape of its horns against the wall as it thrashed.

I limped as far as the stairs and stared up them. They might as well have been a thousand feet tall. I couldn't climb the stairs on my feet, surely.

Fine, I thought grimly. *If I can't climb, then I'll crawl.*

I went up on my hands and one knee, a step at a time. The brief half second on each step when my bad knee had to take weight was like an electric shock. Red flared beneath my eyelids, briefly drowning out the willowlight.

The fur-bearing trout, a joke played on gullible tourists, flapped against its plaque. The jackalope groomed its antlers with its paws. I did not look at the Genuine Feejee Mermaid, but I could hear a dry snapping in the shadows.

It's the mermaid's teeth. You know it's the teeth.

Stop it stop it stop it!

I crawled on. The jackalope turned to watch me go. The snapping was drowned out by the wheeze of breath in non-existent lungs, the sounds of horns and antlers clicking, and hooves pawing against the walls.

It took a hundred years of agony, but I reached the top and looked over the steps.

The giant otter stood in a halo of shattered glass. The hole in its chest gaped open like a wound, dripping silver light.

Too late. I'm too late. It's in the otter.

For an instant, I felt relieved. It wasn't in the grizzly bear. It was an otter. Otters are just clownish water ferrets. This wasn't the worst thing, surely?

Then it turned its head.

Glass eyes moved over me. I froze. My heart stopped in my chest. Claws as long as my fingers. Teeth even longer. It could take my throat out in a single bite, as easily as Beau dispatching a mouse.

The eyes moved over me and it looked away. I did not concern it.

When it leaped down from the remains of the display, it moved like oil. It had none of the awkwardness of the fisher. The carving fitted into this beast's chest like a key in a lock.

God help me, I would have preferred the grizzly bear. The grizzly bear couldn't have walked, with the bad leg. The otter was eight feet long, and even if the muscle was gone, the skin *remembered.*

Apex predator. *Water jaguar.* The pattern of white on its chest shone sickly silver, like fox fire in the dark.

If it had come toward the stairs, I would probably have pitched over backward and broken my neck, saving it the trouble. But it did not. It walked on silent feet to the patched back wall.

The great otter reared up on its hind legs. Its body was too long, too snake-like, a beast from the age of dinosaurs, not the age of mammals. It shoved the Bigfoot statue aside with careless strength and raked its claws against the wall.

Skrreeeeeeeeeek.

The batik tore. Claw marks scored the metal, but it held. I could see the dull reflection of the willowlight in the surface of the metal.

I remembered the hole in the grizzly bear, the hole that I'd thought had been rats. Had the corpse otter tested it out, realized it was short a leg, and decided not to bother? Or had it lacked some other intangible quality that the carving required?

The otter dropped to all fours, then stood back up again, moving its head bonelessly from side to side. It moved its paws over the metal and I realized suddenly that it must be blind.

That's why it didn't come after me. It couldn't see me.

Questing paws found the edges of the metal, and it sank its claws into the wall with a crunching sound.

Oh God.

It doesn't need a human to open the way anymore. . . .

It must have tried before, as the raccoon, but it wasn't strong enough. It couldn't move the statue. The fisher was just temporary, until it could get to the otter. Then it had done . . . whatever it did. Cast a spell or invoked its alien gods or called the willowlight to it.

The willowlight had come, the light that brought things

to freakish, alien life, and it had been strong enough to wake everything in the museum.

It had been strong enough to break into the otter's case as well. I could see the fisher, a deflated rag of fur, lying in state on the bed of broken glass.

The monster got its claws under the metal patch and pulled.

The screws tore out of the wall. The metal squealed as it bent. Cold air rushed past the otter and brought the scent of water and gravel and willows to me.

The otter dropped down and investigated the hole. I saw the whiskers working. It might be blind, but it could still sense the edges. It rose up again, grasped the metal, and pulled to widen the hole.

It'll go, I told myself. *It'll go away and it'll be gone and we'll fill the hole with concrete and the carving will be back where it belongs and that'll be the end of it.*

Please, I begged the monster silently. *Please just go.*

It set its paws on the bottom of the hole, shoulder deep in the other world.

And then something touched me, something soft and furry, and I let out a muffled shriek and Beau the cat locked eyes on the monstrous otter and began to yowl.

My cat. My stupid, valiant cat who never lost a fight in his life and didn't realize he could and who was not going to let a monster twenty times his size get away.

My cat who had probably just doomed us both.

The monster's head snapped around. Blind it might be, but there was nothing wrong with its hearing.

Beau punctuated his yowl with a hiss.

The otter turned in that narrow space like it had no spine. It might be enormous, but it was still a weasel. I snatched Beau up and fled.

My knee couldn't handle the stairs, but that was fine. I went down on my ass, in a fast, bumpy slide, and it hurt like the devil, but it was a lot faster than trying to limp down one step at a time. Beau sank his claws into my shoulder, but I'm not sure if that was to hold on or in outrage that I was taking him away from his prey.

I looked over my shoulder and the otter was there. It came down the steps like a river of oil, eight feet of sleek, monstrous predator. A more dangerous host for the carving I couldn't imagine. The carving had found the worst possible thing in the Wonder Museum.

And it was silent. So very, terribly silent. The Feejee Mermaid snapped her teeth at it as it went by, and I heard the clicking, but I could not hear the water jaguar's paws on the ground.

I rolled to my feet and ran with a desperate hobbling stride toward the back of the museum. My bedroom door was open and I threw myself inside and slammed the door closed. I fumbled with the lock, looking around for anything to jam against the door—the chair, the nightstand, anything that might stop the monster for a few seconds.

The door rocked on its hinges as the otter hit it.

I flung Beau down on the bed. He resumed his yowl unabated.

The door banged again, higher up. The otter was on its hind legs, raking those gigantic claws along the door. I grabbed the chair and jammed it under the knob, the way they do in movies, then learned immediately why they only do that in movies.

There was a loud *crack!* of breaking wood. This plain old interior door was a flimsy little hollow-core number, of course. It would stop someone like me. It wasn't going to stop the otter.

It was also the only way out of the room.

Oh God, why had I run into my room? It was instinct, pure stupid instinct. I'd run to the bedroom and locked the door because some part of me believed that it was A Safe Place and surely the corpse-otter would respect the ancient rules of privacy and not open the door.

Completely absurd, of course, but I hadn't been thinking. I'd just run. If the bathroom door had been closer, I'd probably have locked myself in there, instead.

Splintering, cracking noises came from the wood. I heard the bolt squeal.

I had a strong urge to get under the bed, the same urge that had sent me running to my room. Monsters can't get you there. I fought it back. All that would happen would be that I was a sitting duck for the otter to reach in and haul me out. And Beau would never consent to sit quietly until it went away again.

"Oh God," I said out loud. "Oh God . . ."

On the wall, Prince moved.

There was no shock left in me, only horror. I watched him turn his head, animated by the terrible power of the willows. His antlers scraped against the wall behind him and he bent his neck forward, as if surprised.

"Not you, too," I said. "Oh God, Prince, not you, too."

I didn't know if I could bear it. I loved that elk. His nostrils flared and he turned his head to look at me.

The otter hit the door again, and Prince jerked sideways, ears going flat back. His mouth opened and he gave an enormous huffing snort, despite having no lungs.

The doorframe gave way.

I think the sudden lack of resistance startled the otter as much as it did me. The door slammed inward, sending the chair flying and tearing out a chunk of the doorframe as the bolt went through the wall and the otter tumbled forward into the room.

I snatched up the lamp, still attached by its cord. I didn't know how much good it was going to do, but I'd lost my cane somewhere along the way.

The otter stood up, shaking itself off. It turned its head back and forth, whiskers sweeping the air, then triangulated. Not on me. On Beau, who was still wailing like the damned.

Oh, shit.

The otter lunged forward, and two things happened simultaneously.

With an absolutely stupid courage I hadn't known I

possessed, I jumped in front of the cat and brought the lamp down—and Prince ducked his great head, twisted sideways, and raked his antlers along the otter's side.

My blow was ineffectual. Prince's wasn't. His antlers jammed into the otter, and Prince lifted it up, half-impaled on the points, while the otter writhed silently. Silver willowlight oozed through the spots on its belly.

Beau, seeing the enemy brought low, launched himself from the bed and onto the otter's face, wailing like a police siren. He tore at the otter's eyes, a commendable effort, but given that the otter was blind, not terribly useful.

The otter tried to swat at its attackers but couldn't quite get leverage. It squirmed on the antler points, got free of one, and its hindquarters dropped to the floor.

Beau raked out one of the huge glass eyes and sprang free. Apparently he felt this was enough for his part of the fight, because he bolted through the doorway and into the museum.

That struck me as a very good idea. I flung myself past the squirming otter just in time, as it finally was able to brace its feet and begin to tear itself off the antlers.

I was frightened that it might hurt Prince—insomuch as taxidermy that shouldn't be alive can be hurt—but sticking around seemed like a very bad idea.

I had to get away.

Think, I said to myself as I staggered down the hallway. *Think! Where can you hide?*

The animals tossed their heads on the walls. The bone snake struck ineffectually at the glass.

What would happen if we left the museum? What if I ran and it chased me? What could it bring to life outside?

I had visions of the silver light settling over the trees of my own world and turning them into willows. Willows growing from the cracks in the street, filling the windows of the Black Hen and the boutique with the scented candles, overrunning the gutters, everyone in Hog Chapel surrounded by willows, and Them coming through, not just one but hundreds of Them, once the willows had their roots in.

It wasn't enough to hide or to get away. I had to stop it. I needed fire or an axe or . . .

No.

The corpse-otter carving was the animating force behind all of this. It had been trying to get back into the willow world. It had been trying to get itself home, before it had seen me.

Oh, God, it must have been so frustrated! I could imagine its small carved paws paddling at the ground, shoving itself along like an overturned turtle, and then who would come along but the bumbling human, picking it up and putting it back, over and over. No wonder it wanted me dead. I was its jailor and torturer. For all I knew, the power to animate the skins was a last-ditch effort, something that had taken years off its life (if it was even alive) or hurt like hell or some other alien emotion that a flesh-and-blood mammal couldn't possibly understand.

But I understood wanting to go home. I had been trapped on the other side of the hole, in an alien world, and I would have sold my hope of heaven to go home again.

I knew where I had to lead it.

My knee had stopped hurting in the red stabbing way and started to hurt in a strange, ominous numb way. Whatever I had done to it, it was getting a lot worse, fast.

It made going up the stairs much easier, but the knee also buckled on every step if I tried to put weight on it, so I was hopping and hauling myself along on the railing. Nothing subtle about it. I could hear the thudding noises as the otter and Prince fought below me. I was terrified for Prince, but I just needed the elk to hold him until I got up the stairs.

The Feejee Mermaid clacked in my ear as I passed. The trout flapped. Was it my imagination, or were they moving slower? Was the power winding down?

I couldn't take the chance that it would wear out before it did something horrible to my own world. I snatched up a rainstick from the display at the top of the stairs. It wasn't a good crutch, but it was better than nothing.

It also made the rattling-rice sound whenever I took a step. *That's fine. It's fine. I need the otter to follow me.*

Was it going to follow me? The thumping sounds had quieted from below. Had it gotten loose from Prince? Where the devil was it?

I had just barely had that thought, when I heard a sound

much closer at hand. A clack, a scrabble, then a heavy thump, as if . . . well, as if a Genuine Feejee Mermaid had just tried to take a bite out of a large animal that had swatted its attacker off the wall.

I looked over my shoulder, and God help me, it was *right there* on the stairs. One glass eye was gone and the other was dangling from its skull by glue and a rag of hide, like a handmade optic nerve.

But it wasn't alone. The mermaid was hanging off the otter's whiskers, and the jackalope had leaped down from its shelf and was goring the otter in the leg. The fur-bearing trout was flailing so violently that its plaque rattled with every movement. A mallard came off the wall, still attached to its mount, and began flopping across the ground, hissing like a snake, wings beating violently against the floor.

The museum's protectors, as strange and dead and ineffectual as they were, were buying me time.

I stopped dithering and lunged for the hole to the willows.

The sounds of the museum faded as I scrambled through the hole and into the concrete corridor. All I could hear was my own breathing and the rattling of the rainstick. It was broad daylight outside, but if I could just get the otter to chase me out the entrance and circle back behind, then . . . uh . . . okay, the metal door had been smashed, but it was still blind, so maybe I could hide out in another bunker until it passed. Or something.

Look, it wasn't a good plan, but I'd like to see you do better under the circumstances.

Anyway, if I could just get it out there, into the willows, maybe it would care less about catching me. It would be home. Then I'd come home myself and go crawl up the steps to the Black Hen and Simon and I would weld a dozen steel plates into the doorframe, fill the corridor up with concrete. I didn't even care how hard it would be to lug the bags; I would sell blood to hire somebody to carry them up, if that's what it took.

But that was in the future. Now I just had to move.

Get on top of the bunker, I thought. *Get on top and when the otter comes out, you just lay low and wait for it to move off. It's blind. Even if it wants to kill you, it'll have to catch you first. And once it's out and away, you drop back down into the bunker and get the hell out of this world forever.*

Sure. Piece of cake. I routinely dodged eight-foot predators that had claws like knives. What's a functioning knee between friends?

I could hear the otter's claws clicking on the concrete as it moved. I scrambled up the steps, no longer trying to be stealthy.

Up. Up on top. Just get up behind it.

I stepped into the sunlight. The glare blinded me, and I prayed that the boatman wasn't right there, waiting for me, while black spots danced in front of my eyes.

If he is, there's not a damn thing you can do about it. Get up on top of the bunker, quick!

I turned and tried to scramble up the grassy slopes. I

remembered that they were grassy. I remembered it being smooth and green and . . .

My hands met branches. I blinked away tears from the brightness and saw willows.

They can't be here . . . but remember you saw them before that's why you didn't realize this was the way home the willows grew up overnight because they were looking for you and Simon or they're looking for a way into the world they know there's a hole there the otter told them it made the hole and they want to get their roots into your world and grow and grow and grow . . .

It didn't matter. I'd moved through the willows before. It hadn't killed me. The thing that was chasing me—*that* would kill me.

I scrabbled at the willow branches, trying to make headway. I could get through. I could. It shouldn't be this hard. They were only branches, they *had* to bend, except they *weren't* bending and I was going nowhere quickly and the otter was coming up the stairs, or at least something was coming up the stairs, who the hell knew anymore, and I had to get out of here *now*.

I abandoned my attempts to claw through the willows and tried to turn away, but the willows clawed back.

I don't know why that surprised me. You would think that I would have expected it by now. A light that could wake the negative spaces between branches could certainly wake the willows themselves. But I looked down at the thin branches hooked into my clothes, tangling in loops of thread and digging into my hair, and my skin crawled even more and I yanked myself back.

My shirt ripped. My scalp stung as the willows tore my hair out, but compared to my knee, it barely registered. I staggered backward and half fell, half leaped into the water.

The cold felt like heaven on my knee. That is all that could be said for it. Water went up my nose, and probably I was going to get brain-eating amoebas from it. I snorted and coughed, lumbering through the water, mud squelching underfoot. My sandals were instantly heavy. I kicked them off. My lounge pants soaked through in seconds and molded to my skin.

Well, if I hadn't wanted to make any noise, I was doing a piss-poor job of it. The otter had to know where I was now. I was splashing and spluttering and choking and making more noise than an injured duck.

Stop making noise. I tried to slow my breathing. *Don't kick. Don't splash. And for the love of God, don't lose track of your bunker this time.* I hadn't been able to mark it, but the smashed-in door should be pretty obvious, and the willows on top were decorated with rags that had been my shirt a few minutes earlier. The current tugged at me, and I let it. Downstream. There were more islands downstream, more doors, and some of them were open. If I could get to one, I could close the door. Wait the otter out, maybe.

My original plan, not that there was much of one, had lasted all of five seconds, but maybe now that the carving was home, it would lose interest and go away and I could get out of here.

Don't forget which door it is this time. It has willows. Remember the willows.

Everything in this fucking world has willows, so what good does that do?!

There was a sound behind me. It was not anything so loud as a splash. It was a soft, almost silken noise, the sound of something entering the river as if it had been born for it.

Water jaguar.

I had just made a terrible mistake.

Panic must have guided me. Maybe luck, although you'd think that if I had any luck at all, it would have stepped in much earlier. I swam with the current, my bad leg dangling uselessly, passing two doors, and then I saw one half-open and made for it.

Something slithered past my leg. Something big. I felt a rush of heat, then cold, and then, a distant third, pain. I looked down and back and saw the water blooming red behind me. The heat had been the sensation of my calf being slashed open.

I didn't scream, but I made a rough, strangled noise. *At least it was my bad leg,* I thought, *at least I've still got one good one,* and then the humming noise rang overhead.

They had heard me.

It was close. It was at least as close as it had been when Simon and I hid inside the ruined ship, at least, except this time there was no thin wall of wood and sand to hide me.

it got Petrov and Marco they just unraveled

The water jaguar rose. Its remaining eye dangled obscenely. It moved its head back and forth, whiskers arched. Was it seeking me? Toying with me?

Enemies in air and water. I had one chance left, and it was through the bunker door in front of me. If it was one of the ones filled with water and debris, I was going to die. If it didn't have a door that I could close, a door that wasn't rusted in place, I was going to die.

But at least the otter could only tear me apart. I couldn't take the chance that They weren't hungry.

I threw myself onto the shallow concrete ledge, knee tearing itself into even more horrible useless pieces, and rolled down the steps into the dark.

I lost count of the number of steps. Five, maybe, or six, or eight. Then I hit dark water.

My head went under yet again. Oh, well. The amoebas could only eat my brain once. I rose, treading water, and found myself standing knee-deep. The door behind me was a mass of welded rust. I threw myself against it and it didn't even creak.

Well, shit.

Strangely enough, my greatest feeling was resignation. I didn't scream or cry or fall down. Perhaps I had burned out most of my terror. I had gambled on a door that I could close and I had lost and that was it, shit happens, time to die.

I looked up and the humped shape of the otter blocked out the light.

Resigned I might be, but I was still going to make the damn thing work for it. I waded into the gloom, wishing like hell I were wearing my boots. There was stuff in the water down here, debris, things that felt hard underfoot and might have been broken branches or broken bottles or God only knew what. Things brushed past my bleeding calf—waterweed or algae, maybe.

Was there a doorway? I didn't have a flashlight. I put my hands out in front of me, waiting to hit the wall. If I could reach it, I could work my way along it. Maybe there'd be a doorway deeper in, a room that wasn't full of water, with a working door that I could slam in the otter's face.

The monster took a step down, then another. I couldn't hear its feet anymore, but I could see the light shifting as it moved. Empty eye sockets moved back and forth. I knew it could hear me. I wondered if it could smell me, too.

My fingers touched cold concrete. I don't know why I felt relieved, it's not as if the monster couldn't get me if I was touching a wall. But my heart leaped as I began feeling my way along. There might be a doorway, and if there was a doorway, there might be a door.

I hit a corner. A threshold? No, an alcove. It only went an arm's length back. Could I press myself into it, maybe kick the otter a few times before it got me?

Kick it how? While levitating? Which leg are you going to stand on and which are you going to kick with?

Fine, maybe punch the otter a few times?

It seemed that even that was going to be denied. The alcove was too wide. I followed the back wall to a kind of stone pillar. It was only a few inches from the back. I couldn't have fit behind it. I wanted to scream.

I heard the soft, silken sound of the otter entering the water again.

And then I heard another sound. A familiar one, practically under my left ear.

"Gck! Gck! Gck!"

20

Sturdivant's hand closed over my wrist. It felt like ice-cold twigs. I jerked back, making a noise that might have been a shriek but was probably a squeak of despair. "Let go." I tried to wrench myself free. "Let go!"

"You," said Sturdivant. "You. From before. Still alive? *Still?*"

"I got out. I got out but I had to come back, it was over there, it's here now, it's after me. Let go!"

Something rippled in the water. Was it the otter?

No. It's Sturdivant. You're standing in him right now. If he can grab you, there's probably guts in the water all around you.

I was standing in blackness, but the world started to go gray around the edges anyway. I had not previously realized that fainting in the dark meant that things got lighter. How interesting.

"Bleeding," said Sturdivant. "Blood in the water. I taste it."

"It clawed me." *He tastes the water. How?*

Oh, you know *how.*

Fainting suddenly did not seem so bad, but I tried to cling to consciousness. If I fainted, I was going to die. "It's coming now." Were the spots I saw in front of my eyes from inside my head, or was it the glowing willowlight on the otter's belly? "Please. Let go."

For a long, long moment, I didn't know if I'd gotten through. I waited to hear the hiss of water behind me, to feel the weight of the water jaguar on my back and the claws bearing me down.

"Then get out. Get out! Gck!"

On the last word, he flung me away. I landed in the water with a splash, the world going even grayer. My thoughts came from a great distance away and seemed to echo, as if I were at the end of a long tunnel.

I heard the soft sound of the water jaguar moving near me. Had it heard the splash?

I lay like a dead thing in the water, trying not to faint.

Can't move. Gotta move. Can't but have to. It'll hear me if I move. Move. Move. Things coming. Things in the water with me. Move. Gotta move.

Ripples washed across my face, breaking over my lips. The otter? Sturdivant?

"Gck! Gck!" The sound echoed off the walls and water sloshed over me again. Something slapped my ribs, long and muscled, and I realized that the water jaguar's tail had struck me as it passed, seeking the source of Sturdivant's voice.

Somehow, I don't know how, I crossed the room. I think I mostly floated, hauling myself along on my hands. Every time something touched my legs, I fought the urge to scream, because there were only a few things it could be and none of them were good.

I reached the steps.

I didn't look back out of curiosity. I looked back to see if the water jaguar was coming after me. I wasn't Lot's wife, though I might have been Orpheus.

The light only reached a little way into the darkness. My eyes had adjusted enough to see the surface of the water roiling. Almost, I turned away in time.

But I didn't, so I saw.

The otter erupted from the water, a great sleek shape glowing with willowlight. In the sudden oily light, I saw things wrapped around the otter's body, long black tendrils like hair or seaweed, a kraken wrap of tentacles.

Sturdivant clung to the monster's neck with bony arms, and the otter rolled in the water again and again, getting more and more tangled in Sturdivant's organs, two thrashing figures in a nightmare of water and concrete and darkness.

I crawled up the stairs and fell out into the light.

Even in the willow world, the sun felt like a brief benediction. But I couldn't stay there. I had to get home.

Christ, I thought, making the world's most pitiful dog

paddle. *Christ, we were so close to the way home all along.* But we'd run from Sturdivant, run in the wrong direction, and gotten hopelessly lost among the islands, and it was only dumb luck and stubbornness that led us back home.

I was sure I knew which island to go to now. Pretty sure. Mostly sure. I looked ahead and it was crowned with willows, but it was the right bunker, wasn't it?

I wondered how much blood I was losing, and whether Sturdivant would win.

The hum was chasing me. I was almost certain of it. It was so close that I could pick details out of the sound, a high buzz like cicadas, and a strange rubbery squealing noise. I didn't like any of them.

The water in front of me went *glorp!*

I veered out of the way, not sure what the hell had just happened, but pretty sure that it was bad.

It happened again, a little to my left, a splash as if a rock had fallen into the water, except that there was no rock.

The third time it happened, I realized what it was. The cone-shaped hole They left, cutting into the water, not sand. The water rushing to fill it. If I was in the way of one of those holes, it would cut a hole into me as easily as the water.

you could see his brain and skull all neat lined up layers like a sandwich

"No!" I said, throwing myself forward.

The hum wailed overhead.

"John Jacob Jingleheimer Schmidt . . ."

It is extremely hard to run from something that you are not allowed to think about. I dodged, or tried to dodge, but how do you dodge something invisible that can't quite see you either?

". . . whenever we go out . . . the people always shout . . ."

A water funnel opened up practically under my feet.

I had to get out of the water. There was a sandspit nearby, maybe even the first one we'd waded out to, so very long ago. I crawled up onto the shore, trying to stay in the clear, out of the willows, the willows couldn't be trusted oh goddammit I was thinking about the willows I had to stop thinking about them but they were right in front of me —

The humming wail in my ear sounded triumphant. Whether it was the proximity of the willows that had brought me into Their focus, or if They had simply finally blundered close enough to sense me, I didn't know, I couldn't know *oh motherfucker I was still thinking . . .*

I half rolled on my side and saw one of Them overhead.

It was on the other side of reality, but They were coming through. It was tearing a hole in the sky to get to me, and for a moment I could see the hole and the shape that They made pushing against the skin of the world, like the children in the school bus but not remotely human.

They looked like nothing I understood, like an Old Testament angel, all wings and wheels and eyes. The sky billowed nauseatingly and the hole grew larger, edged with jittery migraine colors. What made the hole was a beak or a drill or a spike, pushing through the back of the sky. The sort of thing that might make a funnel-shaped hole in the water or reality or someone's body.

Seeing Them did not make me more afraid. There was nothing I could hook my fear onto. It was not a shape that my body understood enough to fear. But the sound They made was a hunting sound, a train whistle of hunger, and *that* I understood.

Pain, I thought hazily, listening to the shriek as They descended. What had the Bible said? *She says they hear us thinking and the pain was what saved us.* Singer had attacked Bible and he'd retaliated, and the pain had saved them both. And They had been right there at the mouth of the bunker when Simon and I had fallen down the stairs and the pain in my knee had whited out all my thoughts. And we had lived.

There was nothing else to try, no other place to run. I took a deep breath, raised up as much as I could, and dropped my full weight on my bad knee.

The world slewed sideways and I nearly vomited. I have never felt pain like that before in my life, and I hope to never do so again. My mind went blank. I was suspended alone in a red-shot void with the God of Pain.

I fell over into the sand. I don't know if I screamed, but I know that I bit both sides of my tongue so hard they bled.

It hurt. It hurt unbelievably. I thrashed in the sand like an injured mouse. Waves of black, tinged with red, washed over me. *Knees are the worst*, I'd blithely said to Uncle Earl once, not knowing the half of it.

There was a call in my ears and I couldn't remember what it was from, except that I could hear it and that meant that I had to keep going.

I got up on my hands and collapsed onto my knee again, and that time I think I really did lose consciousness for a few minutes. The waves went from black to white and then they went away.

When I came back to myself, when the pain had receded enough for me to think anything, I was staring at a funnel in the sand less than an inch from my face. I heard the hum, but it was farther away, drifting away over the river, frustrated and hungry.

I was alive.

They had struck blindly and missed.

I wasted no time. The fabric of my lounge pants had formed a crude bandage over the gashes. My knee had swollen, and every step felt like electric shocks were being fired up my thigh. I focused on that. It hurt. God, it hurt. It hurt so damn much. *Think of that, not of . . . anything else.* The pain was safety. So I focused on the pain, swearing under my breath, feeling tears prick at my eyes. So much pain. Never felt anything like that, nope. It hurt so badly that I had a mad urge to laugh, because it made no sense that anything could hurt like that. Agony—

The doorway loomed in front of me. I have never been so glad to see an empty doorway. I staggered down the steps. The metal door lay discarded on the floor. Maybe we could prop it back into place somehow. Later.

Just a little farther, I told myself. *A little farther. That's all. It doesn't matter that my knee's a bunch of useless bits right now. Only a couple dozen feet.*

I put my shoulder to the wall and used it to hold my weight when I took a step on the bad leg. I had to go the long way around the wall to get to the corridor, but I made it, one slow, halting step at a time.

I found the hole and fell over into it.

The silver willowlight was gone. The animals no longer moved. The bone snake coiled motionless in the case, the Feejee Mermaid's face was curled in its usual silent rictus. Still, the museum wasn't dark. Light—cold pinkish gray, not silver—was beginning to filter through the front windows.

the light makes things alive then not alive

I curled up on my side, cheek against the floor, and watched the sun come up over Hog Chapel and the Wonder Museum.

21

It was very early in the morning or very late. Simon bandaged up my leg. I should probably have gone to the emergency room, but I still didn't have insurance. He cleaned everything out, then used superglue to close the cuts. Either I'd die or I wouldn't, which is about as much as you could say about anything.

"So it was the otter carving," he said.

"Yeah. It must have been." #93 - *Corpse-otter carving, circa 1900, from Danube.*

Was it a key? Or worse, a seed?

I wondered if, somewhere along the Danube, a clump of silver willows swayed in a wind from another world. And if they did, if there was a humming sound somewhere above it. If They moved behind the walls of the world, did the willows give Them a marker where to emerge? A guidepost? Were they the vanguards of an invasion and a beacon all at once?

It can't be, I thought. *There can't be willows there. That was a hundred years ago. The world would have been eaten by willows by now.*

"But where did it come from?" asked Simon.

"A friend of Uncle Earl's sent it." Then a thought split my brain like a lightning bolt. "Woody. Woody Morwood." I stood up, nearly fell over, and grabbed for my cane.

"If you tear that open, I'm going to put Little Mermaid Band-Aids on it and call it good," Simon yelled. I grunted an acknowledgment, hobbling toward the front of the store.

Uncle Earl was the last person on earth with a Rolodex. I flipped through it, looking for names. Woody Morwood. Knowing Uncle Earl's somewhat idiosyncratic method of cataloging, I didn't bother with the *M* section and flipped straight to W.

There were three telephone numbers, two of them crossed out. I didn't recognize the area code on the third one. I punched it into the landline and listened to the ringing.

I was surprised to discover that I still had adrenaline left after last night. My hands were shaking. If the number had come back as disconnected, I would probably have thrown the phone across the room.

When a groggy male voice said "Hello?" I realized that what I was feeling was fury.

"Did you send the otter carving here?" I shouted into the phone.

There was a long, long silence on the other end. I had time to think that this might not even be the right number and that I had screamed at a random stranger, and also it might be the middle of the night wherever they were. My reflexive urge to apologize started to fight its way through the rage, and then Woody Morwood said, "Oh, hell," and I burst into furious tears.

"Tell me what happened," he said, once I'd called him every name in the book while sobbing. He was very calm about it. He didn't hang up. He just took the abuse as if he deserved it, because he probably did. So I wiped my eyes and blew my nose and drank the coffee Simon brought me, and I told Woody the entire story from start to finish.

He asked questions, mostly about what Simon had seen, and a few about the light from the willows. I handed the phone over to Simon a few times. As angry as I had been, I felt suddenly relieved. Someone else knew what was going on. It wasn't just Simon and me and a hole in the universe. Someone else understood.

"Why did you send it here?" I asked finally, when Simon handed the phone back to me.

"I thought it had to be near the willows to work," Woody said. "I found it on an island in the Danube. It had made holes everywhere, like Swiss cheese. It was . . . not good." He didn't elaborate, but I got the impression that *not good* was an understatement for the ages.

I tried to picture an island riddled with holes to the

willow world, a place where you turned around and another hole opened under your feet, all dragging you back. *Not good.* Indeed.

"I had figured out that the carving was a key, but I thought the willows were the lock and, if I sent it far away, it wouldn't be able to open anything." He cleared his throat. "I was very wrong. I'm sorry."

"It was trying to get home," I said. "I think."

"Very likely."

"Why didn't you warn Uncle Earl?" Woody had sent us a goddamn bomb and hadn't even told us.

There was a long silence. "I told him to keep it locked up," he said, sounding more baffled than defensive. "In the book. Didn't he read it?"

It was my turn to be silent. Had there been a book in the box? I wrenched my laptop open and punched in numbers. Documented for posterity, there it was. Soay sheep bones, fish-leather mask, a blank book of banana leaves. It was neatly tied with leather cord. Still was. We hadn't even opened the goddamn thing. It was just one more weird object coming into the museum. Why would anyone think to open it just in case there was a warning? I didn't even know where the damn thing was. For all I knew, we'd slapped a price tag on it and sold it to a tourist.

"Are you still there?" he asked.

"Yeah. Yeah, we . . . we didn't see it."

". . . Oh."

I put my forehead on my fist. I wanted to scream, but this, at least, I couldn't blame on him. Hell, even if we had found it, would we have believed it? "All right. You found the carving surrounded by willows."

"They burned. The carving didn't. I torched the whole island, but I didn't want to risk the carving near them if they grew back. So . . ." Woody trailed off.

"But where did it come from?" I tried to imagine the boatman sitting and whittling out a corpse-otter carving. *Surely not. Surely.*

"If there's a way into hell, someone will always find it," said Woody wearily. "The locals said that there used to be a wizard— that's a terrible translation, but it's what I've got—that lived in the water there. Maybe he was a real person who found a way through. Or maybe it was something simpler and stupider. A hole opened and a log got washed through from the other world, and somebody picked it up and said, 'This is a nice piece of wood, let's see what I can make and sell to the tourists.'"

I leaned the back of my head against the wall, trying not to think how horribly plausible that last option was. Tourists. Of course it would be because of tourists. A wood-carver hoping to make a few bucks, puzzled by what came to life under his knife. Maybe he'd thrown it back into the river and it had been opening more holes, trying to get back home.

"I had no idea it could take over a piece of taxidermy like

that," said Woody. "If I had, I'd have done something else. Buried it in a box in concrete, maybe. But I thought that if it was sent far away, it would molder quietly in a box in Earl's collection, along with all the other oddities. I thought it had probably been in a box like that for decades already. That region saw a lot of upheaval. Somebody might have tossed a chest into the river during a war and it took a few decades to finally rot away. I didn't have any idea that the carving had that much power by itself."

I nodded, forgetting he couldn't see me over the phone. "It couldn't do much by itself. It opened the hole, but it couldn't move very much at all. If I hadn't stuck it in the case with the raccoon . . ."

"You couldn't have known. And it was in a box with bones, wasn't it? And nothing happened. There may have been something else it needed. Light or time or exposure to something else."

"No." I took a deep breath and let it out in a long sigh. I couldn't have known, and Woody couldn't have known either. Neither of us had known, and we still didn't know why or how the carving did what it did. Probably we'd never know. It's not as if the carving had left instructions. Hell, for all I could prove, the carving had been completely dormant until exposed to the Thimbles of the World collection. I couldn't logic my way through this. There were too many holes in our understanding, to go with the holes in the world.

Which reminded me . . . "Do you know how to close the holes?"

Puzzled silence came over the line for a moment. "Close them? The ones in the air close themselves pretty quickly. There was one in the ground, but I kicked sand into it, and it filled up and went away."

"The one in the wall sure isn't going away." I tried to imagine how I'd fill the thing with sand.

"It's still open?!"

"Yes! Why do you think I called you?"

The phone crackled with static. "Fill it somehow. But get it closed. Whatever it takes."

✳

"I've figured out how to do it," said Simon. "I think."

"I'm all ears," I said.

It had taken three days, but I'd cleaned up the museum and reported a break-in. I told the police that the otter case had been smashed and the contents destroyed. Insurance didn't cover irreplaceable and not entirely legal taxidermy, but Simon and Kay had both pitched in to help. I was going to have to write Kay into my will. I didn't have anything except the world's largest collection of knee braces and ice packs, but as far as I was concerned, she and Simon could split it.

The hole was covered, yet again. This time, though, it felt different. Quieter. If there was a wasp in the room, it was dead now. I wasn't going to pick that metaphorical wasp up—even dead wasps can still sting—but the source of the malice was gone.

I still wanted it closed for good. I kept thinking about what Sturdivant had said, about concrete buildings the size of parking garages, surrounded by alien humming. And sometimes about the Bible—*This whole goddamn place is a trap.*

It wasn't anything I could ever prove, but in my bones, I was pretty sure that the willow world hadn't always been full of willows. They'd gotten their roots in somehow. Maybe someone over there had found a corpse-otter carving and it had opened a hole—a vacuae—to another place, and the willows had come through after it.

Did the willows cause the walls between the worlds to thin? Were they the first wave of invaders, setting the stage for Them? It would make sense. The willow world was so empty. Nothing but killdeer and fish and the occasional otter. More than that, it *felt* empty. It was hard to believe that there was anything in the world but death and ruined bunkers and the victims of Their curiosity.

The carving had opened the holes. Probably it had been trying to get home, but I wouldn't swear that it wasn't trying to open the way for the willows to get their roots in. Perhaps that was how it worked. A chunk of willow dropped into another world, like a seed. And the reason we weren't overrun by them was the same reason we weren't overrun by willows from this world. Not all seeds fall on fertile ground. The conditions had to be right.

Well. The otter wasn't coming back easily. Sturdivant had

seen to that. But I still didn't want that hole just sitting there, where Uncle Earl might stumble into it.

Where something else might come through it.

"What's your plan, Simon?"

"I've been talking to Woody and reading up on easy concrete walls." He smiled ruefully. "And since your knee's busted, looks like I get to be the one who carries it."

We raided the cashbox of the Wonder Museum. I didn't feel guilty. This counted as cleanup after the not-entirely-fiction vandalism. Uncle Earl had told me to buy whatever the museum needed, and as far as I was concerned, forty bags of quick-setting concrete counted.

It took five trips. My little car could only carry so much. The back bumper nearly scraped the ground each time. But Simon hauled the bags into the hole and built a wall, stacking them up like sandbags. Then we ran a hose from the kitchen sink, up the stairs, and soaked the bags down for thirty minutes.

"And this'll work?" I said.

"It'll take a long damn time for something to get through, anyway," said Simon. "They do it to make quick retaining walls in flood zones sometimes."

"Works for me." I thought briefly of the skeleton at the other end of the corridor. We were walling him up down there. Maybe that's what he'd have wanted. Hell, he'd chosen to die of thirst or starvation or something rather than go out into the willows, and I couldn't blame him.

When the concrete had set up, Simon went to work patching the hole.

"Woody thinks that the holes close if you fill them in with whatever's supposed to be there," he said. He laid mesh over the opening, not the whole thing but about a six-inch patch, then leaned his torso through into the corridor and spackled it shut. "The ones in the air filled in with air. That's why Woody said the holes closed up. The ones in the sand filled in with sand. And this one . . ."

"Fills in with wallboard and plaster. But why didn't it work before?"

"We didn't fill it." Simon's voice was muffled from its position on the other side of the wall. He had one shoulder braced against the bags of cement and looked like a particularly fashionable praying mantis trying to contort himself into position. "We put patches *over* it. We gotta actually fill it up with more wall."

"That makes absolutely no sense."

"As opposed to everything else about this situation, which has been remarkably straightforward?"

I snorted and passed him more spackle. "What stops somebody from punching through the wall here again?"

"Ugh, now we get into theoretical physics or something like that." He emerged and rubbed his shoulder, then laid in another patch of mesh. "Look, Woody explains this better than I do. But this isn't actually a physical passage from the museum to the hallway in the bunker in the willows. It's a wormhole thing that's anchored to this particular patch of wall. If we could change where the wormhole came out, you could go through this chunk of wall to somewhere else."

"The throats between the worlds," I muttered.

"Right. Except the throat in this case is the thickness of a piece of wallboard." Simon stuck his arm through the throat and waved it around. "My wrist's in a wormhole right now. My hand is in the willow world. You see?"

I rubbed my forehead. So the vacuae was . . . what? Like one of those paintings that the Coyote made to fool the Road Runner, a flat wall that looked like a portal, except that the Road Runner could run through yelling, "Meep meep!"

I tried this analogy on Simon, who got a pained look on his face, but didn't argue. "Sort of like that, yeah. And now our job is to repaint the rock flat so that the portal goes away."

I was suddenly glad that we hadn't tried having me watch from the other side while he closed up the hole. "What stops someone from repainting the portal?"

I could only see one of Simon's eyes—the one that belonged to his dead twin. She had a thousand-yard stare for a moment. "Nothing," he said. "Nothing stops it. But whatever portal They make over there could come out anywhere. This world, the next world, any world. If this is the Coyote and the Road Runner, They're inside the rocks and under the ground. We just hope like hell that the hole doesn't come out anywhere near us."

There didn't seem to be anything much to say to that. I handed him another tub of spackle.

Perhaps I had it wrong, thinking of multiple walls getting thin. Say that there were many worlds, but one ran behind them all, like an access corridor for the universe. The crawl space of eternity. If you knew how to do it, you could open a door in the skin of reality and step into it. A small place, without much going on. A few fish, a few otters, a killdeer calling. A quiet place. Maybe there had been more there once, maybe people, maybe a whole civilization. Maybe I just hadn't seen very much of it. Maybe it was vast, though somehow I doubted it.

Say that it was a world full of willows, willows that sometimes shone with light and brought things to life. Perhaps it was the willowlight that made the walls so thin. And then one day They came creeping along behind the sky. Say that the willows and Them found each other and became . . . oh, symbiotic. They fed on the things the willows brought to life, and the willows became . . . what? Somewhere between crops and worshippers?

It was a perfect hunting ground. The skin of the world was already permeable there. They could go back and forth, under and through. The willows could open more doors to more worlds, somewhat haphazardly, and sometimes unfortunate people wandered through. (I imagined a hole opening in a dusty road, a school bus plowing through it and sinking axle deep into the sand, children screaming and the driver trying not to crash. God help them all, they would have been so much better off if the bus had crashed, before They could descend upon Their new prey.)

But say that inanimate objects from that world weren't quite inanimate, either. How could they be, bathed constantly in the light of the willows? The wood and the water wanted to go home. They wanted to go home so hard that if you drank the water, you found yourself sleepwalking, trying to get back. Though I hadn't gone sleepwalking since I got back. Perhaps I'd finally flushed whatever it was out of my system. Although, given how much water I'd swallowed and how much had gotten into the cut on my leg, maybe it had all been the otter's influence. Maybe the carving had latched on to the sleeping minds of the two humans that had been to that other world and tried to force them to open the way again . . . and when that didn't work, it had gone to inelegant solutions, animating dead flesh to carry it home.

I wondered what it would have done if left alone with a living body that could not get away. Then I decided not to wonder about it.

"Simon," I said, after about ten minutes.

"Yeah?" His voice echoed oddly in the corridor, muffled by the impromptu cement wall.

"You should probably look at this."

He pulled back out and looked at his handiwork, then let out a slow whistle.

I don't know what it looked like on the far side, but the drywall on this side was knitting itself up as pristine as if it had never been damaged.

"It's like when you cut the wallboard before," I said slowly. "It cut through the concrete on that side, even though that should have been impossible. Now you're patching the concrete on that side and it's patching up the wall here, even though it's still impossible."

"Well, let's see how small we can get."

It took him hours. I braved the stairs to bring him bottles of water and more spackle. But inch by inch, the wall closed up.

When he couldn't fit his whole body in the hole, he just put in his arm. When his arm no longer fit, he put his wrist in. Eventually he tossed the spackle knife aside and began using two fingers.

"Your hands are smaller," he said finally. "See how much more you can get in."

I nodded, swept up a glob of wet spackle on my index finger, and went to work. In a few minutes, there was only a hole in the wallboard, like a bullet hole, into darkness.

I coated my pinkie in the wet white goop, slid it into the hole, then scraped it back out.

And then there was only a tiny discolored depression in the wall, as if someone had driven a nail in and then patched it up again. If there was an opening to the other world at all, it was the size of a pinhole.

I sank back, groaning stiffly, and rubbed my back, not caring that I got spackle all over my T-shirt. Simon exhaled slowly. Beau wandered by, saw that my fingers were dirty, and disdained to be petted.

"Hey, Carrot?"

"Yeah?"

"Bet that Riley chick couldn't have done all this."

I started laughing. "Come on. Let's go get Chinese food and get drunk."

"That's the best idea I've heard all week."

✳

The wall was dry. The wall was smooth. After about two weeks, I couldn't take it anymore and drilled a small hole and held my camera up to it.

The flash illuminated drywall and studs. The hole was closed. At least for now.

I told Simon. He was less surprised than I thought he'd be. "I didn't see anything," he said. "With the eye, I mean. Before, there was something there."

"You could have told me."

Simon scratched the back of his neck. "Sorry. I didn't really put it into words. It wasn't like a huge neon sign. It was just the wall was a little deeper than it should have been."

"So it's over," I said. "For now."

"Hopefully forever."

"From your lips to God's ears," I said, which is one of Uncle Earl's phrases, and then a customer came in and we didn't say anything more about it.

22

And that, more or less, was that. Except that my grip on sanity is not quite what it was. I have nightmares, obviously. It would probably be strange if I didn't. But they're still less vivid than the dreams where I was sleepwalking and being called back to the willows, so even in sleep, I am not as troubled as I could be.

Waking is harder. When I'm awake, I think too much and sometimes I see things out of the corner of my eye. A particular type of streetlight—not the big orange cobra heads, but small ornate ones with caps like acorns—leaves a silver smear across wet pavement in the rain. The silver is just close enough to the color of willowlight to set my heart hammering in my chest. I've nearly run off the road twice.

There's also a willow in my mother's neighborhood. I went out there for dinner a few weeks ago and saw it in the neighbor's yard. I don't think it's actually an evil willow, I think it's probably just a plain old ordinary one from the garden center. But the first time I saw it, I ran the car up on the curb and missed a mailbox by a couple inches. Then I had to sit there, gripping the steering wheel and gasping for air, while my throat closed and my knee throbbed and the world got hot and tight around my head.

When I was recovered enough, I drove down the street to my mom's house and went in. Dad grunted from behind his newspaper. My mother fluttered and panicked and made me sit three different places in an effort to make me comfortable, until I told her that my knee wouldn't let me get up again, and then she brought me dinner on a TV tray.

Uncle Earl hugged me and apologized for not being there for the vandalism. "I'm so sorry, Carrot. I'm sorry. I had no idea that would happen. I shouldn't have left you there."

"You should have," I told him firmly. "You're looking so much better now."

"I feel better."

"I'm just sorry that I lost your . . . exhibit." I couldn't bring myself to say "otter." I was bombarding myself with memes of cute sea otters holding hands whenever I went online, because if you panic when you see an otter, the internet is a dark and terrible place. Then Kay told me that sea otters are actually adorable monsters who kill dogs and drown baby seals while dry-humping them to death. That set me back at least a week, but it wasn't her fault.

"It's okay," said Earl. "You know how the museum is. Stuff comes, stuff goes. I got a line on an ichthyosaur skull that'll take that space up nicely."

I pictured an animated ichthyosaur skull snapping its bony jaws as it slithered after me. *Eh, no legs.* I could probably outrun it, even with my knee.

"Simon says hello," I said, lifting my wineglass, and Uncle Earl sat down next to me and I filled him in on all the latest gossip and it was good.

The day that Uncle Earl came back, I put my ear to the wall. Was there still a pinhole-sized wormhole? Had we really closed it all? I moved around, trying to catch any sound. I don't know what I was listening for. Knocking. Hammering. *Humming.*

Only silence.

I stepped back from the wall. The front door jangled, and I went down to welcome Uncle Earl home.

Is it strange that I stayed at the Wonder Museum? Perhaps it would make more sense if I fled, leaving Uncle Earl and Simon to deal with whatever remnants might be left behind. But the museum saved me. The beasts inside saved me. Prince bought me time, and the others flung themselves onto the otter as it went by. Later, I found bits of otter fur in the jaws of other beasts, along the path to the stairs.

Do objects that are loved know that they are loved? Did Prince know somehow that a little girl had loved him with the intensity that only a small child can muster?

The Wonder Museum was full of taxidermy, but taxidermy is only skin and bone and stuffing. If animals have souls—and I will fight anyone who says they don't—then the souls of those beasts departed long ago. I cannot believe that the spirits of the elk and the otter and the wildebeest hung around for decades, seething with rage at having been killed. That would be a cruelty worthy of the willow world, not this one.

The Wonder Museum, for all its strangeness, was never haunted. If there were ghosts, they were benevolent ones.

But perhaps skin and bones have a little memory to them, even after the soul is gone to greater things. And the bones in the museum had spent decade after decade marinating in my uncle's fierce, befuddled kindness.

So my best guess is this: The carving was capable of limited movement, just enough to find the host and work its way inside and animate what it found. But the otter was too large for it—or perhaps simply it needed it to wake up and smash the tempered-glass display case—so the carving worked a great, uncontrolled awakening upon the animals' bones.

The malice of the next world over was profound, but it faltered before Uncle Earl's influence. When the bones woke, they woke as objects that had been loved for many years.

Who am I to say that such objects, given brief life, would not fight to defend their home? Who am I to say that Prince could not recognize a child who had loved him and try to save her?

Well. There are more mysteries in heaven and earth, as

Uncle Earl is fond of saying. Normally I get mad when he does that because he's talking about something that's easily disproven, but in this case, I think it might be appropriate.

If nothing else, if the portal ever does open again, there is nowhere else that I would rather be than in a place where I already know that the inhabitants will fight to protect me. And if the willows do try to get their roots in, better to have someone on hand who can explain what's going on.

The taxidermy mostly went back to the way it was before, not stretching into some unusual positions or climbing down out of the cases. I'd almost think I hallucinated the whole thing, or that it was a strange illusion like the negative space in the willows, except for Prince and the cane toads.

Prince's head is tilted to the side, looking up, as if listening to footsteps on the stairs. I think when the strange animation left him, he was listening to see if I was coming back. And if bones and hide were aware enough to try to protect a little girl who loved him, I believe he must know that I did come back, particularly when I threw my arms around his neck and cried.

The cane toads are . . . well, I don't know if cane toads really care if they were loved. All I know is that the damn things got everywhere during their few moments of pseudo-life. We are still finding them under the display cases and behind doors and in boxes of T-shirts. It's enough to make you sympathetic to Pharaoh with the plague of frogs.

(I also have some suspicions about some of the tiny mice in

costumes. I keep checking the photos I took for the catalog and they look right, but I can't shake the feeling that something in their position changed or possibly keeps changing. Simon says I'm hallucinating, but he also doesn't say I'm wrong.)

I made Uncle Earl get rid of the Feejee Mermaid. The memory of those clacking teeth would keep me up at night if I weren't already being kept up by all the other memories. I can't swear it didn't help me by attacking the otter on the stairs, but I'm pretty sure that it would have bitten the crap out of me, too. Uncle Earl sent it to a nice little start-up museum in Charlotte that needed one.

The doctor at the low-cost clinic says I am a definite candidate for knee surgery and that I absolutely shredded some important tendons and membranes. He also says that he realizes it's not an option without insurance. So I have a brace and some generic pain pills and I do my exercises and stretches religiously and mostly I hobble around the museum the way Uncle Earl does. We joke that we should get matching T-shirts.

He says he's going to leave the Wonder Museum to me in his will. I laugh and tell him he's going to outlive me. The catalog is nearly finished, anyway, which is probably as close as it will come. Skulls keep coming through the door, and cane toads, and bits of fish leather that Beau tries desperately to eat.

Woody came to visit once. I don't know what I pictured from a man who had described the willow portals as "not good." Someone like Allan Quatermain, maybe, fresh from

King Solomon's Mines. Instead he was short and bald and had wire-rimmed glasses, but when he met my eyes, I saw a familiar haunting. Simon's eyes looked like that. Probably mine did, too.

I usually go over and sit in the coffee shop with Simon in the evenings, and sometimes afterward we hang out in the back of the museum and watch badly dubbed anime and terrible movies about Bigfoot and throw popcorn at the screen. We don't talk about the willows much . . . or at all . . . but it helps to have someone around who's been there.

Anyway, here I am. I keep thinking I'll get an apartment, but then I don't. Nowhere else in the world would I be surrounded by so many valiant, if unliving, protectors. And the rent is nonexistent, and I get all the coffee I can drink.

What can I say? It's bizarre, it's sometimes tacky, but it's mine. It took me a few years, but I found my way back at last. The Glory to God Museum of Natural Wonders, Curiosities, and Taxidermy, open nine to six, six days a week, closed Mondays. The Wonder Museum.

I wonder what happens next.

Author's Note

H. P. Lovecraft wrote that "The Willows" by Algernon Black-wood was one of the most terrifying stories ever written. Before I read it, I assumed that this probably meant some people in it weren't white, and I began it preparing to roll my eyes a bit. But "The Willows" is a genuinely disquieting story, for all the occasional excesses of the prose. Some lines stick with you — "the frontier of another world, an alien world, a world tenanted by willows only and the souls of willows."

Frequently, a line from a story that sticks with me is what eventually spawns a book. My first horror novel, *The Twisted Ones*, was derived from the line in Arthur Machen's "White People": "And I twisted myself about like the twisted ones." That line stuck in my head, and eventually I had to write a book to unstick it.

With *The Hollow Places*, I found myself thinking about this alien world, tenanted only by willows, and by strange alien forces that seek to change humans, who make funnel shapes in the sand and who are attracted by human thought . . . and by otters and corpses and boatmen and a number of other elements. It seemed like an interesting place. Not a good place, but an interesting one.

Giant Amazonian river otters do exist, though they are endangered. If you look them up on the internet, you may find a video that records their vocalizations as they hunt. They make a high-pitched giggle, like feral children, and it is deeply unsettling. Nevertheless, they are extraordinary creatures, and I hope we have the sense to find a way to preserve their habitat. The world is richer and stranger for having such creatures in it. (Much gratitude to my friend Eve Forward, who spent time swimming with giant otters and was able to tell me things about them.)

As for the Wonder Museum, which has no place in Blackwood, it is a mash-up of a dozen fascinating little museums that I have visited over the years. I love few things so much as an incredibly earnest tiny museum that is deeply passionate about its focus and wants to tell you all about it. The Rattlesnake Museum in Albuquerque; the Museum of Creation, Taxidermy and Tools and the sadly now-defunct Serpentarium in my own North Carolina; the Mothman Museum in West Virginia; the Voodoo Museum in New Orleans and, down the street, the Pharmacology Museum; the Museum of English Rural Life;

and possibly the single most earnest place on earth, the Butter Museum in Cork, Ireland, are all profound delights of my heart.

Well. Every book has to come from somewhere. I spend an inordinate amount of time at my own beloved coffee shop, writing books such as this one. Infinite gratitude to Ducky, the barista, and Emmett, the owner of Café Diem, for coffee and surreal stories of their childhood that gave rise, eventually, to the character of Simon. (If anything, I toned him down! I have heard things.)

Thanks as always to my husband, Kevin, who read the book at various points and assured me that it was at least semi-coherent, and my editor, Navah, who made it even more coherent, and my agent, Helen, who bears up under the strain of my increasingly idiosyncratic writing. You are all quite lovely people, and I am grateful for your patience.

T. Kingfisher
October 2019

About the Author

T. Kingfisher is the adult fiction pseudonym of Ursula Vernon, the Hugo Award-winning author of *Digger* and *Dragonbreath*. Perhaps best known for her children's fiction, she is an author and illustrator who has been nominated for the Ursa Major Award, the Eisner Awards, and has won the Nebula Award for Best Short Story for "Jackalope Wives" in 2015 and the Hugo Award for Best Novelette for "the Tomato Thief" in 2017. Her first horror novel for adults, *The Twisted Ones*, won the RUSA Award for Best Horror, and was nominated as one of *Library Journal*'s Best Horror Book of 2019.

For more fantastic fiction, author events,
exclusive excerpts, competitions, limited editions and more

VISIT OUR WEBSITE
titanbooks.com

LIKE US ON FACEBOOK
facebook.com/titanbooks

FOLLOW US ON TWITTER AND INSTAGRAM
@TitanBooks

EMAIL US
readerfeedback@titanemail.com